Pollen in the Wind

To Joyce, with much appreciation for her friendship and interest in my efforts

love, Dave

David K. Richards

Copyright © 2006 by David K. Richards

All rights reserved. No part of this book shall be reproduced or transmitted in any form or by any means, electronic, mechanical, magnetic, photographic including photocopying, recording or by any information storage and retrieval system, without prior written permission of the publisher. No patent liability is assumed with respect to the use of the information contained herein. Although every precaution has been taken in the preparation of this book, the publisher and author assume no responsibility for errors or omissions. Neither is any liability assumed for damages resulting from the use of the information contained herein.

This is a work of fiction. Names, characters, places, and incidents either are the product of the author's imagination or are used fictitiously. Any resemblance to actual events or locales or persons, living or dead, is entirely coincidental.

ISBN 0-7414-3048-7

Published by:

INFINITY
PUBLISHING.COM

1094 New DeHaven Street, Suite 100
West Conshohocken, PA 19428-2713
Info@buybooksontheweb.com
www.buybooksontheweb.com
Toll-free (877) BUY BOOK
Local Phone (610) 941-9999
Fax (610) 941-9959

Printed in the United States of America
Printed on Recycled Paper
Published April 2006

Dedication

To our children and our grandchildren,
who, without knowing, have taught their parents
a great deal about life.

Table of Contents

Dedication i

Index

Acknowledgments v

Preface 1

New Beginnings 3

Small Packages 10

The Broach 14

The Eagle's Feather 23

The Trail of Tears 33

Where the Heart Is 41

Mountain Man 44

Snake Oil 55

Miss Margaret's Chalkboard 61

The Learning Pool 78

The Piano Player 87

The Singing Wire 95

The Preacher 107

Pulling Together 120

Dance Hall Girls 129

iii

Helping Hands 137
A Thread of Truth 143
Old Hands at Poker 149
Discovery 157
The Trunk 168
Hallowed Ground 173
The Iron Horse 190
The Conquistadors 198
Doc Who? 212
"Waicu" 217
The Measure of a Man 228
"Teach" 235
A Wise Choice of Words 244
Perspective 253
Thoughts in the Autumn of Life 264
Branded 267
Where the Trail Narrows 277
Where the Past is Present 283
A Look of My Own 292

Acknowledgments

This collection of short stories grew out of a course at Keene State College, a program named CALL (Cheshire Academy for Life-Long Learning), designed to serve un-matriculated persons interested in broadening their interests and extending their educations as well as enjoyment. To Kate Phillips, Professor of Communications and Films, our teacher, I express my appreciation for her thoughtful guidance, encouragement and generous sharing of her time. Kate was a movie actress and script writer and is currently active in the Keene Theater Program.

To my wife, Mary, I say thank you for your patience, your proof reading and criticism as each story was prepared for my next class and re writings became appropriate.

I also want to thank Joyce Robertson, long time family friend, who also lent criticism and encouragement to my efforts.

Each story, in most all instances, offers some subtle suggestion as to how one might live, viewed from the author's own entirely personal and admittedly biased viewpoint.

Preface

The Nation is healing from the trauma of the Civil War, as resolute groups of pioneers venture westward to build new lives. The voices of these hardy souls are recorded in a varied collection of tales that span a number of years of the expanding nation. The voices and natural flowing dialogue of each story briefly paint the events of that special time, bringing to more intimate life, a significant chapter of American history. Effort has been made to be historically accurate and morally enlightening without being pedantic. "Pollen in the Wind" chronicles the sowing of the American spirit across the land in a personal collection of stories that can be enjoyed by all ages.

There is one story, however, that I have left to the end of this volume. "A Look of My Own." It raises a serious question of relationships that across contemporary America have been poorly addressed and sadly needs to be fairly and honestly reconsidered. I see the good and the bad within all of us. Too often our youthful memories of the American Indian are of brutally violent responses to what was European incursion into their native homelands. It has been, sadly, as much a problem in our Democratic nation as in other lands with other peoples. Human history is not without parallel in other areas of the one world we share.

New Beginnings

I am standing looking out of our one open window. Off in the distance, blue mountains reach dramatically up into the bluest sky I have ever seen. Closer to our sod home there are a few tall pines and several slender aspen. The light shimmers off the new green leaves of the aspen as they quiver gently in the ever present wind. Our two children play noisily but happily in the shade amongst the trees. Beyond the grove toward the slight rise in the land I can just picture where we hope to build a real house, one with wooden floors, glass windows, plaster walls and a roof that doesn't leak in a heavy rain. My father used to caution me that good things take time.

Off to the left of the trees my husband, Nathan, labors, encouraging our oxen to pull an old single blade plow. The soil is rich and dark, the furrows long and deep as he struggles to hold a line. He will work there all day turning over the rich earth and come in, his muscles aching, and I will gently wash him down with hot water from our cast iron stove. He intends a harvest of wheat by the end of the summer. He said this year's plowing would be easier than the last. I hope so for him. He's a strong good man, and I love him more than words could possibly express.

I don't recall how long I have watched him, for my mind has been going in its own direction, raising questions I'd already asked myself several years back. Goodness knows, I have enough to do myself, canning things from our garden, pounding last year's corn into flour and baking bread. But for the moment bigger questions have pushed their way into my thoughts. What am I doing here? Why was I born? After this, what comes next? Is this all there is? Right now the last question seems the hardest to answer.

I had grown up in Philadelphia, a lovely home with crystal chandeliers, beautiful furnishings, a grand piano in the music room, nice china, so many things that my dear parents had provided for my brother Charles and me. At least some of the questions seemed to have easier answers then than now. It is obvious to me today that we work and serve.

The city of Philadelphia was an exciting place to live, the birthplace of our nation, with sparkling entertainment and numerous social opportunities. By the age of sixteen I'd learned to read and write as well as play the piano. With help in the house, preparing food had been done by others, all a far cry from the need here to can and store foods in our root cellar as our summer season rolls by. Now it was for me to learn and do. In my mind I could see the pained expression behind my parents' smiling faces when I told them of Nathan, the man just now mopping his forehead and licking his lips as he momentarily halts behind the plow. He said he likes the salty taste of his perspiration. When together, we told my parents about moving west. Father bit his lip and when alone, I'm sure my mother cried. When we shared our plans to travel west to homestead and tried to explain what we wanted to do, they both listened and quietly hoped otherwise. Letting go of your children must be difficult, even though necessary for them to grow. They had wanted so much for me, could have and would have given freely.

Nathan had come home with Charles from one of

the Army training centers. That was how we'd met. His home had been in Maine before the war with the south. I loved the gentle way he spoke and the flat sound of his words. He was quiet and seemed somewhat overwhelmed by the abundance that our family enjoyed. To me he was the most handsome man I'd ever seen and the most wonderful. Before he left and the two of them went on to one seeming military disaster after another during the war, he said he'd write. Father chided me that he'd held my hand much longer than needed for a simple goodbye. He did write, often when he could and two other times he came to Philadelphia for the military, he spent several days with the family and one time brought word of Charles' advancement to someone's staff, evidently an important step upward. He was pleased for him and pleased too for the comradeship they had shared.

Over the years I learned that my brother was a person of incredible inner strength. It was when word came that Charles had been killed at Atlanta that I began to see what life was all about. Charles had been on the staff of General Sherman as they marched across the south destroying and burning everything in their path. He wrote of railroad tracks that they had torn up, heated and twisted into great loops, of crops burned and all the sustaining elements of rural and community life that the people had, wantonly destroyed. I'm sure, as with Charles, and what they were ordered to do, that he came to know grief in ways too intimate for words. Typical, I'm told, events of such awful days are not ones veterans often share. Without speaking, I know he was sick of the waste, of the killing and destruction. Our exchange of letters repeatedly probed for answers to the same questions I was asking of myself again as I stood by my window.

David K. Richards

Charles' last letter, which I treasure, shared what for him was a turning point in his life. It had come to him slowly as such moments often do, but for him it was an encounter with a black man who had been wounded or somehow injured as he'd struggled to help his master escape the city. Yes, he'd been a slave, a house slave, the kind that are not relegated to the greater hardships of the cotton fields, but as one that served a fine family and benefited some rudimentary education. That slavery business I'm not sure I understand, at least to appreciate the differences. To me it is wrong that one person be beholden in that way, bought and sold. It was different than being indentured as many in this land had done in order to start a new life. Charles found the man by the road, his wagon overturned, his master dead, and he himself was near to dying. Charles gave the man water and gently moved him to a shady spot beneath a tree. As he set him down, making him more comfortable, the man looked up at Charles with tears in his dark eyes and asked simply, "why? Why?" Then he closed them forever.

It was such a brief encounter but it brought to fruition a turning point in Charles' life that had been slowly seeping into his awareness. His encounter was such that he could no longer remain neutral. It was a point where he found it necessary to take sides if he was to reveal his humanity. After that, he requested a transfer, but did not live long enough to receive it. He had written that the riches of life are not to be found in an endless accumulation of things, but that the riches in life come with a commitment, a point where one shoulders a responsibility and discovers why he was born into the world. He had discovered the meaning of real service to others. Charles had grown in wisdom, understanding and compassion. How I loved him for what he'd shared with me.

In time, the years of conflict ended and Nathan, my Nathan, said he had come home when he knocked at our door and then waited for me in the parlor. My heart ached at the experiences he had had and could not or would not share. But he too, had reached a turning point, a decisive choice and willingness to make a new beginning. We both knew it would not be easy. So here I stand, not regretting even a single moment.

We had traveled west with others, all seekers for a better life. We were just one of many homesteaders. We cut sod from the earth and built the walls of our home, had cut pine to span our single room and damp packed the earth for the floor. A neighbor showed us how. Neighbors all worked together here in the west. It was slow and hard work and our hands were raw from the effort, but we did it. We even created a small area for the few animals we had brought with us. As architecture, what we created would hardly fit in Philadelphia. One day, later in our first summer, a small group of Indians came by, looking curiously at our strange house and we fed them. A few days later we awakened very early at the sound of ponies outside, but by the time we had stirred enough to open the door we found only the fresh killed body of a small antelope. Kindness and love are so vulnerable.

Each day has been a hardship and the cold of our first winter was almost more than we could bear. Our wood supply had not proved enough and if it hadn't been for the deep snow piled by the wind against the sides of our home and the animals brought inside, I do believe we'd have frozen. The following summer we had our first child, followed too quickly by a second.

David K. Richards

Nathan rode across the valley to our nearest neighbor and an older daughter came to care for me during the last few days. We have been so lucky.

A rider came through one day several months back and asked our name. When Nathan replied, he said there were letters waiting for us back in Dodge. He would have brought them had he known. It was time to get supplies, sugar, coffee, salt and cloth, so we welcomed the journey, at least one way. Coming home a range fire swept across our route, started by lightning or someone's carelessness. It took us miles out of our way but we learned a lesson that small defensive fires can be used to save larger areas. The letters were from home and one contained a check that was most welcome. Nathan insisted I buy a bonnet I'd admired in a store we passed, and I knew he thought highly of some red suspenders. Of course we bought each of the children a small toy, a doll for Geena and some marbles for Cameron.

Somehow I don't miss the abundance of my earlier years. I do miss family and know that across the miles they miss us. It is good to stand out on the prairie at night away from the light of the oil lamp and look up at the stars and be mindful that the stars overhead are the same ones that looked down on Homer, on the shepherd David, or the brave men who crossed these plains guided by the north star. And yes, they are the same stars that look down on my parents and Nathan's.

We've had other visitors. Why, just last month a rider passed our way, got water from our spring and shared a meal. He wasn't with the Pony Express we've heard about. But he did have news that a great rail line would soon be crossing the country and that all kinds of new scientific discoveries were being made back

Pollen in the Wind

east. Our part of the country was now an official state, he believed, and more people were continuing to move west. Off to the north we heard of Indian problems, but so far we'd seen none of it.

So, as I look out my window at the efforts of my beloved husband, I know of two important beginnings in our lives; the day we were born into the world and the day we discover why. I know the answers to my big questions and that, as individuals, families or even a nation, we have the potential to evolve from our inner being. We need but to make a worthwhile commitment to make it happen.

Small Packages

"If she could only see this valley now!" Clyde Hanford eased his strawberry roan to a stop and gazed out over the fertile valley that lay before him. "Flowers and color as far as the eye can see. She was somethin' alright!"
"What'd you say, Clyde?"
"Huh? Didn't realize I'd spoke out loud, Sam." He removed his wide brimmed hat and mopped his forehead. "Been over this trail a dozen times now an' every time we trail this way, the view from here gets prettier."

For so many miles the trail behind them was desolate, rocky, and with only scattered patches of grass and scrub growth. Sam relaxed one leg over his saddle horn, pulled a small bag of tobacco from his shirt pocket and began to roll a cigarette.

The valley that lay before the two men, and on into the distance, was covered with brightly colored flowers; Columbine, Black-eyed-susan, Yellow daisy, Bluebell, and so many others. The view was breathlessly spectacular.

Clyde Hanford smiled a kind of inward smile to himself, lost in his own thoughts. He said nothing as he reflected for a whole minute, looking out across the colorful valley, lost in thought.

Clyde was a clean shaven, strong and powerfully built man and recognized for his integrity and knowledge of the trails west. His parents had died years earlier in a tragic wagon disaster as his family had started west themselves; an accident on a long and difficult decline. Their wagon had rolled over crushing the life from them. As a boy of twelve he'd continued his own way west with another family; adopted. The years of growing up had been lonely and desolate for him. The loss of his family had proven most difficult, yet Clyde had never been known to complain.

Eventually, he retraced old trails and searched new ones to lead many homesteaders successfully across the raw plains into Oklahoma, typically with a high degree of success. Yes, there had been times, however, with losses, breakdowns and Indian attack; occasionally painful reminders. Each journey had a story to tell and Clyde sometimes enjoyed swapping travel experiences. Sam Johnson had made several trips across the plains with him and knew that. And he knew just the right way to get Clyde talking.

"Peaceful this time o' day and just look at them wild flowers. The whole valley is patches of color from one side t'other, like one of them oriental carpet rugs."

In his mind, Clyde Hanson had already reached back into memory.

"Yup," he said . . . "wer'nt always this way." He shook his head at the thought. Some memories just don't go away.

Sam looked back over his shoulder at the wagon train stretched out in a long lumbering line behind them. It would be more than a few minutes before the first wagon topped the rise where they sat their horses. He knew a question or two might clear the way for Clyde's sharing. They had come this way before and on this trail he had some time back suspected there was a very special story here. He didn't have too long to wait.

"Yup, if she could only see it now. Let's see! It was fifty-two when we first come this way; sixteen wagons;

the hopes and dreams of sixteen families brave enough to risk starting over."

He slid off his horse, letting the reins fall loose, and bent over to pick a handful of blue bonnets and daisies. He held them to his nose. Then he pointed to a gentle mound a short distance below them.

"T'was right about there we'd formed up fer the night. Fact is, we had to hold up two whole days. A couple of major repairs; the tongue on the Carleton wagon had split and Harley Daniels had broke the spokes out of a wheel and he didn't have a spare. We'd been pushin' just a mite too hard. It was only my second time across. We talked it over, took a vote and all the folks decided to catch their breath. I was too green myself to realize the possible consequences."

"Indians?"

"Sally Daniels was eight or nine. Long golden hair, she had, and a smile that was like a refreshin' breeze, bright blue eyes that smiled along with her smile; not big in size, but then some of the sweetest things do come small. She decided, with everybody catching up on repairs, laundry and what-not, that she would plant a garden. She was so anxious to put down roots; like so many. She knew we'd be moving on but that made no difference, no how. She had gathered a small packet of seeds before the family had left New England and she just couldn't wait to give some of them seeds new homes."

"Yup, Sam. It was Indians; not many, but by surprise; my fault. I hadn't posted nobody to keep watch. It happened so quick! An' Sally . . . she was so full of life an' wantin' to do so much. One of the wagons was destroyed, and several folks wounded, but Sally Daniels . . ." He pointed toward a small area of red columbine where the late afternoon sun seemed most intense. "We buried her right there, beside her garden."

Clyde Hanson turned away to blow his nose. Sam didn't have to guess the real reason. He'd ridden with his boss long enough to see more than the toughened hard driving task-master that he appeared to be. He knew that inside the man was a haunting loneliness; more than a few memories that he'd never really talked about. Never married, no family beyond the one that had taken him in; living since from one day to the next. There was an emptiness in him that seemed to drive him.

"Pretty little girl. She put down roots where I pointed and look at this valley now . . . she never saw the results. . . just started the seeds . . . flowers in bloom now as far as you can see. Spectacular! Ya' know Sam, all the years I've traipsed back and forth across this great country, I don't have a thing to show for it. Not one worthwhile thing to leave behind. And look what a nine year old little girl left behind."

Clyde Hanford picked up the reins of his horse and hoisted his weight into his saddle. There was that deep sadness in his face that Sam Johnson recognized when they had come this way. . . . recalling times past.

"Sam, she was one little girl I'll remember forever. Every time I come this way, I cherish the memory of her." He took one more long look before turning away. "Yup!" He paused. "'mazin' what a little nine year old youngster could accomplish in her short life." He cleared his throat. "I've heard folks say that only special things come in small packages."His mouth was grim as he turned to meet the lumbering line of wagons behind them. "Yesser, Sally Daniels herself was sure one them small packages."

The Broach

Jeff Blair had gone off to war and not returned home as he might have. His problems were of his own making. He missed his family. He now sat with two other men huddled around a small campfire. They were dressed in what appeared to be various articles of military clothing, a shirt, a cap, a belt. They all wore guns, pistols they had possibly stolen or used in the war between the States a year or so back. It was obvious that their stop was to be a brief one, a rest for their horses, a pot of coffee.

"Any more coffee in the pot, Clay?"

"You filled the pot. If they ain't none it's yer fault." The man who spoke had long unkempt hair and a shaggy beard. He lay back against his saddle and looked up into the night. "That stage goes through in the mornin?"

"Yesseree! And we'll catch her just as it slows to the top of the rise." The man who spoke was apparently their leader and wore the cap of a Confederate Army officer. Of course it carried no real authority at this point in time beyond the three of them. These were men who after the war had decided to prey on the traffic of new settlers as they moved west. The third man, who sat quietly off to the side was the younger fellow named Jeff. He just sat watching and listening. He was thinking serious questions and finally put one of his thoughts into words.

"You're sure there'll be no killing, Jake? We can do what we have to without that, can't we Jake? Besides it would put a price on our heads." The younger lad was obviously nervous about what had been planned for the next day.

"Kid, we got this thing all planned out. You just do as I say . . . we just needed one more person to pull it off."

"That's why you wanted me? This is not . . ."

"Sweepin' stalls at the livery is no way to get ahead," interrupted the older man. He looked to his partner and chuckled. "We're expanding our business, ain't we, Clay?"

"Big time," said, Clay, grinning stupidly. With the back of his hand, he wiped his mouth. He was missing a finger on the hand, an ugly scar, suggesting a possible wound during the war or carelessness on his part. Not having gone beyond the fourth grade had limited his opportunities.

"Well . . ."Jeff hesitated, but didn't argue further. He was by far the youngest of the three and quite hesitant to go along with a venture he didn't really subscribe to.

"You ain't really cut out for this business, kid. We'll all do what we have to! An' you'll do just fine." It was Jake, the man with the Confederate cap speaking. He shifted his overweight body away from the edge of the fire and took a finishing swig of coffee from his tin cup. What was left he splashed into the fire. "Clay, you git some water an' put the fire out, it's time to move on. Kid, you git the horses." Of the three, Jeff didn't seem at all fit for the role of a highway- man and bandit. It had been circumstances that had brought the three together. He felt uncertain about what he was letting himself in for, and it showed.

The make-shift camp was quickly secured, the fire, ashes scruffed aside with a boot. Blankets were rolled and tied down behind saddles. It was quickly accomplished, born of long practice with the Confederate cavalry, having been continually on the move then and since. It was somewhere after Vickesburg that Hank and Jake had decided to leave the army before the war ended. They saw it as a lost cause. For a year and a half they had roamed the country-side. They had been taking advantage of whatever opportunities they came across. With word of a stage coach making a run into Carson Creek, Jake suspected this might be a rich one. More and more money was moving back and forth across a growing and healing nation. They needed the third man to pull it off. Jim made the threesome. They had met in a hospital and run into each other sometime later.

"Cash box ought to fix us for a time, eh?" said Clay, rolling his eyes in greedy contemplation. He swung a leg up over his horse and mounted up. In minutes the three were moving on.

Aboard the stage the men had in mind, a family of three was traveling west. This was the Blair family, a middle aged couple and their daughter. There was also a salesman pushing medical supplies and a middle aged woman who sat quietly in the corner, her lips tightly pursed. Occasionally she would remove a letter from a small bag and carefully unfold a worn picture which she would look at over and over. It was a letter from a man in Denver who was seeking a bride. She had responded to his ad, written and had received an answer. She was going to him at the end of their journey. When she finished rereading the letter she would carefully put it and the accompanying picture away. Then she would smile to herself, push the little curtain aside and stare out the window.

The salesman across from her talked a lot. It didn't

seem to matter what the subject was, he seemed to be an expert. He was clean shaven, wore a derby which now sat on his lap. His coat hung neatly on a hook at the side of the small coach space, so in the heat of the day he sat in his striped shirt and colored garters half way up his shirt sleeves.

The small family of three tended to sit quietly, as if they really had much chance to do otherwise. They were the Blair family and had come from West Virginia. They were also on their way to a destination somewhere around Denver. His business had been in banking and he hoped for a position in one of the growing banking opportunities of the west as things developed. His wife had her head down. It was bobbing back and forth, up and down, as the stage moved over rutted roads. There was a deep sadness about her, but the man, her husband, Mr. Blair, seemed to be a very comforting fellow. They had lost a son in the war between the States. He had been killed or was missing in one of the many battles. They were never sure. She'd never gotten over it. Mr. Blair would pat her gently from time to time and whisper comforting words of assurance. The young girl was about fourteen, too old for dolls, but holding onto one that had evidently been a favorite for a long time. Her name was Emily. She was pretty in a blue flowered dress, soft blonde hair tumbling down over her shoulders. She wore a small broach at her throat, an heirloom from her grandmother that she now wore and treasured.

"This will be one of our longest days," said the salesman."And most likely over the roughest roads," he added, suggesting some knowledge of what lay ahead. "We go up through some mighty rough country. Yes, siree!" The woman in the corner just smiled politely.

It was on toward noon when just ahead there was some kind of activity as the stage climbed toward the top of a rise. There it came to a complete stop. It was the salesman who leaned out the window to see what was going on. Up ahead were two mounted men holding guns.

"Oh, no! he gasped.

"What . . . what?" stammered Mr. Blair, suddenly holding tight to a small leather package he'd held securely between his feet. He tried to lean across the lady in the corner to see for himself. She just put her head in her hands and shook her head. For her, the trip was proving demanding enough. When the stage rolled to a stop, the two drivers were ordered down. One of the drivers started to make a move toward a rifle beside him. As he turned, a third masked fellow rode up along the side of the stage. The driver wouldn't have had a chance if he'd tried to reach the weapon.

"Under the box up front!" ordered the one with the Confederate cap, pointing a rifle where he meant. Without a word, Hank climbed up and pulled out what he believed was the cash box being sent west. He tossed it to the ground. There, the lock was shot off and the box opened. Sure enough, it held coins and bills and other important looking papers. Hank jumped down and began raking the cash into a small sack. Unable to read, he paid little attention to the folded and ribbon wrapped papers.

"Look at this! Man!" Hank's eyes were bright with glee and greed.

"Kid, get the people out'ta the stage," ordered the man with the Confederate cap.

"Right!" Jeff dismounted and opened the stage door. One by one the passengers were ordered to step to the ground and to line up along the side of the stage. "Empty your pockets and handbags, folks." He holstered his pistol and moved from one person to the next, accepting what the frightened passengers offered. The salesman held back and when Jeff dropped his hand to his holster, the salesman changed his mind. Mr. Blair emptied his pockets and protectively put his arm around his terrified wife. His attention was with her.

Hank, meanwhile, unhitched the team of four horses and with a swat on their rumps sent them galloping back along the road they had just traveled. Mr. Confederate cap nodded his approval. "Now tie the driver's hands and feet. We don't want no hidden guns to be dug out from somewhere too quick-like. Move!" He turned back to Jeff who had gathered a little cash from the salesman, a gold watch and the couple's rings. It wasn't much.

Jake glanced at the young girl and reached toward the small broach he spied at the neckpiece of her dress. It was an attractive little cameo of obvious value. Quite naturally she pulled away and hunched over to prevent its loss. Jeff stepped forward, also bending as he reached out to take it, following his orders. As he bent over and tore off the broach, she looked right through his mask and whispered, "Jeff?"

Jeff gasped! "Emily?" He recoiled quickly and smacked her across the face, hoping to mask his obvious surprise and sudden confusion. He looked again! There was no question, this was his little sister and the couple were her parents, his parents. On edge, he quickly turned away from the line-up, avoiding further confrontation, and put what he had in a cloth bag as Hank had done. He had to do something!

"Let's get outta' here!" he yelled. Responding,

Hank and his partner mounted, wheeled their horses around and as suddenly as they had appeared, the three masked bandits were gone.

Mr. Blair fumed about the loss, but when he looked inside the stage, his leather packet that he'd held secure at his feet and had kicked under the seat when he was ordered out, was still there. This was his savings for a new business. Relieved, he proceeded to untie the drivers. The lady with the letter and picture of her mail-order husband just wept softly, while the salesman talked the whole time about justice and what should be done as well as how to go about it. At that point he didn't have an audience.

Emily, now very much in shock and in disbelief, saying nothing, ran to her mother's open arms.

The question remained, what to do next. As it turned out, the drivers did have another gun hidden under the leather strappings of the stage, which they retrieved. The older driver stuck two fingers in his mouth and gave a shrill whistle. Then he sat down and waited. He whistled again. Shortly, the horses appeared, not having been run off so far that they'd kept on running. Given a little time, one by one the horses were hitched and then everyone was told to climb aboard.

That night, in the next town the passengers were lodged in the local hotel. Of course the local sheriff wanted as many details as possible, the salesman magnifying their tragedy and even offering information nobody else could recall. Within an hour, or not much more, the sheriff had a posse together and was ready to ride back along the road.

Settled in for the night, but not sleeping, Emily lay quietly, revisiting what she thought she had by accident learned back at the stage hold-up. It had been her brother, she was positive of it. He had even spoken her name. How had he come to this? How had he taken up with those other two bad people? There was no way to know the answers. Why had she not said anything about this to her parents or to the sheriff who questioned every one of them. As she lay there while her parents slept soundly on the other side of the room, she was startled by something outside their window or against the wall. It sounded like a small pebble hitting the side of the building. It happened again! She slipped out of bed and tip-toed to the window. Standing below on the ground was a man. He was dressed as she had seen the man on the road. This time he wore no mask. It was her brother! She leaned toward the open window. When he saw her, he motioned to her and whispered to unlock the door to her room. "Jeff!" she gasped under her breath. She was sure now that it had been him. It took a few minutes before she was ready to comply and even then was hesitant. A moment later she very quietly stepped out into the hotel corridor. Jeff saw her down the hall and joined her. At first they just stood there wondering what to say or do. He held out his hand and in it the little broach he had taken from her dress earlier that day. Emily accepted it and slowly reached up to put her arms around her big brother.

"I ran out of money and got in with some bad people. I was along with others when we had been hospitalized. It wasn't what I really wanted to do."

"Why didn't you just come home when the war ended? Mom has felt terrible not knowing. We never heard. The folks have missed you so much. I've missed you. How did you find us? How did you get away?"

"I pretended my horse went lame and couldn't keep up. They got what they wanted and didn't need me. It was a mistake to get involved." In the dim light of the corridor Jeff's face was wet with tears. "It was a guess to come looking . . . I asked the night clerk at the desk. Sis, I'm so sorry! With the war over, I've tried to work my way toward home. I just don't have enough words to explain . . . I don't know now what Dad will say . . . after . . ." Head down and sobbing, he moved uneasily from one foot to the other.

The door to the Blair room slowly swung open behind the two young people standing in the hallway. "Jeff, boy." It was a gentle caring voice that broke the silence.

"Just tell your mother how sorry you are, son. The war is over and we're together again. We'll work out the problems as a family. That's what families are all about."

The Eagle's Feather

Pa and me hadn't been gettin' along peacefully for some time. Growin' up don't seem easy for me or my Pa. He argued that I didn't use good judgment, I was gettin' too big for my britches. At fourteen I was physically doing the work of a man and felt I should be given the same consideration received by any other man in the wagon train. Ma stayed out of the arguments, but I could often catch looks between the two where Ma wanted one or the other of us to back off. Ever since we had left Council Bluffs, Pa seemed to be down on me. To be starting life all over again in a strange place made a number of the folks in our wagon train more edgy than might have been normal. I guess Pa was no different.

Mr. Beasley, our wagon master, had a lot of things to be responsible for, but somehow he seemed to be aware of how each of the families was doing along the way. He knew I was workin' as hard as any man and he knew Pa was ridin' pretty rough on me. It was none of his business. But, I had a feeling that in his mind he would have liked to make it so. One time he dropped in at suppertime. I'd just spilled a plate of beans and Pa jumped me. Mr. Beasley saw it had been an accident and in his deep resonant voice had suggested so to Pa. Somehow Pa saw it as wasteful and careless on my part.

"We have little enough for you to go spilling our grub over the landscape," he'd shouted at me.

"Tighten up the leg on that table and it might not

tip so easily."

"Beasley, you just stay out of this! That boy has spilled table food all his life. He'll be the death of us yet."

"Well, now Jeb, Jeffrey's few spilled beans aren't a matter of life and death."

Pa had more to say on the matter and Mr. Beasley said no more and very shortly drifted off to the next wagon. That wasn't the end of it for me.

A few days later, always moving further west, the country began to lay down flat. We were making fifteen to eighteen miles a day so long as it didn't rain. Back in Pennsylvania the land south of Erie had seemed flat. This was different and beautiful in its own way. You could see for miles in every direction. And the sky was more blue than any I'd seen. One bright morning Mr. Beasley dropped by, checking to see the last of our breakfast gear stowed away and the wagon ready to roll. I'd just had my head chopped off by Pa for some reason and been sent off to gather wood while we still had the chance.

When I came back, Pa and Mr. Beasley were havin' at it, arguing.

"I'm sure you can spare him for a few hours and it'll do him good to have something special to do," Mr. Beasley was saying.

Pa chewed at his upper lip, a thing he seemed to do when Ma was about to win an argument and he had to figure out how to give in without seeming to. "He's hardly dry behind the ears. Besides, aren't we getting into Indian country?"

"It'll be the same from here on west. I'd judge he's able enough."

The gist of the debate was that Mr. Beasley had suggested I ride out along our flank and possibly add

Pollen in the Wind

some fresh meat to our supplies. We'd had little enough fresh meat and we had occasionally seen elk or some kind of small deer off away from our route. Pa had to admit I could shoot well enough and in the end bit his lip and agreed. He gave me a handful of shells and I started off. It made me feel good inside. Now I had to deliver!

I untied Nel from the back of the wagon and put the saddle on. Pa put his Winchester in the saddle boot. As I rode off, feeling good, I thought about Beasley. He'd never married or had any offspring that I'd heard tell of, but he did seem to get along with the young people in our group. He'd taken trains through several times before our's and most everyone had confidence that he knew what he was doing. I felt sure he did. I had a funny feeling Pa agreed with Beasley about me, just hated to admit it. Some parents seem to have difficulty letting go of their kids.

Some days Mr. Beasley would ride off to a rise along our route and with a glass search the horizon around us. Some said it was because of Indians. He never said. He knew the route. And like Pa had said, we were already into Indian territory. Mr. Claxton, Mr. Beasley's hand, had told me some about the Sioux, not to frighten us, mind you. They'd had problems a time or two. They had never lost a wagon yet though they'd had to dicker some. So, don't you think the thought didn't put some caution into my leaving the train trailin' off in the distance. I tell you what!

I'd been gone perhaps two hours, roughly six miles from the others. I was following the small hoofed track of a deer or elk. Mr. Claxton had pointed out tracks to us so I was trying to put new knowledge to work. The tracks led me down into a kind of gully or draw, so I was not hurrying my mare along what was rough goin'. Low branches of small trees tore at my sleeves making it difficult to see very far ahead. The tracks moved along on what I was beginning to see as a small trail. Mr. Claxton called that readin' sign.

I followed the trail. A little further along, Nel's ears pricked up and she began to prance a bit. She smelled water. I held her back and a few minutes later we came to a small stream. There on the far side was an elk. Without having realized it, my approach had been from down wind, so the elk was taken by surprise when I appeared across the stream. Without waiting, the elk turned to run. Having seen it first, I was ready. I aimed carefully, squeezing the trigger slowly, and put a bullet where it hurt. The elk went to its knees and fell over. I'd never cleaned one, so with a little effort, I got the body loaded in front of my saddle, across Nel's back. I sure hoped Pa would speak kindly of my success. Pleased with my good fortune I decided to move a bit further along the stream before I turned back. The sun was well up and the gully was hot. Picking my way amongst the brush and rocks was difficult. At one spot I refilled my canteen and let Nel have some water. Then I decided to work my way to the top of the slopes that formed the gully. It was time to head back.

I hadn't gone too far when, of a sudden, I saw a dark mass up ahead. It took only a few more steps and I realized it was a fallen horse and not one from our wagons. The horse was hurt or dead and on the far side was a person pinned down and not moving. Turned out it was a boy. I'd guess he was about my own age; an Indian boy. If he wasn't dead he was sure hurt bad. I'd never seen an Indian up close, so I wasn't sure just how to deal with him.

Evidently, his pony had caught a hoof in a gopher

hole and flipped them both against the rocks, pinning the rider beneath. I tied Nel to a nearby tree and cautiously circled the fallen horse and rider. I put down my rifle and felt the boy's body. He wasn't dead, but his horse was. No tellin' how long they'd been there. I poured a little water from my canteen on the boy's face, allowing a little to trickle into his mouth. He opened his eyes, surprised at my appearance and being there. He struggled as though he could pull himself free and defend himself. He was far too weak. Five hundred pounds of painted pony held him fast. For a whole minute we just stared at each other, not sure what to do. Finally, I decided.

Nel was no cow pony, but she was strong and with a rope looped over a limb and her pullin', it lifted enough weight for me to ease the boy from under. One leg was all bent out of shape and his breathing was difficult. It was like my Pa when one time a log rolled onto him and he'd had a number of ribs broken. Ma and I moved him back to the house and it took weeks before he was back to normal. The Indian boy's twisted leg was another matter.

At first he didn't want me to touch him. Once he began to sense I was trying to help him he gave in a bit. I wondered if he was a Sioux. My big question was what to do next. I'd been sent off for fresh meat and surely wouldn't be expected to return to the wagon train with an Indian. I could just imagine how angry Pa would be and what he'd say. With the boy out from under the horse I wondered how he would do on his own. Would his people find him way out here or even come lookin'? I put myself in his place and knew I couldn't leave him. At least Ma would understand.

I looked over his twisted leg. It was a bad mess. Carefully, I washed the blood caked mud and began to straighten it. The flesh was torn and the stark white of a bone below his knee was sticking out awkwardly. He nearly yelled out as the pain must have been fierce. Fortunately, he closed his eyes and relaxed into unconsciousness. Slowly, I eased the leg into a normal position. Then the bleeding began again, so I used my belt around his leg to cut off the flow. I believe I'd read that somewhere. With the leg finally straight and the bleeding stopped, I cut and wrapped a piece of my saddle blanket around his leg, along with a couple of small branches the size of my wrist. Splints is what they'd be called.

Lookin' over my doctorin' there didn't seem much more I could do, so I went back to the stream and refilled my canteen.

When I got back, the Indian's eye's were open. From the look on his face I could tell he was hurtin' something awful. He drank a little water and we just sat there, me puzzling what to do next, him wondering what I intended next; neither of us able to communicate with words. I leveled an area on the ground beside us and drew a picture of our wagons and pointed in the direction I believed them to be. With the sun so close to straight overhead I wasn't entirely certain. He seemed to understand my picture and held up nine fingers, actually one more wagon than I'd drawn in the dirt. He was right! He was more aware of us than we had been aware of his people, though I'd bet Mr. Beasley knew they were watching.

As we sat there, the boy didn't take his eyes off me for more than a second. Sittin' quietly, we each gained confidence in the other. I pointed to myself and said, "Bobby," several times. After a few tries he repeated my name and I nodded. Then he did the same. His name sounded like Sakota. At least he nodded when I said it. Stretched out as he was, he was a few inches taller than me, well built and I would guess quite strong, at least before his accident. I put my canteen to his lips and he drank. The water seemed to help. By now I'd decided to somehow get him back to the wagon train where Doc Simpson could do a better job patchin' him up than I could, fer certain. I'm sure Mr. Beasley would agree with me. I'd have to deal with Pa later. My next problem was how to move Sakota.

Remembering a picture I'd seen once, I cut a couple of long poles with my knife. Using what was left of my saddle blanket and rope, I shaped a thing Nel could drag along behind her. It took a while to get it rigged and pointed in the right direction and then get Sakota onto it. We moved slowly out of the gully, but not without my having to tie Sakota so he wouldn't roll off. Up on the grassy plain it was easier. In spite of the smoother going my patient had spells where he passed out and thrashed in discomfort and pain. Yet he never once cried out. With the sun high up and hot, I covered him over as best I could. We moved in a direction that I felt sure would intercept the wagon train. After two hours of slow going we came to a rise in the land where I could see across the open plain. What I saw sent chills through me.

About a mile off the wagon train had been brought into a circle. Off to the west there must have been a hundred mounted Indians. Between the wagons and the Indians there were several riders. They seemed to be returning to the wagons after some kind of meeting. I recognized Mr. Beasley and Mr. Claxton, but not the others. I watched for several minutes imagining what was going to happen. I didn't have long to wait.

The Indians gathered together around two or three leaders who began pointing in directions to the right and left of the huddle of wagons. There were a few whoops and several fired guns into the air. They were going to attack!

I'm not exactly sure why I did it, but I just fired my rifle in the air also. Immediately several Indians turned their ponies in my direction.

Something was said as the Indians spread out and two rode toward me. Now I'd really done it! I stood even less chance than the families preparing to defend themselves behind the wagons. I looked in their direction, thinkin' Pa had been right about a lot of things and when I'd left earlier we'd not been too happy with each other. As I watched, I saw a quick flash of light, something I'd seen before and recognized for what it was. It was Mr. Beasley's glass and the flash was the sunlight reflecting off the end. Well, at least they had spotted me and knew the kind of trouble I was in. I decided to be like Sakota and be as brave as I possibly could. I stood straight and tall as possible, holding my rifle upright beside me. Two Indians, riding bare-back, dressed in animal skins and feathers, their faces daubed with stripes of colored earth, jumped from their ponies and came at me. I leveled my rifle at them and they held back. Curious about the travois behind Nel, one went behind me and lifted a corner of the covering that protected Sakota from the hot sun. Speaking excitedly they seemed to believe I had taken him prisoner and had tied him there. They didn't look further to see his condition.

Rushing me from two sides I suddenly became their prisoner and altogether we were pushed and pulled back to the knoll where they'd had their pow-wow. By now all the Indians had spread out into a long curving line that cut off the route of the wagon train. At the front there was one Indian with a feather fringed

Pollen in the Wind

lance held high over his head. I guessed that his signal would start the attack. When we arrived he whooped loudly and turned in my direction. I had never been so scared in all my life. When Pa took the strap to me, it hurt, but after a while it hardly scared me. Not like this! But, like with Pa, I wasn't going to show how I felt inside. I stood as tall as I could and held my head up.

One of the Indians pointed to Nel and the drag behind her. He spoke to the warriors and they uncovered Sakota. For a moment they just looked. They spoke rapidly to their leader and he went to look for himself. As they untied Sakota's arms he opened his eyes and spoke. The Indians crowded around him. I had no idea what was being said.

Across the plain between the wagons and the Indians a rider galloped toward us. It was Mr. Beasley. He rode right up to us like he had no fear at all and spoke powerfully to their leaders. I hadn't known he could speak their language. Then he turned to me and quietly assured me to stand firm. The group spoke together for several minutes before he spoke to me again.

"Jeffrey, take my horse and ride to the wagons to fetch Doc Swanson. Don't take time to explain anything. Now git!"

"Yes...yes, sir!"

He didn't have to urge me. I rode hard. I found Doc Swanson and he mounted up. Pa saw me. I couldn't hear exactly what he called out but I knew the tone. Ma was clutching her apron and lookin' scared. I thought of Mr. Beasley out there all alone. They pretty much left my doctorin' as it was. There was a lot of talk back and forth. Mr. Beasley didn't back off one bit. Finally the leader brought up two ponies and pointed to me. Mr. Beasley told me on the way back to the wagons what had been said.

"Boy make fine trader and better than Beasley." He laughed his deep laugh and smiled. I sure felt a lot better when we arrived at the wagons.

We ate fresh meat around the campfire that evening and Mr. Beasley told everyone how it had all worked out; how I'd saved the life of the chief's son as well as the wagon train. By then, of course Pa simmered down and both Ma and he took a second look at my growing up. We didn't actually see any more Sioux as we moved west, but I'm sure from a distance they saw us and saw the eagle's feather the Chief had sent to be stuck in the band of my hat when we parted.

The Trail of Tears

I heard the door close gently behind where I sat as my young visitor departed. My son, having just said good-bye, left to continue his return trip to the Indian territory of Oklahoma. He was in his last year in law school and spoke enthusiastically about what he believed the future held. At my age of 73, I wondered what potential the year 1871 had in store for him as well as for his people. We had a good visit and I felt proud and pleased that he had accepted opportunity provided to attend law school and that he was doing so well with his studies. With the Civil War ended I felt sure the surge of settlers to the west would not be without problems for his native American brothers.

Reaching for my cane, I rose from my chair and hobbled to the window just in time to see my young protege, my adopted Cherokee son, hail a carriage and climb in. He looked up toward my window and waved just before he disappeared inside. There was snow on the ground, a wet heavy snow and I observed the thin tracks of the carriage wheels as it moved over the cobbled pavement on down the street. The snow and the tracks reminded me of a time long ago.

It was when he was born. His parents had somehow slipped away from the long column of the Cherokee as they traveled west. A trooper had been dispatched to find them and bring them back. He found them in a barn, and in the process of capture, the father was killed. The mother, having given birth without proper assistance and attention, was slowly bleeding and freezing to death. She died quickly.

The trooper reported to me that no further concern was needed. Unsatisfied, I followed his tracks in the snow, found the barn, the lifeless parents and a bewildered old farmer and his wife. They had been aroused by the noise of a scuffle and had cautiously approached the barn to investigate. They found the crying baby. Uncertain on what to do other than care for him, I was able to persuade them to care for the child until I could return. It was then that I fully realized the tragic injustice that was being committed. My life was changed!

I did return within the year. I located the infant, thanked and compensated the couple who had cared for him. I entered the legal profession seeking to determine the justice in what had been done. The government, I found, has problems treating all human beings as equals. In time, with the help of a young woman, I was able to complete my preparation for the law and later to see my young man through school and into law school. It hadn't been easy.

Back in my chair I thought over our conversation of days past; matters that related to his Cherokee ancestry, their history, as well as my own shortcomings as a person during, for them, a tragic period. It is both strange and amazing how in memory events just days ago are less clear to our minds than those that happened many years long passed. I closed my eyes and let my mind drift back to that dreadful and trying time in my personal life. There had been snow on the ground then and tracks, endless tracks. They were tracks I will never forget.

For years following my discharge from the military in 1839 I had sought a truth that hung over me like a dark cloud. Like the pages of a water-soaked book, I have since then gradually peeled back each soggy page to add to my information and understanding, yet, also to my pain; pain that should be more than only my own.

I had been only sixteen at the time I joined the military and in 1814 served General Andrew Jackson. I fought in the battle of Horseshoe Bend in March of that same year. It was a battle on a bend in the Tallapoosa River that runs through Georgia and Alabama. The fight was against the Creek Indians. Jackson was loved by his troops as Old Hickory and there was not a man who would not have died for him. It was not a major battle as conflicts go, but it was the participation of some 500 Cherokee Indian allies that turned the tide in our behalf and saved our command. Even to historians the details of the battle have long been dimmed, but not so for me. Young, hardly dry behind the ears, at the time it was an event that came into sharper focus for me 16 years later when I was bucking for a commission as Captain in a cavalry regiment.

In 1830, then President Jackson the politician, no longer the General I'd known as a fighter, unbelievably signed the Indian Removal Act. For many years a public attitude had persisted among white immigrants from abroad, supported even by our government as early as 1802, sanctioning the removal of Indians from their native lands. The attitude for removal evolved further as a consequence of discovery of gold in Georgia and the continuing encroachment by whites in their unquenchable thirst for expansion. Since my discharge from the military I have over time learned that Senators Daniel Webster and Henry Clay spoke out vigorously against removal and also a Reverend Samuel Worcester. He was a missionary to the Cherokee and carried his objections to the Georgia Supreme Court in 1831. I sat in that courtroom and was crushed when the verdict was read. Unfortunately, he lost his case to the State of Georgia. Powerful public interests had exercised their influence. It was as coldly simple as that! So it was that the Cherokee Nation vs Georgia became a major decision relative to all issues of Indian sovereignty.

In 1832, however, in the case between missionary Worcester vs Georgia, the courts properly affirmed Cherokee sovereignty. It was a decision that President Jackson, I say again, unbelievably, in an act of outright defiance of the court, established the government's precedent for the removal of many Indians from their ancestral lands.

With receipt of the Captain's commission I had sought, along with a command, I found myself a part of a 7,000 man force that would escort some 17,000 Cherokee men, women and children west for resettlement in the Oklahoma territory. I dutifully carried out my orders as part of my command. My decision to leave the military followed that heart rending experience.

Before the year was out I returned to the gathering of the reestablished Cherokee territorial nation as they sought recovery of some of the lands taken from them. What I had experienced then was beyond belief, as hunger, death and soldiers with bayonets, prodded the defrauded Cherokee from their lands to cross five States to a land they did not know. What brought me back to Fort Gibson, to Tahlequah, their new capital, was the moral anguish I suffered, the pain of not doing more in their behalf at the time.

When I arrived in Oklahoma in the fall of '39 I recall that the ground was hard and again covered with snow. I was met by a tall dark eyed lad and shown into a long pole framed structure. It was crowded, members of the council sitting along each side. The meeting place was a far cry from what earlier had been one of the nation's most prosperous and progressive tribes in the U.S. I have learned of large plantations and the holding of numerous slaves to work them to be not uncommon. Theirs was, as a nation within our growing nation, a republican form of government, with schools, churches and an alphabet of their own.

The young Indian led me to a place where I could see and hear. He stood beside me and whispered in English that I had arrived just in time to hear the old Chief of the whole Cherokee Nation speak to the gathered elders. He translated in my behalf as things progressed. When the Chief stood to speak, the room fell silent. He stood proud and straight, though his hair was gray and his sharp features greatly creased by weather and the passage of time. It was a whole minute before he spoke. He spoke slowly and I remember so clearly what he said.

"I am weary and my heart is heavy. Our journey has been a long one and with little understanding. As a youth in the forested hillside of Georgia, I saw the white man come and fight his war of Revolution and felt even then the pressure of the white expansion. Their ways have not been our ways, for they burrowed into the mother earth for the metal they call gold, and when they found it, their words became forked with hidden meaning." He paused.

A murmur ran through the gathered elders. They knew as I did too, that the Congress of the white man in the Treaty of Echota, signed in 1835, had ceded 7,000,000 acres of land to the white man under fraudulent reasoning that the Cherokee could occupy the land but never own it. For a nation of people organized into a democratically tribal state with representation and an economy based on farming corn, squash and beans, there was little possibility that the waves of new settlers would be inclined to share. I sat, ashamed as the old chief spoke again, his words like the straight shaft of an arrow stabbing where my pain was greatest. In my mind I can hear so clearly his every word. This, too, is what he said as he continued.

"It was our former friend for whom our warriors fought and died, President Andrew Jackson, who later as President and great white father to all the people of his nation, defied the decision of the courts and extinguished our sovereignty. It was his word and his orders that began our removal in the summer and autumn of 1838 to this new territory. It was his deed that defied the white man's own laws that placed our people on that trail of tears, costing the seven clans of the Southern Allegheny and Great Smokey Mountains some 4,000 painful deaths; freezing cold."

The old Chief's voice faltered to a whisper and he steadied himself by the small table beside him. There was a lump in my throat as I recalled that dreadful march; the weather gradually turning bitter cold and the driving snow that followed. As an eager young Captain I was not then fully aware of the infamy that I was implementing on my fellow man, but I was certain a great wrong was in the making. I clearly remember the problems with food supply and the hunger that led to starvation of so many. Yes, I was a part of it and so few escaped from us along the trail.

Looking back, as I have so many times since, I should have been a help to those who opposed the march. I should have stood for what was right and just. Once again as I sat comfortably in my chair my thoughts returned across the years and miles to that cold day in the lodge of the elders as the old Chief began to speak again. His voice was filled with deep emotion that I, too, felt then and even now in behalf of his people. I could barely hear his words.

"We are gathered this July to adopt our new constitution. We are a peaceful people and will rebuild and educate our nation's young on the same democratic principles of the Great Law of Peace of the Iroquois Confederacy, so long ago admired and drawn from by Thomas Jefferson (see below *)for his new nation. It is you who will begin the rebuilding of our government, our businesses, our schools, for as a people these things are not new to us. The fires within me have burned low but as an older nation our spirit of survival will persevere."

At this point the lodge was again silent as the old Chief stepped aside. Without comment he knew his time had come. Others then came forward to further the workings of their council.

It is strange how we remember such things in clear detail. I rose once more from my chair and moved to my window to look down. The tracks in the snow had been covered over, yet I knew my son would carry on where I'd left off. His was an undaunted challenge to make right a great wrong for his people as well as for me, for again Cherokee rights and land as a consequence of their persuasion to the side of the Confederacy was now being denied. I knew the young man would give answers that fit his native experience. If we as a Nation are to survive and be respected in the world, as today our expansion sweeps westward, surely the opportunity to be just must be raised. I admired his optimism but am barely hopeful about the future.

---

* "ACT of UNION, JULY 12, 1839

WHEREAS our Fathers have existed, as a separate and distinct Nation in the possession and exercise of the essential attribute . . . of sovereignty, from a period extending to antiquity, beyond the record and memory of man.

AND WHEREAS these attributes, with all the rights and franchises . . . remain still in full force and virtue . . . it has become essential to the general welfare that a union be formed, and a system of government matured, adapted to (our) present condition, and providing equally for the protection of each individual in the enjoyment of his rights.

THEREFORE WE, the people composing the Eastern and Western Cherokee, in the National Convention assembled . . . do herby solemnly and mutually agree to form ourselves into one body politic under the style and title of Cherokee Nation."

Sadly, it was Mr. Van Buren, who as President at the time, did not recognize their new nation.

Where the Heart Is

As the wagons rolled west day after day, the land before us changed. It had been flat and wide open for days after passing beyond Lincoln. Now it was beginning to roll and there were mountains in the distance, big sharp pointed ones, blue, and not at all like the worn off hilltops of New England.

Our guide, Mr. Marshall, knew right where our group was going and had been there before. He described it as a wide valley with several small streams, lots of aspen, tall pines and places where rock jutted right up out of the earth. After a long day, sun-up to dark, takin' turns walkin' with my sister, ridin' the mare, Mr. Marshall would circle the wagons. Then when chores were done, water and firewood gathered, folks would collect 'round a big fire in the center.

Sometimes an old fella in the Johnson wagon would play a fiddle, but mostly we'd sit relaxin', telling stories or talkin' 'bout what our new homes was going to be like.

Our family had moved a lot during my fifteen years, so we'd more or less gotten used to the shiftin' and makin'-do with new places. That never bothered me none. I see it this way.

Over a lifetime of places there is only one place that holds any deep rooted attachments for me. It is in feelin's, not a place at all, but all the places known by me that have been called home. Physical things in life can be bought and sold, can grow, can change, wear out, or be destroyed. But home to me is different.

Home is a constant because of the people, family, love, trust, concern, workin' together and sharin'.

I carry images of activities undertaken individually or collectively, shared secrets, of happiness, teasing, tears, work and conflict. I carry images of illness, grief and funny things that have happened amongst our family. They are of warmth and caring, tenderness and support.

My attachments include the smell of good food in preparation; the Thanksgiving turkey, chocolate cake fresh out of the oven, sticky buns laden with warm brown sugar; of cut flowers picked after a spring rain and carefully arranged on the family table; of fresh mown hay with a rich smell all its own. I easily recall the fall when leaves were burned or the smell of maple syrup fresh out of the big tins. I can smell apple logs burnin' in the fireplace, offering the added visual delight of copper sulphate's flickerin' blue patterns amongst the logs.

I can close my eyes and feel the excitement of a kiss on cold cheeks fresh in from a winter snowstorm. I can hear the stampin' of snow-covered boots in the little room off the kitchen after slidin' on a hill or diggin' out. There is a peaceful silent sense of isolation when too much snow has buried all the roads and trails, and we are snug inside the house before a cracklin' fire.

Garden rows, freshly cultivated; beds weeded or finished labor in the fields; laid wall, dry of mortar, true and sound. These are images that carry beyond their locations. New curtains, slip covers, a pretty dress, cut, sewn and modeled, hold stories of their own, as does the long ago struggle of homework, chores and thank-you notes after Christmas.

Memories of games, of laughter, a shaggy dog

who wanted to lick, but was taught otherwise. "Tippy" tried so hard to be a person. These memories too, are part of the pictures I call home.

Home is where the family is. No matter where it is or where it has been, home is the place of encouragement, council, and supportive guidance, love expressed. Yep! I look to those blue mountains ahead with anticipation. For me, geography is not involved at all, but home is without question a very real place.

Mountain Man

War changes people. Not only the men who do the fighting, but everybody it touches, young or old. David Bigelow lived on one of the big plantations outside of Wilmington in North Carolina. At that time, he had just reached the age of fourteen. Home had been a lovely old two story plantation house with tall Corinthian columns, gardens and great oaks that spread their huge branches over a curving driveway.

Off beyond the main house there were other buildings where slaves made their quarters or things were stored that were necessary to the working of the cotton fields that stretched off in the distance toward the Cape Fear River. It was a gracious way of life that for the whole south came to a tragic end. Davey, as he was called, saw it all burned, totally destroyed and the bewildered slaves told they were free. Blue clad troops seemed to be all over. With his younger sister and a big black man named Sam, the three had had to run as hard and fast as they could to the edge of the river bank to escape.

There, still fearing pursuit by troops out of control, they huddled together in the bushes on into the night. In the distance they could see the flames of their home rising spectacularly into the night sky. They hoped their mother, who had gone into the city, was safe at Aunt Caroline's. It was a frightening time.

"If papa were here, they wouldn't have gotten away with that," insisted little Mary Beth.

"Hush, chile," whispered Sam.

Pollen in the Wind

"I don't know, Mary Beth. There are so many." Davey put his arm around her shivering body.

It was January 20th, 1865 and with the fall of Fort Fisher, just days before, the Army of the North under the command of Brigadier General Terry and supported by the warships of Admiral David Dixon Porter off the coast, accomplished control of the entrance to the Cape Fear River. For too long it had been the water avenue to the important Confederate port city of Wilmington. Control of the surrounding area had followed, causing country wide devastation and the burning of the Bigelow plantation along with many others.

When daylight came with the cold damp mist of the river, all three lay shivering, cold and hungry.

"The road to your Aunt's home is that way," said Sam, pointing as well as suggesting they leave their mosquito ridden hiding place.

"You think it's safe, Sam?"

"Yasuh, Master Davey. At least we's best leave here. Little Mary Beth is all bit up an shiverin'."

So it was that the three cautiously started out, scooting into hiding at any sign of blue uniformed troops moving about. At the edge of town they waited until dark before approaching closer. They were finally able to get to Aunt Caroline's house and she was there. She was glad to have them safe with her, but worried about their mother. She had gone to the fort. Aunt Caroline quickly fed them and put Mary Beth to bed where it was warm. Sam was a big help and was generously appreciated. When thanked he asked several times what it meant to be free, a question waiting for a better answer than Aunt Caroline's.

In the morning, with the bombardment of the huge fortifications over, Davey insisted that he, too, was going to the Fort to find his parents. Sam went with him, fearful of what they might find. Originally garrisoned by only five hundred men when Major Butler initiated his first attack, Mr. Bigelow, already a wounded veteran from battles further north, had responded to the call. Davey's father was in a group of nineteen hundred men that had gone and like so many at the battle's end would be listed amongst the casualties. Some women, including Mrs. Bigelow, had also gone to help with the wounded. With the battle over, the interior of the fort, from the vicious hand to hand fighting, was a blood chilling horror.

The shelling from the ships off the coast had caused horrendous wreckage. It was there in the shattered rubble that Sam found both of the parents in a tangle of twisted bodies. He tried to prevent Davey from seeing the frightful sight but was unable. There was nothing they could do.

Defeated, angry and bitter, Davey stopped off only briefly at Aunt Caroline's to say he was going south to join General George Picket guarding a vital crossroads at Five Forks. As he prepared to leave, Sam handed him a tattered little volume that had been for him a clandestine step toward learning to read. It was his Bible.

At first Davey hesitated but the look in Sam's eyes caused him to change his mind. He seemed sure Davey would find meaning in its worn pages. Aunt Caroline wept and promised to take care of little Mary Beth. So off he went. At this point in the retreating Confederate forces nobody questioned his age if he could properly handle a weapon.

At Five Forks, Picket was taken by surprise by the attacking Major General Philip Sheridan whose forces inflicted staggering losses against the defenders. For the Confederate forces, their fate was then sealed and the war came to an end April 9th at a place called Appomattox Court House. Davey was relieved it was all over. Though brief, for a fourteen year old , it had been a devastating walk through the valley of the shadow of death; too much for a young lad. He wanted to be away from the horror as well as the error of the whole conflict.

He was glad that Sam would be free, but to him he'd never fulfilled the northern image of what a slave was; he was Sam, one of their collective family. Sadly, not so for all. Davey could not face returning to Wilmington and his very personal losses there. If he were absent, he felt sure that Aunt Caroline would look after Mary Beth. He wanted to run away, to go west, to somewhere find solace and inner peace from the experiences that he feared would shape his life from that point forward. Someday he might return.

By the age of twenty-three he had traveled most of the way across the expanding nation all the way to the Rockies, with their huge rugged mountains rising in stately emptiness. There he traveled alone through the mountains seeking in their solitude and silent trails some meaning, some restoration from the horror of his early years. He hoped that one day when the ashes of his fire were cold that his haunting memories and loneliness would somehow end. He wanted nothing more.

As it happened, in time he came to reach less often into the shadows of his brief war experience and for that he was thankful. There, high in the mountains of western Colorado he made a home. Tucked neatly on the high point of a ridge and shaped amongst a tumble of huge boulders, David Bigelow, like a weary soul on a quest, found peace.

He learned how to survive and in time, from his secluded hideout, he would take a staff and venture forth to man trap lines, resetting sprung traps and snares. He would collect his catch and retrace his steps to his carefully concealed refuge. After a time there was one such day that he noticed an animal following in his footsteps, always just barely out of sight. It was not the first time he had suspected something was following him at a distance. Some days he would cover twenty miles or more, seeing no one, passing no one, feeling comforted by the hills.

And not far behind would be that solitary animal at a safe distance. Yes, he believed it was limping.

At home he would skin the game he'd caught, carefully preserving the edible parts and working the furs to a soft pliable condition for later trading.

Another day he would spend putting his quarters in good order, cleaning, repairing, ever improving. With mallet and froe he shaped shingles for his roof and in to the roof he'd gone even further. One day, frustrated by the darkness inside while the sun outside was so bright, he cut a square hole and made a lid that fit down over the hole's surrounding curbing. By lifting it off with a long pole he could let the sunshine pour in and he could see the blue sky above. He liked that! The side walls of his home were rough plank that he had hewn from tall pine well below his rocky promontory. Against the exterior surface of the plank he'd secured into place for walls, he piled up stone for concealment. Brush and native vines added further to disguise the obvious, though he yearly had to cut them back at his two small window openings.

Inside was divided into an area for food preparation where the bladder of a large animal provided a reservoir for water. There were antlers overhead that held a few pots and cooking utensils and dried herbs. Below the rack he built a work counter in which were stored containers of sun dried berries and strips of jerky. Adjacent this area and facing into the central space was a fireplace, carefully built of smaller stones mudded together. At the side of the fireplace opening he fashioned a crane from the metal rim of an abandoned wagon wheel that he had scavenged and hammered into its new shape. Many of his tools had been found at sites of other wagon breakdowns or disasters. He wasted little of what he came across.

Off in the end in a small alcove formed by the huge boulders, he built a place for sleeping, its surface softened by quantities of furs that he had gradually accumulated from his hunting. Above this sleeping area was a shelf and there neatly placed were his treasures, a collection of a few books, the well thumbed Bible that Sam had so generously given him back in Wilmington, The Rise and Fall of the Roman Empire and a tattered Oxford Book of English Verse. Each year when he'd trekked north to Jackson Hole for the annual round-up, he'd return home with a few coins gained by exchanging furs.

Over the years his furs became recognized as some of the best, so there was always a ready market as word had been passed around. The coins he saved, hoping to find other books for his shelf that he could purchase.

Not far from his retreat Davey created a small garden plot where the soil was rich and with a small spring and still waters near by. There he grew corn, potatoes and typically root plants that would keep over the winter in the earthen pit in the kitchen area. He'd brought a few wild strawberries to his patch but they had not done well with the altitude or the winters of the high country. Picking berries in the valley in season and sun cooking them, as had been done back home for jam, had been a better answer.

Around the perimeter of his garden Davey created a stockade of brambles hoping his efforts would not be found by either man nor beast. So far from any settlement, he'd had little to fear. Someone would have had to be lost or searching to have come this way.

Davey had added other conveniences to his home and in the process of daily living had come to a fairly regular schedule of activity with whole days set aside for attendance to specific chores. And out of each day he set aside time to read or sketch the wildlife that he observed or came to his area, curious about his intrusion. He traveled the mountains, occasionally meeting others, sometimes assisting, many times avoiding contact with passers by, and almost always, that strange limping animal that followed. He knew the Indians who seasonally established their village camps along the streams down in the valley, and he learned their ways and tongue. Sometimes they would speak together of the endless streams of people coming into the area and together share their concerns as to what it all meant for their way of life, his own included.

Only once in a great while would Davey venture into a settled area or town. He would take with him his findings from mountain streams, small attractive stones, a nugget or two that he recognized to be gold. They were enough to barter for salt and a few supplies he could not otherwise obtain.

One time he added a book to his shelf of treasures, a dictionary. Sometimes, too, his trading had been with the Indians from whom he had already learned so much.

In town people would look at him, a big husky,

Pollen in the Wind

fierce looking fellow dressed in skins, leather leggings and moccasins, a string of animal teeth around his neck and wearing a wide brimmed hat and feather. At his waist he wore a knife, carried in a beaded sheath. At his hip he carried a small pouch for shells for the Sharp's rifle he used for hunting. He didn't mind their staring but typically made short his visits. Seeing people dressed in their store-bought clothes only brought back memories of a way of life he'd left behind and what their ways, at least to him, had led to. He long ago had considered it a way of life he would not return to, though at such times in town, he did think of little Mary Beth and Aunt Caroline. His sister would be a grown young lady by now.

One time when he saw a little girl he was so strongly reminded of Mary Beth that he asked her name.

"My name is Jenny and my mommy is . . ." the end of her reply cut off by a hand that grabbed her and pulled her away. Another time a sheriff strolled a short distance behind him, visibly assuring the town that their safety was not in jeopardy.

In one town where he ventured to visit for supplies, he ran into a rowdy pair of blue uniformed horse soldiers. They were badgering an old fellow who wore a gray jacket, obviously a keepsake from the days of the confederacy.

On December 8th of 1862 President Lincoln had long ago issued a Proclamation of Amnesty and Reconstruction that restored full rights to any Confederate who took an oath of allegiance to the Federal government. Following that in his second inaugural address on March 4th of '85 he had reaffirmed his commitment to a peaceful reconciliation . . . "with malice toward none; with charity to all . . ."

It was sad to see the two bluecoats and it became an occasion that brought Davey to a point where he lost control. He grabbed one of the fellows by the uniform collar and threw him bodily into a nearby horse trough. The other started to loosen the flap of his holstered pistol and received a quick kick that sent the weapon flying. Fortunately, before the two could recover and redress their assailant, a young lieutenant appeared and ordered a hasty retreat. He obviously recognized that even the three of them were both out of order as well as physically outnumbered. The clerk at the hardware store that Davey entered didn't linger to visit as he did with other customers.

It was only the girls above the street level that leaned over the porch railing on the second floor of the saloon who attempted conversation. Davey would smile and nod to them in return but without changing his stride. Lust was not in his make up.

He did get his hair cut and trimmed each spring, revealing a pleasant face beneath and providing the tonsorial artist a source of conversation that he would share for days. He would look back at his face in the looking glass and wonder what of his youth he was preserving against the encroaching years. He began to realize his thoughts more frequently turned to Mary Beth.

Generally, Davey was glad to step into and beyond the fluttering aspen at the fringe of town and be swallowed up by the pines as he worked his way upward into the hills and across the miles toward home. On one such day when he returned home he was met at his door by a gray wolf. He stood still and watched as the wolf limped toward him. Here was the shadowy figure that had for so long kept its distance and now limped cautiously toward him. He kneeled and held out a hand which the animal sniffed, then licked. Perhaps wounded at some time in the past, he had now found a friend. Perhaps they had found each other. Davey took him in and fed him and cared for him.

In time, tenderly, carefully, Davey re-broke the leg that caused the limp and set it right, allowing his companion to run. From that day forward, they lived and traveled together, he and Little Sam, as he called him.

Of all the things Davey pursued with diligence when home, were his books. Best of all he loved the poetry of Sam's tattered gift, in particular the Psalms. He tried each day to read something, or memorize, but most of all to understand. Here were stories of the struggles of people, the problems they had faced and through them all the foolishness of vain pursuit of power, of one man's efforts to control another.

What had the wars between the States accomplished or all the fighting and destruction that become the history of mankind? So many times when Davey had closed the pages of one of his treasured books, he weighed in his mind the choices mankind had made from the beginning of time. And he weighed his own. And in his thoughts he wondered if he had been the shepherd or had the real shepherd been Little Sam. Had other men like himself run away from past experiences? Because of what he'd read over the years he'd come to the realization that he was simply going through the motions of living, possessed by a wanderlust, an escape. Man was not intended to live alone. His reading had shown him that, and the solitude of the mountains had provided the peace he needed to see and find himself. And there was Little Sam who shared each day. He admitted finally that the solution was outside of himself.

Alone in the quiet of the mountains David Bigelow realized an inner hunger had finally caught up with him. He realized that what the shepherd does for his sheep is not unlike what man's Creator can do for his children. What had for years been none of his business he admitted had always been his business.

By now his Aunt Caroline might be gone and little Mary Beth just might need a big brother. Davey looked around his refuge; it had been so secure, so comfortable. Would other men who traveled these mountains alone find their souls restored as he had? He wondered. He put some treasures in a pack, took one last look and closed the door. With Little Sam at his heels, they headed east.

Snake Oil

It was about noon when the wagon rolled into town. It was a colorful rig, not large, but pulled by a beautiful team of well groomed coach horses. The driver was a middle aged man, rather well dressed, wearing a colorful vest, suit coat and a derby hat. He looked like he might be a professional man of some sort, or perhaps that was the impression he wanted to create. Supporting that thought, on the brightly painted side of the wagon was emblazoned in colorful bold letters his name and a brief commercial, "Doc Hadley and his Elixir to Health."

Beside Doc Hadley on the front seat sat a younger man, clean cut, dark curly hair, a rather handsome young fellow. He was neatly dressed and smiling as they arrived.

When the wagon rolled to a stop in front of the hardware store, he jumped nimbly to the ground to attend the horses and then proceeded to open a panel at the side of the wagon. It was somewhat larger than a window might be expected to be, appearing more like a diminutive stage.

By this time a number of shoppers had, out of sheer curiosity at this strange new arrival, gathered to see what was going to happen next. They didn't have long to wait. Doc Hadley had removed his coat and added an apron to his attire. He then moved into the wagon and appeared at the window.

"Greetings, my friends, greetings! As you can readily see by the announcement on the side of my conveyance, you are in the scholarly company of Doctor Alexander Groveland T. Hadley, MD, MMD, LBD, etcetera."

People looked at each other, some smiled, a few winked at friends, while others watched with a ho-hum expectancy. Doc Hadley went on.

"Coming from the higher academic laboratories of our more progressive, and advanced medical institutions of the east, I have invested my modest resources in an alexipharmic solution I have humbly named the Powerful Eleven. It is, in simple layman's terms an antidotal treatment for a wide variety of medicinal and physical incapacities."

Response was again mixed. Some seemed doubtful, others interested, but by and large still curious.

"Now before I go further I want to introduce the young man who is now assisting me in passing amongst your numbers with an informative little folder I had prepared for just such a responsive and intelligent assembly. Ah, I see your good sheriff has added his interest to our gathering. Good to have the judgment of the law nearby. Now why don't you come right up front here where I can keep an eye on you."

There was a moment of light laughter, a few turned to look. Doc's young man continued to circulate until he was motioned to the front. He turned and smiled at the growing crowd. No question, he was handsome! Doc took hold of his arm, raised it and asked, "Now just how old do you think this fellow is? His name is Jethro."

There were half a dozen answers, "twenty, twenty-six, thirty."

"Although astute as you are , all your observations are incorrect. He is actually fifty." He waited for the protestations to die down. "Fifty and as fit as a fiddle."

Pollen in the Wind

He paused again. "Now what we'd like to do is challenge any man in this fine audience, yes, even you sheriff, to engage in a brief pugilistic competition. I will reward any single individual the munificent sum of fifty dollars if he can stand against Jethro for one solitary minute. If, at the end of the minute he remains on his feet I will declare him to be the winner and generously reward him."

Now a murmur ran through the crowd and names were suggested by small clusters of the audience. Finally someone shouted, "Why, Doc, why a fist fight?"

"Ah, I'm glad you asked that question my good man. You see it's in this way that I can not only tell but show you all the marvelous consequences on my Powerful Eleven. I certainly will not share a proportional itemization of its medicinal ingredients, but rather that subscribing to a regular daily dosage by any one of you, you would look younger, be of better health and avail yourself greater strength than you can currently muster. A spoonful or two each day and by the end of a week you will feel the difference. Jethro here has been under my specific care now for hardly six months and with your own eyes you may judge his physical condition. I found him a physical derelict in New York's filthy bowery. Today, he is as you see him, slight of build, quick of eye and reflex and I would venture as strong or stronger than any man here."

Again there was a murmur that ran through the swelling crowd. The sheriff edged closer to make his own inspection of Jethro's arms, the look on his face reflecting substantial doubt.

"Doubt?" said Hadley. "Then let your champion step forward, let me have a taker. My reward stands, fifty silver dollars to the victor. Stand back my friends and form a ring and by all means select your man."

Now there was a response as several candidates were urged to the front and finally the number reduced to a single contestant. The ring was formed, a timer chosen and the sheriff asked to be the sole judge of the winner. Each man removed his shirt and stood facing each other. The crowd waited in anticipation. The fellow opposing Jethro was about the same height, broader shouldered and quite well built. The big fellow's name was Jake, and he worked in the blacksmith's shop down the street. He grinned and rippled the muscles of his arms and shoulders. The crowd fell silent as the sheriff nodded, signaling the timer to begin. There seemed little doubt as to who the winner was going to be.

Jake moved to the center of the makeshift ring, swung a few times at Jethro, missing each time as Jethro skillfully weaved and dodged and incidentally placing a quick hard jab against Jake's head. They circled and as Jethro backed away, Jake swung again, the blow glancing painlessly off Jethro's defending arm. This was repeated a time or two. Jake charged, his arms flailing the air and unable to land a solid blow. Then another blow by Jethro to Jake's stomach was followed by a lightning quick blow to the jaw. Jake blinked and backed off, dazed as Jethro followed up with another sharp punch to the head, two more fast jabs followed. Jethro advanced forcefully now and with a sharp punch to the chin, you could hear the crowd gasp. He truly was fast, very fast. One more swift punch landed on Jake's jaw. At that point Jake's knees gave way and in less than the limiting minute the contest was over.

Friends brought water from a nearby horse trough and when he regained consciousness Jethro stepped forward, his hand extended. He apologized if he caused Jake real harm. Still dazed, Jake took his hand.

"That was quick! Wow! He's half the weight of Jake. Never seen anything like it!" There was a whole chorus of admiration. "An he done it all fair," said others. "Man, what is that stuff he's been taking?"

By now it seemed as though the whole town had gathered. Doc Hadley thanked Jake who slipped away somewhat embarrassed as Doc offered a new challenge. There were no takers.

Jethro returned to passing out folders extolling the virtues of his health program and moving slowly through the crowd. It was then that Doctor Alexander Groveland T Hadley began his sales pitch.

"Aches and pains, no problem, rheumatism, chronic cough, persistent headaches, blurring of vision . . . " he went through a long litany of ailments including even the removal of warts. He further explained the limits of availability, since he'd so fortunately oversold at an earlier stop and would have to shortly return east for a new supply. So it was one to a customer! He was a real drummer.

During this entire time my ninety-one year old grandfather listened and smiled as people feverishly pushed forward with their money in their hands to make a purchase. Like so many others, we had been curious too. There were many in the audience, whose facial expressions continued to show doubt and made no effort to take out their change purse or wallet to make a purchase, or for that matter reveal where they pocketed their money. Had they reached for their wallets, they would have discovered that careful observation and nimble fingers had deftly relieved them of most of their resources and carefully returned it somewhat lighter.

It was about then that the Marshall from a nearby town worked his way forward through the crowd, spoke quickly to the local sheriff and turned to Doc Hadley and Jethro. The snake oil business was ended. The implied fifty year old boxer was actually twenty, a city trained pick pocket able to gather substantially more than the offered fifty dollar reward by working the crowd. It was a small iron bar in his fists, a concealed brass knuckle, that provided a powerful addition to his lightning fast jabs. The crowd, as word spread, was naturally furious.

Grandfather, lovingly put his hand on my shoulder as we walked away. He was chuckling aloud.

"The right attitude and right relationships, my boy, are better than any medicine," he said

As I look back, he's been right.

Miss Margaret's Chalkboard

Schools in western towns in the early days seemed to be located beyond the expanding activity of main street, which was usually a small unpainted collection of front buildings. Typically, the school in Iron Horse was a one room building about a mile east of the town. At twenty - six and her first teaching opportunity, Miss Margaret was still learning that there are not enough hours in a day.

She had been working on vocabulary and had decided that it was time to test all the grades with a list of words; how to spell them and what they meant. To her, words were like keys, keys to so many things worthwhile. The normal school day had just ended. The children had all galloped out of the school yard and she was concentrating on what she was doing. Evidently she didn't hear the door open behind her. It wasn't until a board in the floor about ten feet from her desk made a familiar squeak from somebody stepping on it. She turned from the chalkboard to see who had forgotten something and had returned.

Standing there between the benches was an Indian. He startled her, taking her completely by surprise. Trying to remain calm, she was determined not to show fear. Inside, at this moment, she was terrified.

This, however, was not her first experience with Indians. Years earlier, she had come west from Illinois with her family. Their wagon master had given a small war party some gifts in order that the wagons might have safe passage on one occasion and later, further on, the wagon train was actually attacked by others.

The white man's relations with Indians was having its difficulties. As she stood before this Indian in her classroom, trying desperately not to reveal her feelings; a flood of terrifying remembrances passed before her eyes; the pain and screams of people dying; flaming arrows that set fire to wagons and the few treasured belongings they carried. She could remember so clearly, as a little girl, being pushed under an overturned box by her father, while the fighting continued, until the sound of a bugle and arrival of help ended the attack. It was at that time that her folks had been killed. The Svensons, her adopted family, were very kind to her.

She stood now about as far from her desk as was the Indian. He stopped and was cautiously watching her. The drawer of Miss Margaret's desk contained a .44 that she knew very well how to use. She eased toward her desk and sat down. Her knees could not have held her up much longer. She was trembling, hopefully not visibly. Seated, the desk was now between them. Slowly, she moved her hand toward the desk drawer that held the gun. She didn't want to use it, but would if it became necessary.

There had been recent reports of Indian raids against other towns in South Dakota where people had been killed. Many people worried that Iron Horse would be next. Fort Wadsworth to the west was having its hands full with the efforts of Chief Red Cloud resisting construction of a wagon road. It was the Bozeman Trail into Montana and being built across Sioux lands. There had already been raids and skirmishes with people killed as a consequence.

Carefully watching each other, the Indian raised his open palm in a sign of peace. It was evident that he wasn't armed. Miss Margaret then raised her hand and said the word "Peace." He watched her lips shape the word , so she repeated it.

He moved his lips to shape the word. For several minutes they looked at each other. Gathering courage, Miss Margaret rose and returned to the chalkboard and pointed to one of the words she had written moments earlier. It was the word "Peace." When she turned back, the Indian had seated himself on one of the benches. The two continued to look at each other, both wondering what to do next.

This was a time of the year when the Indians normally migrated toward the mountains off to the north. Settlers from Minnesota and the east were continuing to force relocation of the Sioux westward before them as they came, so traditional migration had been disrupted. Miss Margaret guessed this man to be a Sioux or Oglala. He was full grown, middle aged, though it is difficult for one race to easily tell the age of another. Typically, his eyes were dark revealing little of what was going on behind them.

The Indian grunted a deep guttural sound and pointed to the chalkboard where Miss Margaret had just pointed. He slowly repeated the word "Peace." She almost smiled in relief, though she was not to be put off guard. She pointed to her upraised hand and said the word once more. From his reaction it was evident to her that he made the connection to the written word. His response was almost childlike. He stood up, raised his open palm and said "Peace" a number of times. Then he rushed toward her as she stood at the board.

"Oh, no!" she gasped. What had been a moment of communication and achievement suddenly became a moment of real panic. He had successfully maneuvered her away from her desk drawer and her only defense.

He came toward her grinning. When he raised his arm as if to strike, instead he pointed past her to another word on the chalkboard. Miss Margaret gasped for breath and turned to look.

The word was "music." She momentarily closed her eyes in prayerful relief and tried to smile. Before she said the word she pointed to the row of benches and motioned him to sit down. He looked at her for a moment uncertain of a woman's authority over a man, but he did seat himself. She went to her desk, only briefly considering the gun it contained. Instead, she took out her pitch pipe and blew a note before she said the word. He smiled childishly as he repeated it. Together they hesitantly tried other words. For "horse" she had to draw a picture that again he smiled at and for the word "teacher" she pointed to herself and said "teacher", then "Margaret." By trial and error she learned that his name was Agakota. He seemed pleased when she addressed him by name.

The word games continued for some time as they traded words in each other's language. Margaret wrote several of his words on the chalkboard much to his amusement, seeing how the sounds in his language were translated into English. She turned to the chalkboard to add another word to their growing list and when she turned back, the room was empty.

Miss Margaret put aside her chalk and suddenly realized she was exhausted. She sank into her chair for a moment feeling both exhilarated and drained. If only all students were as eager to learn. Inspite of her fear now and the frightful loss of her parents, she realized she was not filled with hate. Her new experience was proving to be a one person to one and exciting. In her mind she began to imagine the possibilities of the boys in her classroom actually playing games or competing with the boys in Agakota's village. What a learning experience they each would have. Could such a reality be possible? Her mind filled with such thoughts, she gathered her cloak, and turned the key in the door. With her tongue curled against her front teeth, she whistled the way her father had taught her. "Mrs. Lincoln" whinnied in response from a small grove of aspen where the children and Margaret picketed their horses while school was in session. There was no sign anywhere of Agakota.

At home, as she helped Mother Svensen put supper on the table, her thoughts returned to the surprise experience at school. She wasn't sure if she should speak about the incident. The Svensens themselves had lost a child in an Indian raid and though the family read the Bible daily, Mr. Svensen's memory was stronger. She wondered what other districts were doing, if they were doing anything at all. Mr. Svensen's attitude was no different than that of others in many small communities. Mr. Svensen had already expressed concern about prevailing Indian problems. Uncertain, she decided to say nothing for the time being. The evening passed quietly with no more serious questions than those about one boy or another, how they were progressing and so on. Sleep came easily when the oil lamp was finally turned down and Mr. Svensen's chores in the barn were completed. Iron Horse was not a large town and the major efforts of the settlers were wheat and other small grains in the open lands beyond the town itself. There were a few outlying ranches, but no great herds as there were to the south and further west. Svensen and their three boys, who were out of school, worked about two hundred acres, all of it in crops.

Bright and early the next morning, Mrs. Lincoln

and Margaret rode off for school, hoping to get there well ahead of any others. When she arrived, there were already two horses picketed in the grove. The McNally boys, Kent, ten , and Cameron, eleven, were already at the door step. Kent had a question.

"Did you say yesterday that we were going to have a word test today, Miss Margaret?"

"Well, yes, I did, Kent. Do you think you can handle that?"

"See, I told you so, dummy!" He shoved Cameron out of the way so she could unlock the door. They all entered. Miss Margaret had pulled down the wall map to cover the words on the chalkboard so immediately every effort was made to peek around it to view the list of test words. Off to the side there remained a few Indian words that she had forgotten to erase. She quickly realized she should have done so earlier, so proceeded to do so. It was Kent who noticed and asked about them.

"Are those going to be words we're expected to know?"

"No, Kent, that was something I was doing after you all left school yesterday. You won't be asked to know them." She realized immediately that that wasn't going to be the end of the questions. Fortunately, the Olson Boys burst in the door and asked if there was time enough to play some ball before school. Miss Margaret said there was and sat down to organize her thoughts. She really wanted to share her experience, but as with Mr. Svensen, wasn't sure what the reaction might be. There were people in town who felt pretty edgy over the whole matter of Indians. Tempers had already flared when towns just north had a group pass close by and the Fort had refused to intervene. She decided to face whatever came and do so as naturally as possible. As anticipated, it happened just before recess, after the word test was over and their initial anxiety had passed.

"What were those words on the chalkboard that Kent saw, Miss Margaret?"

"Well, Geena, they were Indian words or at least the phonetic sound of Indian words."

"What did they say?"

"You mean, what did they mean?"

"Yes, ma'am."

"Yesterday, I had a visitor, after all of you had gone home. He was an Indian. His name was Agakota. Yes, he really was an Indian and wanted to learn a few words in our language."

"Will he come back again today?"

"I don't really know, Jerry."

That was the end of questions and the rest of the day went along according to her lesson plan. First and second graders sat in a circle and they read together while the next two grades worked at their numbers on their slates. The rest of the grades practiced their writing skills. Of the eighteen students there were only a few beyond the fifth grade. Work on the farms took them away too early. They were all well behaved young people and it was a privilege, she felt, to be their teacher. When it came time to go home the classroom emptied with its usual urgency. She sat down to think through plans for the next day. In the back of her mind she had also been asking herself the same question Jerry had asked. As it turned out, she was disappointed. The two McNally boys had hidden out beyond the aspen grove, waiting to see if Agakota would return. Even the next two days passed with no comment of her after school visitor.

On Friday, she worked a little later than usual and

typically was working at the chalkboard when the loose board in the floor groaned slightly. She turned to face not Agakota, but Agakota and two others. All three held up their hands and spoke.

"Peace, Miss Margaret."

For an hour on Friday and the following Tuesday and Wednesday the same three appeared. On Thursday there was a fourth. It was exciting for all of them to so eagerly trade words and actually begin to form sentences. They were all such attentive students and did not seem to require words to be written down to take with them. Each night Margaret took home her own workbook, being careful not to say anything or let it be known what had been occurring. Unfortunately, the younger Svensen had heard of Agakota's earlier visit and asked if he had ever come back. It was an innocent question, yet her answer did not actually avoid the truth.

"Wouldn't it be something if we could speak each other's language?" she replied.

Mr. Svensen mumbled, "I've had all the Indian I ever vant and da sooner vee move dem on a reservation the better off vee'l all be. You surprise me Margaret." He stuffed a biscuit in his mouth and glared at her. "Make friends mit dem und vun day find yourself surprised they did so for a reason. Ve'll all vind up mit our hair dangling from da end of a spear . . . dammed savages!"

Margaret didn't reply, but busied herself with the food on her plate. When she looked up, he was still glaring at her, even through her. He didn't speak of the matter further, though Margaret was sure that was not to be the last of it. She was not so sure what to do and gave the whole matter a great deal of serious thought to arrive at a decision. Fortunately, no one else asked her any more questions. Mr. Svensen usually had the last word and his message had been clear enough.

Monday was rainy and cold all day. Miss Margaret's Indians did not show up, nor did they for the balance of the week. It was quite a let-down after the days they'd had. She tried to dismiss the matter and was glad none of the students asked further questions.

During the next two weeks and part of the following, Margaret's Indian friends did show up. All of them had practiced their words and could pronounce them, still without anything written down. She was quietly delighted. Together they began to distinguish between words, identifying subject and object words; nouns. Next came action words; the verbs. Agakota liked acting out the new words, like run, stand, sit and speak. They, in fact, began to communicate with each other. The process became a thrilling experience.

On into the fall of 1867 Margaret continued to enjoy her students, each learning from the other. Agakota had said, "We need learn talk each other," and Margaret agreed. Before long, as they continued meeting, they were able to carry out simple conversations and from these Margaret came to recognize that Indians were not all the same. Their word, honesty, seemed to be very important to them. Their Creator was very real to them and many places were considered sacred. They did not like the white man crossing sacred grounds. They did not appreciate the killing of so many buffalo. Their anger was not without Margaret's understanding. "Why kill all buffalo?" was a question Margaret could not answer. At one point her visitors began to ask her questions about the Great White Father, Ulysses S. Grant in Washington. In turn, at home, she had many questions that she tried to explore at the supper table. She tried not to raise suspicions, but in time Mr. Svensen began to give her questioning looks or too short answers, none that cast the Indians in a favorable light. His mind was too firmly fixed to allow change. She wondered if he suspected anything. He must have!

On Friday morning as Miss Margaret excitedly prepared for the day ahead, earlier than her usual school time, she was visited by four men of the Town Council. Their faces betrayed their intent.

"Miss Margaret, we want what you are doing to stop! We are aware that you have been entertaining savages here in a public building and that is not what you are paid to do. You must be aware that there have been terrifying raids against several surrounding towns and people were scalped and tortured."

"Mr. Prince, I am aware of what has occurred in other towns and just wonder if the reason we have not suffered is because we have treated the Indians as people. They are certainly fine students . . ." They didn't let her finish.

"We have told you what we expect of you and that is the end of it."

With that said, and no opportunity to discuss the issue, Margaret sat down at her desk. The Town's representatives filed out the door and wide-eyed students filed in. The day turned out to be a disaster from beginning to end. She was relieved when the school day was finally over, but also nervous about the possibility her Indian students might arrive. The McNally boys and two Olsons attempted to conceal themselves in the aspen grove to await their arrival. For some reason her Indian students did not show up. Perhaps they were aware there were boys hiding nearby. When Margaret arrived home, Mr. Svensen was more pleasant and talkative than usual. He finally asked at the dinner table if there had been visitors. She admitted that there had been visitors.

"And vwat do you propose to do?"

"Now, Judd, let the poor girl eat her dinner. She looks wore out." Mrs. Svensen hustled the boys to the table and sat down. "She'll tell us about it when she's ready."

"Thank you ma'am," was all Margaret could say, much relieved for her intervention. She had no answer for her family and was not sure also if she could make herself understood to Agakota and his friends. Nobody was surprised when she slipped off to bed earlier than usual. She dreaded the arrival of Monday. Unbeknown to her, Monday was going to be quite different than she could have imagined.

The day began normally and her small reading group was hesitatingly sounding out words from a new storybook. The older boys in the back of the room were solving some subtraction problems and working multiplication tables. About ten thirty, a horse, traveling at a very fast pace, raced into the school yard. The rider made no effort to tie him, but simply jumped off and burst through the door.

"Indians . . . the Indians . . ." he shouted, out of breath. "They have taken over Mr. Anderson's store and are holding people inside. They shot at several men who tried to go in after them. The town is preparing for an attack!"

The classroom was immediately a confusion of children, some screaming, all questioning, all frightened that somehow they would be involved. It took several minutes to quiet them down enough for them to listen.

"You've got to come, Miss Margaret. I was sent to get you." The man's face was filled with his fear.

"You've got to come, now!"

"Wait, let's start at the beginning. Who sent you? And what am I expected to do?" Margaret needed to know a lot more before she was ready to leave a schoolhouse full of young children. Could this whole business with Agakota be a trick as Mr. Svensen had suggested? "You're Mr. Haskel, Billy's pa, aren't you?"

"Yes, ma'am, now please come."

"And who sent you? Let's have first things first."

"Mr. Prince sent me." Mr. Haskel nervously fidgeted with his broad brimmed hat and shifted from one foot to the other. "A whole band of Indians sneaked into town and into Mr. Anderson's store. Nobody really knows how many or why. But they won't leave and they're holding Mr. Anderson and several customers prisoner. We have the store surrounded . . . the whole town is up in arms." Mr. Haskel continued with a few more details, obviously anxious to get moving.

"Kent, will you bring Mrs. Lincoln to the front of the school, please." Sick inside, Margaret turned to Mr. Haskel. "Are you armed?"

"Yes, ma'am, this Colt and the rifle in my saddle boot outside. And you'd better be armed too!"

"Cameron, will you get Mr. Haskel's rifle, please." She went to her desk , removed the .44, spun the cylinder to make sure it was fully loaded and handed it to Charlie Burns. She was quite sure he knew how to use a pistol and was looked up to by the other boys. "Now, Charlie, I want you to stay by that window there and watch the aspen grove. You know what we are looking for, but don't shoot unless you are fired on . . . do not! . . . unless you are fired on," she repeated. "Do you understand?"

"Yes, ma'am, I sure do." His eyes were wide with excitement. "If those dammed Indians come here, we'll

Pollen in the Wind

sure take care of 'em."

"You do just as I've said, Charlie. Mr. Haskel will be on the other side of the room and when Kent returns, he'll be at the front door. I can't believe the school and you children will be attacked, but if I'm wrong, you'll be ready."

All this time, Margaret tried in her mind to find an answer to her question, "Why me?"

Mr. Haskel had an uncertain look on his face and started to speak. Kent ran through the front door and ran smack into him.

"Now, just where in town will I find Mr. Prince?"

A minute later, Margaret ,on Mrs. Lincoln, galloped out of the school yard toward town. She quickly found Mr. Prince and was confronted by a whole group of armed men. She got the answer to her question.

"This is all your doin'" he said. "Now you talk to those Indians in there an tell them to clear out. If they didn't have prisoners in there, we'd go in there ourselves. Now you talk to them . . . tell 'em!"

"But Mr. Prince, I don't speak their language . . . at least not yet." I meant "not very well," but it didn't come out that way. He was furious and like the rest of us, scared too. "How do you propose I go about this?"

"Lady, I don't have any idea. You've been having those savages in your classroom day after day in the school and now we've got them right here in our midst. . . and I'll wager torturing the people inside. No telling what they're doing in there. So you go talk to them!"

The two debated back and forth a bit, Mr. Prince getting angrier by the minute. Miss Margaret wasn't sure just what she could do; what a woman could do or the words to use. What could she say? She felt obliged however to try. She walked toward the front of Anderson's store with her open palm upheld. About twenty paces from the building she stopped. A shot rang out and dirt kicked up at her feet. Evidently, that was as far as she was being allowed to come. Her heart was pounding furiously. She called out to Agakota and repeated a few words in his language. There was no answer. She took another step toward the store and was stopped again by a bullet at her feet. She stood still, terrified! Again, she called out, again and again. Slowly, she backed away and returned to the side of Fray's store where Mr. Prince and a group had built a barricade.

"You just march yourself back there and try again. We don't intend to see any scalps tied to any Indian lances this day. Word has been sent to the Fort, but they may already have their hands full as well."

Miss Margaret looked from one face to another, but there was no sign of friendship or concern for her in any one of them. She had brought this on the town.

"You caused this by trying to befriend them. You end it!"

"Whatever you taught them," someone said, "you'd best put it to use. Mrs. Jensen and her two little girls are in there! You and education!"

"One person has already been wounded and that is Bill Anderson's horse lying dead out there in front of the store. No tellin' what they've done to him!"

Margaret was close to tears, but knew crying was not the answer. This had not been her doing and they knew it. She was somebody to blame. Margaret bit her lip and returned to the front of Anderson's store. Again she called out.

This time she got close enough to see faces as she adjusted to the tension of being so close to danger and under fire. She noticed that the Indian who had done the shooting from the broken front window was not Agakota. In fact, the face was one entirely new to her, not one of her four students. She stood waiting for something positive to happen, her legs stiff and shaking, tears streaming down her cheeks.

As she stood there, out of the corner of her eye she saw a rider coming into town. Whoever it was, they were in a hurry. The rider came from the direction of the school. She didn't see where he went, but just dreaded the prospects of a message from the school and bad news.

She called out again for Agakota, hoping that he might still be one of the men inside. From a short distance behind her she heard a low grunt and then a voice she recognized.

"Agakota here, back Miss Margaret. Stop school. You not there. Boy tell Agakota."

Agakota held himself close to the side wall of Hardy's Saloon in the narrow space between the buildings. He had obviously taken note of the armed men nearby and determined it best to not be seen as he approached town. He came up beside Miss Margaret.

Agakota called out in Sioux to the Indians in the store. One, then two appeared, cautiously at the door. He argued with them in their own language. Then he stepped out into the street and motioned Margaret to walk with him and approach the store.

"They say we steal from them, so only fair they steal from us. You leave Agakota talk my people."

Agakota did talk to the Indians in the store and described them to Miss Margaret as bad Oglala's, drunk in fact, and somehow wanting to get even with the white men pushing into their hunting grounds and forcing people into reservations. When before the white man came, they were free to roam over great areas. "Much mad. Too much greed," said Agakota. "They not understand," he paused, "not any my people understand you take from earth."

"Nor I, Agakota." Margaret looked back toward the store. "Please try again, Agakota," which he did.

There is more that many of the residents of Iron Horse can now tell. They tell of Agakota who went into Mr. Anderson's store and shamed the renegades who had come to town to steal supplies and found it was easier to get into town than to get out. It was touch and go for a few tense minutes , but in the end it all worked out.

Yes, there were raids further west and some fierce fighting . For a time it did seem endless. With three military outposts along what had become known as the bloody Bozeman trail, the stream of settlers was cut off, yet still they came. Finally, the forts were abandoned. This was Indian land and their hunting grounds; they would defend it. Yet, everyone knew the situation could not go on as it had and finally it was decided that it would be less costly to feed the Indians in preference to fighting them. As a realist himself, Chief Red Cloud recognized the limitless capacity of the military. With his forces melting like snow on a hillside, he was being confronted by forces that increased like spring grass. A few months later news came through Agakota to Miss Margaret that on November 7th Chief Red Cloud signed the 1868 Treaty of Laramie that was to assure peace between the whites and the Indians.

Miss Margaret was already planning for school opportunities for the Indians in the area of Iron Horse. Her chalkboard would share more new words; they would all learn.

When it was all over Mr. Prince did the hardest

Pollen in the Wind

part of all . . . he apologized to Miss Margaret. Pa Svenson just grumbled, but the subject never came up again around the supper table. Perhaps in his own way he realized it's pretty easy to dislike people you don't know or understand, particularly if you don't make an effort. He wouldn't have said so, but I believe he would have agreed that sharing words together is just a good first step.

The Learning Pool

My chores were done and the afternoon was proving to be a warm one. I passed through the kitchen wondering if there might be a slice of pie or a handful of cookies I could eat as I left the house.

Ma was out of the kitchen at the moment, so I thought this would be my best opportunity. Pleasantly surprised, there were four cookies already waiting on the kitchen table. I had decided to meet Rich Cunningham at the bend in the river. We'd already figured if we could get off from the farm we'd enjoy a refreshing swim together.

I slipped a halter on Partner, our old mare, and together we eased around the far side of the barn. Pa would be somewhere out in the corral or riding a fence line somewhere. I found my little brother Noel laying in a mound of our first cutting of hay. He was watching clouds. When I said I was going swimming, he was quick to climb up behind me on Partner.

"Does Ma know where we're going, Davie?"

"Most likely. Now hang on!"

The bend in the river was about a mile away. A bit further north someone had noticed a small number of Indians had made a summer camp along the river. We did not intend to go that far. We'd been told by Pa to steer clear of 'em; no telling what they might be up to.

Rich Cunningham lived on the far side of the river and evidently had been told the same thing. The water at the bend in the river was a lot deeper than where it stretched out into a line. Pa said it was the way the currents worked, creating a sand bar on one side and a deep pool on the other. Some days we fished the area below the pool where the river seemed to flow faster again. By the time we got there, Rich had already skinnied down and was wading in. It didn't take us long.

"Cold!" he yelled. Rich was bigger than me, the benefit of being a whole year and two months older. He had sisters instead of brothers in his family. He always asked them if they'd like to come swimming with him and they would shriek and run for the kitchen. He got a big chuckle out of it.

"Hey, it won't be cold once you get in," I answered.

"This was the hard part," he laughed and with the heel of his hand sent a spray of water in my direction. He always did that so this time I was ready and ducked under the water. It was not all that cold.

"Did you bring the rope?" I asked.

"Yup, it's up on the bank there. I figured to get wet first."

There is a big old sycamore tree at the river's edge and we'd figured last summer if we could get a rope, we'd tie it to one end of a big branch that stuck out over the water. What a great swing it would make. Rich splashed in my direction again, but I'd ducked and it caught Noel a good one. He screamed.

"Hey," he yelled, "no fair!"

We laughed and minutes later we were all up to our chins in the cool water, expecting more splashing. That didn't last long. Rich went under, his feet kicking up in the air as he disappeared under the surface. When he came up he spit out a mouth full of water and held up a smooth white stone. He tossed it in my direction, but about ten feet short.

"See if you can dive for it," he sputtered.

I turned my backside up and went down. It was even a lot cooler deep down, but I spotted the stone and surfaced with it in my fist. Noel was now paddling around in the shallow water.

"Can I come out where you are, Davie?"

"You learn to swim first," I yelled back at him. He was making progress, but I didn't want him in over his head yet. It had happened to me and it was a long time before I had any interest again in swimming.

"Rich, is the rope on your horse?"

"I told you it's on the bank. Do you want to do that now?"

So, we climbed out of the water and slipped into our pants. We figured they'd dry from the sun by the time we were ready to leave. Rich gave me a boost to where the limbs started to branch out, tossed me the end of the rope and I shinnied out on one of the big limbs.

"That looks good," Rich said, so I tied a number of knots with a couple of half-hitches and worked my way back down the tree. He had tied a number of knots in the lower length of the rope and when he tested where it would swing out over the water, he tied a loop.

"Who's gon'na be first?" he said.

"It's your rope. Let's see you go."

He did, pulled it back well ashore, grabbed hold of a knot and ran toward the water. He made a big splash where he dropped off into the water and came up laughing. "That's great!"

Unnoticed by the three of us, a canoe had quietly drifted from up stream around the bend. There were two Indians in it. They appeared close to Rich's age or perhaps my own eleven years. They slowly paddled holding the canoe steady as they watched our playing in the water. I motioned to Noel to get out of the water and both Rich and I did the same. The three of us stood on the bank wondering what was going to happen next. They were doing pretty much the same.

Then they stopped paddling and let the canoe drift down into the deeper water. When they reached the dangling end of the rope, the one in front took hold and swung up and out of the canoe. He climbed the rope, hand over hand, almost to the top. The boy in the canoe had drifted on beyond the rope and darned if the kid on the rope didn't let loose and twist into a dive.

"Gee whiz, that was great!" shouted Rich.

On the far side, the boy in the other canoe beached it on the sand bar and loosened his loin cloth.

Noel noticed and giggled. Turning to me he whispered,"They look just like us, Davie."

"Yup, what'd you expect?"

By then the first boy had climbed up on the bank and stood as far back as the rope would reach. With a short run he swung off the bank way out over the water again and twisted into a dive. Rich grabbed the rope as it swung back and prepared to do the same. He swung out alright, but his dive was a belly whopper, kasplash! There was laughter as he came sputtering to the surface, but before many more attempts, we, all excepting Noel, had it down. We had great sport, taking turns, each trying to outdo the other. After a while we all lay on the bank in the warm sun and began to try to communicate in more than hand motions and exclamations.

"Me Rich," said Rich, pointing to himself.

"Little Elk," the boy responded. He pointed to his friend and said, "He, Bird Claw," and jabbed him in the ribs. Then he pointed at me. "He make iron horse road?"

It took a minute to figure out his question and surprised us that he knew a few words in our language. But, then Rich figured that he was asking about the rail line that was being built a few miles south of where we lived. A lot of people had been brought in to do the hard work. Some, it is said, came from far away.

We all shook our heads. Pa had said that was off limits too. I plowed my hand in the dirt and pretended with some grass that I was growing a crop. "Farmer," I said. They understood the motions and tried the word, "farmer."

We continued for over an hour and took one more dip before heading for home. It had been a great afternoon. That is until Noel asked a question.

"Can we tell Pa, Davie?

"About the Indian boys? Golly, no. I hadn't thought . . . man, he'll be hopping mad. No, we'd best not. We don't tell Ma either, Noel."

So for several days we kept our mouths shut and continued to return to the bend in the river. The Indian boys appeared several times and we continued to swing off the rope into the refreshing water as well as add a few Indian words to our vocabulary. To me, it was a lot more fun learning their words than Latin during the school year. It was Noel who finally got us into trouble. He used a word at the supper table that was an Indian word and Pa wanted to know what it meant and where he'd learned it. Noel looked at me and burst into tears. Very shortly, the whole story came out. Pa was furious.

"That's enough, no more swimming at the bend. I don't want to come up there one day and find you've been scalped."

"Aw, Pa!"

Pollen in the Wind

"Has Rich told his parents? We've told you often enough these people are savages, not to be trusted."

"But . . . but . . ."

"No buts about it! That's it!" Pa's fists were clenched and we knew he meant business. It was Ma who came to our rescue, later. The rest of the supper was pretty quiet. We heard the two of them arguing about it after we'd gone to bed but were not asleep.

A few days later we really had a stretch of hot weather. The far stretches of Nebraska can get really hot toward the end of summer. We approached Ma and teased a bit. She's already made up her mind, but wanted us to be very careful.

"You look out for Noel, Davie."

The Indian boys didn't show up that day, but they did the next. We had a great time together. Before the day was out one of the Indian boys was doing flips off the end of the rope. I quietly shared our experiences with Ma and shared a few Indian words we had learned.

"Ma?"

"Yes, Davie."

"They pulled Noel out when he got in over his head."

"Were you watching out for him?"

"Well, yes, but I was on the rope and the Indian boy saw he was in trouble. He didn't hesitate, Ma. There wasn't anything I could do. . . . he just reached out to him and pulled him into shallow water."

"I'm glad it wasn't more serious and that at least one of you boys was looking out. Now, I suggest you just not take this story any further. You know how your Pa would react."

"I already told Noel to keep his mouth shut, that I'd do the explaining."

"You've done the right thing by telling me, Davie. I'll take it from here. I'll tell Pa and give him a little time to turn it over for himself. Then I want you to tell him yourself. We'll just not say anything right now."

"Thanks, Ma. We've really had fun with the Indian boys. And they seemed to like the idea of learning more of our words, Ma."

It was by accident late one afternoon that we had returned from a swim and Ma had a few cookies for us in the kitchen. Pa came in the back door. He'd been in town.

"Ran into Bob Cunningham in the hardware store. He'd been down along the river where they're starting some bridge work for the rail line, He watched for a bit, said some of the laborers they brought in really work hard. You boys would be interested in what they are doing."

"Can we go there and watch, Pa?"

"Better we go together, one of these days." Pa looked over the kitchen table and what had been set out. "Cookies enough to go round?"

So, we all shared in the brief afternoon treat. A few more comments about the rail line people were exchanged and Pa, just about to go back to work, ruffed his hands through Noel's tousled hair. It was still damp.

"Is your hair wet too, Davie?"

"Yes, sir." When Pa asks a direct question you just don't lie. We'd been told not to go there and now we'd been caught.

"Pa," said Ma."It has been hotter than usual. I said they could go. They've had such fun and the Indian boys have been no problem at all. In fact, I think the experience has worked well in both directions." That was when Ma nodded in my direction. I understood

Pollen in the Wind

what she expected me to do and told what had happened with Noel. I told it just the way it had happened and the Indian boy had done just what any brother would have done.

Pa was mad. When even his ears get red from the explosion building up inside him . . . he's really mad. But, Ma defended us and her position.

"I suppose Rich was there too? Do his folks know what you three have been doing?" He went on for several minutes about how the savages live and what they do to people. When he began to sputter some I realized when he did this he was close to losing out to whatever Ma had to say. More times than he would ever admit, she got in the last word.

"Yes, Rich was there," I replied. "And he brought along a funny lookin' kid from the railroad construction camp. We couldn't understand anything he had to say. 'Wong' was the closest we . . ."

Pa slammed his fist down on the table. He was all cranked up again . . . and mad! Mad all over again. "And those construction people are no better either," he shouted. "They may work hard, but that's what they're hired for. As for their kids, who knows what kind of mischief-makers they might be. Everything about them is different. Their faces don't show at all what's going on inside."

Noel and I expected the worst, but again it was Ma who came to our rescue. She seemed to think things through differently.

"Erwin!" she said. She didn't call him by his first name very often, only when she was gettin' her own back up. "Erwin, they're just boys getting to know each other and about each other. I hope in time more of us can be both appreciative and understanding. Too many of us go through life with our minds already made up."

We were allowed to swim, thanks to Ma, and before the week was out there must have been a dozen of us, Indian, Chinese and a couple of Italian kids that joined in. It was almost funny, everybody shouting and laughing in a different language. Oh, we exchanged words too.

Pa listened to what we shared at the supper table. Said again that one day soon we'd drop over and see how the bridge work was coming. Ma just served up our plates full of baked beans and smiled.

"Erwin," she said. "I suspect these kids are already learning a bit of bridge building."

Pa looked at her funny-like, almost agreeing with her. He didn't respond, but I'm sure he was thinkin' some. In her own way, Ma was right and he knew it. As usual, she got in the last word.

"Those kids have simply been building bridges for all of us," she said.

The Piano Player

Genuine humility is like an unfound gem that you have to dig for, and is a rare find.

It was late in the afternoon in Bountiful, a small ramshackle wooden town in Utah. The sun's rays slanted steeply through the side window of the Emporium, one of the town's watering holes, and streaked across the floor and empty tables. Isaiah Wright stood behind the long highly polished bar, a graying dish towel in his hand as he wiped the insides of all but the last of a stack of shot glasses. He enjoyed this time of day, the temporary peace and quiet that it afforded a few hours before the big room would fill up with men off the street and ranches.

Isaiah was a quiet man, a good listener as many bartenders seem to be. It was relaxing just to be in his company. Sometimes we didn't even talk. Just sat there. But, when he did, he could draw some fine stories out of his own past experiences. He'd seen a lot over his fifty odd years; not one to complain. He was like that.

Here was a man, bereaved of parents by an accident at the age of ten, signed on as a cabin boy to a China bound clipper ship, seen most of the world, even shipwrecked at sea one time, and in '63 served the nation in the war between the States. A lot of water over his dam, I'd say.

As I say, Isaiah is a bit over fifty and weighs only three times that. His hair is graying mostly around his ears; not much left on top. He has a genuinely friendly way about him, a quiet humility. I've found him to be a most engaging fellow and at this time of day when I can slip away from the store, I spend some time listening to him tell stories or share experiences. He is never negative, a man who could always see the potential of something good in a situation if impatience didn't get in the way of a person's understanding. You have to encourage him some to get him started, but he generally obliges. I feel privileged.

"Well, let's see," he would say, as his eyes would roll up and he'd reach into memory. Some of his stories were sad ones as were some of his experiences. Isaiah wasn't what you'd call a religious man. He would acknowledge something beyond the life we know and certainly was sufficiently familiar with the wisdom of the 'Good Book' and other sources to quote a few lines now and then, though never in a preachy way. Some folks that have all the benefits of a college education, he suggested one time, might actually have been educated beyond their intelligence. He'd scratch his head and chuckle, a characteristic prefacing gesture, before putting both hands on the bar in front of him. "Ayah," he'd say. Then he would begin.

"When the Civil War ended, we had all kinds of people coming west," he said, "particularly when the railroads were being built north of us. I was up to Ogden in May of '69, when they drove the last spike, Promontory, it was. Completion of the transcontinental rail line is a great material accomplishment for eastern business interests. I came out here in '68, came from Maine, so I guess I was one of them, eh?" He looked right at me and smiled, remembering.

I noted the muscles of his mouth for just a second, tighten slightly as he spoke. His choice of words. 'material accomplishment', suggested an opinion,

Pollen in the Wind

perhaps another story I hoped he'd share sometime. I knew he felt the native Americans had already gotten the short end of the stick.

"There were a few coming west who couldn't accept that the war was over, weren't there?" I said.

"Ayah, some of the southern boys came this way with a chip on their should'a. To them the war wasn't over or one thing or anoth'a. To them the war was really something that was still going on inside themselves. Ayah."

He smiled at how he agreed with himself.

"Oh?" I said. I had long ago found that a simple questioning 'oh' was all it took to encourage Isaiah.

"Ayah," he said, his Maine roots showing through again. "Had a young lad come in here, not too long ago, should have been drinking Sasparilla, but he wanted a shot of whiskey. I hesitated but went ahead and poured a short shot for him."

"Drink it?"

"Yes, siree, he did! Put his head back and down the hatch. He'd seen some of the older ranch hands drink that way. He nearly gagged, his face got red and his eyes watered. All I could do to keep a straight face."

"Hadn't he ever had a strong drink before?"

"Not here. He came off one of the new ranches that was lookin' for hands . . ." He paused . . . "gun hands, that is."

"He wore a gun?"

"Ayah, had all the trappings, gun tied down . . . you know the type . . . smart mouth to go with it. That kind usually drop out of school before they're dry behind the ears. Not too smart."

"So what happened?"

"He became belligerent . . . insisted he knew good

liquor and that I'd passed off some cheap stuff."

"But that wasn't so?" I asked.

"Of course not. He had no idea what he was talking about. He left mad, evidently had a few drinks someplace else, and still mad came back to the Emporium. I wish he hadn't."

"Oh?"

"You've been here when old Bill Plunket was sittin' at the pianah. Like a lot of black men he has a lot of music in him. He'll sit all evening and play, his right hand makin' the music sound just like one of them player pianahs. Plinka, plinka, plinka, with the right hand while the left hand works out the tune."

"Sure, I know the sound."

"Bill is a harmless old codger, burying a good bit of his past memories in his music... Ayah... fought for the north in the war, he did, the 54th Massachusetts."

"Oh?"

"Ayah... the 54th Massachusetts."

"I'm not familiar with that outfit."

"It was a regiment recruited from some twenty states and under the command of a Colonel Robert Gould Shaw, one fine man. There was also a handful of other white officers. The black troops got paid $13 a month, $100 bounty for volunteering, State Aid to their families, food and clothing. It was a way for them to share and they did willingly. They did so even under white command."

"So there actually was a black regiment?"

"Ayah," Isaiah shook his head slowly, picking his words carefully.

I was beginning to wonder how this smart kid was involved with old Bill, but didn't want to interrupt. A minute later he went on.

"At first the Colonel's regiment did all kinds of lab'ah, behind the lines, menial jobs, no fighting. Can't say for sure but evidently higher up the chain of command didn't seem to have a lot of confidence in the black men's fightin' ability. Colonel Shaw complained. He had more confidence than those above him. The men respected him and liked him. The men wanted more than kitchen duties and hauling freight."

"I don't believe I was aware of many black troops being involved in the war."

"Oh, yes. By the end of '62 Mr. Lincoln authorized recruitment to make up for shortages in military manpower. More than 170,000 black troops served in the Federal army."

"And fought?"

"Ayah, like tigers! Absolutely no question of loyalty." He scratched his ear and looked over at the piano in the corner. Old Bill wasn't there at that time. He would come in later and sometimes a fellow with a banjo would join him. If you could hum a few bars, old Bill could handle the rest . . . a natural . . . with a real knack for it." Isaiah enjoyed company and with afternoons a bit quiet, he took his time with his stories. "Ayah."He looked over at the piano again. "Folks like him . . . have made him feel welcome in Bountiful . . . like turning a new page for some of us."

Again, I began to question where this story was going. Somehow, I suspected there were things he might be avoiding.

"The 54th fought, a place called Fort Wagner near the mouth of the Charleston River in South Carolina was one place Bill was at. July 18 of '63, I rememb'a.

It was a large earthwork fortification stretching across Morris Island, a strategic location. Federal forces had to take the place to tighten the shipping blockade against the south. There was some question how to attack the place and nobody wanted to volunteer the best approach across the open terrain. Colonel Shaw got his opportunity . . . led, yes, led his men across some 200 yards of open beach. 600 men made the bayonet charge. A bayonet charge isn't pretty, you understand. Colonel Shaw's forces took the fort, but at a terrible loss of brave men.

Old Bill lost a lot of friends . . . nearly half of the regiment were killed, but they sure proved they could fight. He later fought in the Battle of Olustee, in Florida in '64. It isn't the kind of thing he talks much about. Can't blame him. Nobody that's been there," he hesitated and didn't finish . "Some grief is just too close to home for understanding.

"Once in a while he gets drunk trying to blank out his memories. That's one way I know what he won't talk about otherwise. He sobs and it comes out a little at a time. He lost everybody he knew. Combat brings men close together. Had few to start with. I usually put him to bed to sleep it off."

"Well, how did he get way out here?"

"Running away from memories," said Isaiah. "As if that would work. Not unusual," he added.

"And the smart mouthed young lad who should have been drinking Sasparilla?"

"Him! Oh yes." He rubbed his chin hesitating, but I think we'd visited together often enough for him to finish what he'd started.

"He got himself liquored up, paraded around braggin' 'bout a few skirmishes back east in the war; ambushes, I've heard tell. Before long he called old Bill a good for nothin' "niggah" when he didn't play 'Dixie' for him quick enough . . . physically dragged him away from the pianah . . . shouted that he was the cause of the whole Civil War and only free because others had done the fighting that gave him his freedom. He simply didn't know what he was talking about or wasn't smart enough to learn.

As a southern'a, he should have known that even Jefferson Davis in March of '65 called for legislation and authorization asking for some 300,000 black soldiers."

"But March of '65 was too late to save the southern cause," I said. "So the kid started making trouble?"

"He did," said Isaiah. "Fortunately the sheriff dropped in about then. He took the kid by the collar of his shirt and tossed him out. Told him he had a thing or two to learn about people. The next day when he sobered up he came back lookin' for the sheriff . . . he was going to get even . . . challenged him and from what they say, his gun never cleared leather."

Isaiah picked up the last shot glass and dried it carefully before adding one more thought. "Smart kid with no character. Too bad! If he'd taken the time to learn a little more, he wouldn't have been buried on "boot hill" today. And do you know, old Bill felt badly . . . real bad"

He looked over at the piano again, as if Old Bill might actually be there. He jerked his thumb in the direction of the idle pianah. "He paid the kid's funeral expenses. Ayah. I've known Bill for a good many yeahs, . . . a good many yeahs. 'No man is wise enough by himself', "he winked and smiled, a sad smile. "Plautus," he said. "Ayah . . . known Bill a good many yeahs."

The rays of the sun by now had vanished from the room. The sun had already dropped below the ridges of the mountains to the west, leaving them a deep blue in place of the red rock just minutes ago.

As I returned to the store I thought about Old Bill and Isaiah. Isaiah was really more than a simple bartender. He had a quiet depth to him that is rare. You sure can't judge a person from appearances. When he shared an experience his role was always forwarded as a minor one; a unique trait. I smiled to myself at the thought and half aloud said "Plautus".

It was quite by accident that I later learned of Isaiah's special respect and bond to Old Bill. Isaiah had also served with Colonel Shaw at Fort Wagner. He was one of the few white officers in the regiment that had survived. I'd also wager he'd been a good officer. Isaiah was what I'd call, a real gem.

The Singing Wire

By the time the telegraph began to be strung across the West, it had already come a long ways from its origins in 1684 as a long distance signal system. It had been the work of an Englishman, Robert Hooke. As a system of signal towers with pivoted beams and arms, the different configurations of the arms represented letters, allowing messages to be transmitted over considerable distances.

By 1830, a Frenchman by the name of Claude Chappe had modified the visual system to a wire where an electrical impulse deflected a needle or pencil. I'm not exactly sure how it works but by long and short deflections of the needle, individual letters can be communicated.

The first long distance line in the U.S. was undertaken between Baltimore and Washington by Samuel F. B. Morse in 1844. He also invented the Morse Code. In 1856 Hiram Sibley founded the Western Union Telegraph Company.

All this information was in a little folder I was given when I went to work for the Company over a year ago. Our line wasn't the first transcontinental line to be put in place. The first was completed back in 1860. As the son of one of the Company's top executives, I'd hoped to get an office job but instead found myself at the bottom of the corporate ladder with a field crew stringing wire westward out of Cheyenne.

Half of the crew was on ahead locating and placing poles where the field engineers had mapped a route paralleling the lands where the Federal grants would be locating the Union Pacific railroad. Bill Tallman and I made up the second team and were stringing bare copper wire to insulators that we first secured to the top of the poles. It was a repetitious job, somewhat monotonous, but I found Tallman not only a capable partner but a most unusual chap.

I suspected early on that he'd had some schooling in one of the eastern colleges some years back, but like so many others had come west. He seemed to be well adapted to this part of the country.

Bill was inches shorter than my five feet nine, about forty I'd judge, broad shoulders, soft spoken and like any of us out here in the bright south Wyoming sun, pretty well tanned.

From the way he climbed the poles we fasten the line to, I'd have to say he was in great condition, a potential athlete. We'd been working together now for some three weeks and expected to go as far as the Great Salt Lake where another crew would take over. By then I think I hoped to be ready for the next phase of my apprenticeship.

"Well, Bill, that about it for the day?"

"Believe so. We need to get a bag of insulators and long screws. We've used up our supply." He laughed. "So I guess we head up the line toward camp." He looked off to the west toward the red sandstone pinnacles and ridges of the Bow Mountains, their ragged shapes and wild color even brighter in the late afternoon sun.

"Some rough country, compared to the basin we've just crossed."

"Dangerous ?" I asked.

"Not to me," he replied, smiling. He lifted the remaining spool of wire into the flat bed wagon and looked around to make sure we weren't leaving anything behind. He was thorough; knew his job.

"All set," I said and climbed to the seat, flicked the reins to set us rolling, following the tracks of the wagons that had gone before us.

"You been workin' for the Company quite a while now." I said it as a statement of fact, so it wasn't really a question, but Bill understood.

"This country is growing by leaps and bounds. Yep, I've been with Western Union and strung wire for hundreds of miles now. There's work here for anybody that wants it. 'Course fellows like me start at the bottom, "he smiled at the thought.

"A lot of people are moving in this direction," I said.

Bill didn't answer. He was looking off toward the skyline, following them with his eyes and our field glasses.

"Thought you said there was no danger ahead?"

"Danger happens when you're not ready for it. My father pointed that out to me when I was a young lad. I wonder if we'll get more than beans tonight?"

He changed the subject, but I was beginning to think of food myself.

Most of the time chow was beans, bacon and hot coffee, sometimes stew made from local game shot along our way, but always hot coffee. Hank Oldfield ran the field kitchen and took a lot of ribbing for what he dished up. Nobody went hungry. He was a pretty smart old timer; knew people.

For years now the movement west had been cutting into Indian territory, seriously depleting the herds of buffalo to the north of us, along with other game that had been the native American food supply from the beginning of time.

But, it had been the pressure of settlers along the Eastern seaboard that had gradually pushed the native Americans further and further west that had changed the game available to them. Sure, there have been fights between newcomers and Indians, raids and so on. The military would one day end all of that now that the Civil War was behind us. Actually the development of the telegraph had made a lot of progress during the war between the States and now with the movements west again there would be more progress; rapid progress. The difficulties with the Indians would subside.

During the War the telegraph had made possible the deployment of troops as had the railroads. It seems to me, at least, that wars have been the impetus to significant and beneficial progress of a good many things; more a consequence than related to the conflict itself. It was a thought that lingered with me back in camp along with Bill's response about possible danger ahead. As any greenhorn will find out, there's a lot to be learned from people you work with no matter where you are.

After chow, not many of the men lingered around the campfire. Most found a quiet place to read, write a letter or play cards. There was another day of hard work ahead. I did ask Hank Oldfield a few questions about Bill; wondered about an incident I'd heard sometime back. He obliged and told how Bill and another fellow had been sent back along the wire to repair a break. It wasn't just a break but rather the wire had been intentionally cut, cut in several places.

Oldfield began to explain. "If the wire's been cut between the transmitter and the receiver there will be no electrical impulse at the receiving end."

"I understand that much."

"So," he went on, "we complete a section of wire and send back a message to a central message switching center. A transmission can go back through several offices before it gets back to the main office or whereever. Messages are recorded on a magnetic drum or paper tape by a machine called a reperforator until the line to the next office is free."

"No, no, I'm wondering who would cut a line. And why?"

"When the wind blows, the wire hums. To the Indians, it sings. You've heard it, a low mournful sound that varies with the wind as it vibrates. There is something spiritual and mysterious to the sound that a shaman can't explain any other way."

"So the Indians cut the line to end it?"

"Yup! . . ." Hank stroked his mustache and looked in the direction where Bill Tallman was curled up in his blanket. "I have nothin' ag'in Bill," he said apologetically. "He's a straight shooter, honest as the day is long." He shook his head. "You know he's part Indian?"

"Bill?" I found it difficult to believe. He seemed quite well educated, certainly a loyal worker, a fine man I'd judge.

"Story goes," Hank continued, "that he caught an Apache before the fellow could climb down the pole, didn't hurt him in any way, spoke to him in his own language and accepted the man's word when he let him go that he'd not cut the singing wire again."

"He's an Apache?" My face must have shown shock and amazement.

"Nope! He's a Paiute, a small Shoshonean tribe in southwestern Utah. You'll find he knows this country. Mother was white, a survivor from a wagon train that didn't get where it was going. Taken as a little girl, she grew up with them. Father was an Indian."

"But his education? He sure seems to be a knowledgeable person . . . "

Hank's comment seemed to end the conversation and I'd already decided to ask a few other questions in Bill's direction. I felt sure he'd square with me. I rolled into my blanket feeling I really had a lot more to learn than I'd anticipated.

Overhead the sky was clear, filled with a million stars. The several campfires were already beginning to burn low and two of the men in the party were already making rounds of the camp. I'd not given much thought before to the fact that they were armed and others would replace them on toward midnight. I moved around in my blanket only long enough to remove a rock under me that I wanted free of, then began to drift off. I watched a shooting star streak across the sky and shortly after was gone.

Bill nudged my foot in what he called morning. The sun wouldn't be up for another hour. At least I was getting used to the routine. The smell of Hank's pancakes and hot coffee was enough to get me moving. After morning chow, loading the wagon and some last minute instructions, we headed back along the trail to pick up where we'd left off the day before. The sun did finally come up and the mountains in all their jagged richly colored layers of tilted sandstone were beautiful.

"Sleep ok?" Bill asked.

I yawned and nodded. He laughed at me. Somewhere along the way he had learned that I'd come out of one of the eastern offices to learn the business. I think he would have shown patience, regardless.

"We have a long day ahead of us," he said.

Fully awake now I began to wonder about my conversation with Hank Oldfield last evening. Was it

Pollen in the Wind

even an appropriate thing to question? Much of the day proved to be a quiet one between us and we finished stringing wire with my questions unasked. As it turned out, I drove the buckboard toward the wiring team's camp perhaps not paying as much attention to the wagon ruts as I might have. Anyway, somewhere back along our way I made a wrong turn.

It was Bill, who having closed his eyes for a bit suddenly commented that the tracks were not fresh ones, nor one of our wagons.

"I think we're heading the wrong way on somebody else's tracks; old ones."

"Oh? So much looks the same along here. There may be a place just ahead here where I can turn us around." I felt embarrassed that I hadn't paid close enough attention. It would take somebody familiar with the area to pick up the difference in such things. Greenhorn!

"There's something up ahead," Bill said.

So there was! It was the remains of a wagon, a wagon that had once been loaded with household goods that were now scattered all around the wagon. It was obviously the end of the trail for one family's travels west, a disastrous one! We pulled up close by and looked around before either of us climbed down.

There was a dresser, drawers all pulled out and contents scattered, a smashed chair, a butter churn, an open Bible box, bits of clothing, now bleached out by the sun, certainly nothing of much value. There was no sign of life and evidently hadn't been for a good many months, perhaps even longer. In the hot sun some things don't deteriorate as rapidly as others.

"What shall we do?" I asked.

"We'll take a look around," Bill said and jumped to the ground.

There really wasn't much of worth left behind. There were a couple of arrows with shafts buried deep into the back side of the dresser and other signs that indicated an unpleasant end to whomever had come this way. Bill looked at the arrows and identified them."

"Apache," he said.

Poking around, looking for something that might identify the names of the people, I found a small book below some of the debris. When I picked it up I found it to be a diary. I hesitated to open it, someone's private thoughts, but realized that didn't matter at this point. I did turn the pages. Toward the back of the diary, in a few pages were a few cryptic lines that told part of the story. There had been an argument with others in the wagon train. Tempers had brought about the separation and without better guidance the party had blindly moved onward. There were a few children's things around that indicated a family. How sad, I thought. The remains of the ravaged wagon told us the rest of the story.

I put the diary in my shirt with the thought it might provide a clue as to who these people were and who back east might need to know. There wasn't much more around to look at.

"Shall we go?" said Bill.

"Guess we'd best be on our way," I replied.

As I began to turn the wagon around I noticed a few yards beyond the wagon, the bleached white bones of a skull, a person's head. As I went over toward it and climbed down to look. Bill suggested I not. When I touched it with my foot it seemed to be fixed in place.

"I suggest we leave," said Bill. . . get back to the right wagon tracks."

I agreed but remained curious. I'd never seen anything like this before. I finally broke the ice.

"You said, Apache back there. Can you tell from just an arrow? Can you be sure?"

Since he had taken over the reins when I climbed down, he pulled the wagon to a stop and turned to face me. "Where do you think the name Tallman comes from? My roots are native American, Paiute. My mother was white, my father a brave. . . but a very wise man."

I just nodded. Hank Oldfield had told me that he was Indian. I just hadn't thought much about his name. Now that he'd started to speak out I wasn't going to interrupt. For a few minutes I was suddenly fearful of where I was and in the company of an Indian. It was the scene at the remains of the wagon that triggered my concern. Bill Tallman seemed to sense the brief look of panic in my eyes.

"No reason to fear," he said. "Let me explain." He let the reins fall and began slowly. "You know my roots. My father for years watched and resisted the streams of people coming out of the east and gradually taking over what had been ours from the beginning of time. Our food supply, the land our creator had provided for our people, was diminishing. For years we fought, fought in whatever way we could. Fighting back was in itself both good and bad. You may find that hard to understand. Seeing no end of people invading and taking over our lands, my father saw no end to what was taking place, no justice in the treaties forced upon us.

My father was fortunate enough to meet a Mormon settler and his family who respected our plight and what was taking place. He, too, was a man of unusual understanding. As you may know, their way of life emphasizes self-sufficiency and hard work as do my people with their efforts undertaken in the services of a heavenly master.

As a consequence, I have benefited a sound education and an understanding of your people. I would judge that you and I are not far apart in many of the things we believe in."

"Where . . . ?" I started to ask, wondering just where he had received his education. His language, his insights, so much about him that suggested more than an ordinary schooling.

"A bluecoat raid against our village took my parents. At the age ten my father's Mormon friends found me and took me in. My awareness of your life began with them. Along with their children I attended an eastern school, a small college in Ohio." He stopped, letting his comments sink in. I sat amazed and confused.

"You are right, I do not understand all this, how you could let that Apache go free and here identify what we've just seen as Apache with evidence even of torture? How cruel can a person be to bury his captive alive?"

Bill Tallman picked up the reins and started the wagon rolling along the old wagon ruts. "You don't really understand, do you?"

"I guess not," I replied, relieved that we were moving in the direction of camp and also that we were talking on matters I did not understand or had no awareness of, as they related to this vast new territory and our presence in it. Here was a native American, a savage by all reports, speaking of philosophical issues beyond my own education. I wanted to know what he meant when he spoke of "good and bad," so asked.

Bill shook his head and stopped the wagon again.

"To not fight back has the capacity of betraying

the very good it seeks to further. By too much trust we give our lands into the hands of the enemy. Yes, I trusted the Apache at the pole and let him go free with the assurance of his word. Trust is a sacred bond between my people. Humankind is not entirely incurable. Appeals to justice and sympathy, however, are inadequate when you are faced with forces lacking genuine concern and trust.

My second family believed that to not fight back has the power to turn enemies into friends, but to get there you must walk boldly in times of trouble and cautiously in times of quiet. There is a time to deny the urgency of a bugle."

I listened in silence; in awe. Yes, Bill Tallman's father was a very wise man, as was his son to have listened to wise counsel and committed to it.

Bill's face was serious as he continued.

"It seems to me that you have to accept or reject a call to arms. If you accept, you may be wiped from the face of the earth. If you reject, there remains potential. All wars defeat the human freedom it strives for. By birth I am both sides of a worldwide problem." He nodded his head visually emphasizing his statement. "I have chosen the path of peace but not with my eyes closed." Bill's voice dropped almost to a whisper. "If conditions are ever to move upward, someone must be ready to assume the risk of beginning. It has been my privilege to learn the difference. We have a long ways to go as two peoples."

Our ride on into camp was in silence. There wasn't that much more to say; a lot to think about!

When we arrived and I stood in line for a plateful of stew and hot coffee, old Hank Oldfield smoothed his mustache and smiled. I suspect he was keen enough to know I'd pursue my questions and would be surprised by the answers.

A month later we completed the section of telegraph wire on into Ogden. When I shook Bill Tallman's hand goodbye to return east to my own next step up the professional ladder, I realized that here in the field was a man at the bottom of the ladder who might never have the opportunity to move up. I knew in the business world that I was returning to, because of my sympathies, I would have to walk cautiously. I'd learned a lot more than the workings of man's technical innovation, the telegraph, the 'singing wire', as the 'savages' called it.

The Preacher

The white heat of the sun directly overhead made an oven of the small hollow where I'd already lain wounded for several hours, and with no means of defending myself. My lips were swollen and cracked and overhead buzzards had begun to circle lazily, watching, waiting. I'd made a mess out'ta my life . . . no real learnin', purpose or nothin'. My escape from the Laramie jail had been a foolish decision. It had been impulse.

Hoping on my own to clear myself of charges that I'd participated in the hold-up of the Overland Stage and the killing of one of the drivers wasn't working out as imagined. By running, I had in a sense confirmed my guilt. It weren't me at all. I had a pretty good idea who had been involved and just because of our similar descriptions I'd been the one nailed.

I'd hoped to slip out of town without being seen, but that sure weren't the way things was turning out. A fast horse, barely ahead of a sharp-eyed deputy and two others had pursued me three days of hard ridin' south and west toward the mountains. Crossing the brow of a hill a chance long shot had winged me in the shoulder. Another had taken my horse from under me. Tumbling, rolling and sliding down the far side of a gully, I'd scrambled and crawled through the mesquite and sage to what I hoped would be a good hiding place. Only the tumbleweed I'd pulled over me screened me from view. If there had been a real tracker in the group, they would have easily found me. From my concealment I could hear their voices as they called back and forth to each other.

"I can't believe he got this far. I know I hit him good."

"This heat'll cook us all if we don't find him soon."

"Stick your head up, Charlie, so we'll know where he is when he shoots."

"The hell you say. I don't know if he's armed and don't want to find out."

"Them buzzards will get more than his horse if we hang 'round here much longer. I say let's head back, Jake."

Pain shot through my body as I tried to shift my legs from their cramped position. With the initial shock of my fall worn off, I realized my difficulty was even more serious. Moving started my shoulder bleeding again.

During the search, one of the men came within a few feet of me and I tried to remain conscious, making every effort to stay silent. But, this too, was a struggle I was losing. I lay there thinking I hadn't really amounted to very much in life anyway. Who in Colstrip would ever miss a no-good runaway kid who cleaned out the town stables? How would it matter to anybody? Slowly a curtain of haze surrounded me. It was so peaceful.

When I came to, the sky was filled with stars. The big dipper was below the north star and holding water, four A.M. I was no longer concealed in the small hollow, my covering gone. My leg was bound by splints and a few yards away the dying embers of a small fire glowed softly in the darkness. I groaned as I felt the dressing on my shoulder and with my stirring a nearby blanket roll came to life. A man rose and stirred the fire, picked up a cup and came toward me.

"Better try get some of this liquid in ya, young fella."

The voice was not one of the ones I'd heard earlier.

"The buzzards attracted me to your horse an' after them fellas left I tracked you to your hiding place. You're hurt some but not so bad you couldn't be moved. Name's Jeb Hawley."

"Where am I?"

"'bout a half mile from where you were. You warm enough? Gets a bit chilly once that sun goes down. Warm enough?"

"Yes . . ." I stammered.

"Then go back to sleep. You're going to be alright."

Still wondering, I did drift off to sleep and the next time I opened my eyes my benefactor was hunched down over the fire cooking some bacon and warming up a pot of coffee. He was a big fellow, dressed mostly in skins, had a huge knife in a fringed sheath at his hip. He wore blue trousers with a yellow stripe down the side like the cavalry troops that pass through town. In spite of the rough woodsman-like appearance he was something cleaner and neater, and he spoke good. The name Jeb Hawley didn't mean nothin' to me.

Jeb Hawley didn't say a great deal. I watched him at the fire and as he prepared to break camp. He didn't waste a move. He hoisted me to the back of his horse. I was surprised that he rode bareback, Indian style, with only a lariat around the nose of the horse. I'd heard that the Indian braves were some of the finest riders anywhere. They could put a horse through all sorts of maneuvers seemingly paying no attention to the horse. But he wasn't Indian. Hawley looked over the countryside around us and at the clear blue sky overhead, then we started off. He walked along side me with long even strides.

"Be home afore noon," he said.

Home turned out to be a small log cabin in a small grove of aspen that backed up against a rock ledge. A small trickle of water spilled down over the ledge and was apparently guided by wooden pipes to the side of the cabin. A large stone chimney could be seen on the back side. As we approached, a woman turned from what I believed to be a garden patch to meet us. She spoke in a native dialect. Hawley nodded and replied, evidently with some instructions.

"This is my woman. She'll attend your needs."

I was gently lifted off the horse as the two people spoke further. I had no idea what they said to each other and wondered how I was fitting into things. Then Hawley hoisted himself up and rode off. For a moment I felt thankful for the rescue but then pretty uneasy about what was going on. I knew I was far too weak to do much for myself. Once assisted inside the cabin I pointed to my chest and spoke my name.

"Henry," I said, and repeated it several times. "Henry."

Jeb's woman smiled and spoke in English. "My name Wild Flower, not speak good. My take care," and she pointed to me.

I was made comfortable in a rope bed that had a sweet smelling straw mattress and was left wondering what was going to happen next. All the moving around from the horse to the bed had started my shoulder bleeding again and the pain was something fierce. I may have even passed out for a time.

When I came 'round again Wild Flower stood by the bed with a bowl. She had mixed a slurry of stuff and gave it to me to drink. It tasted terrible.

Pollen in the Wind

Gradually it did make me sleepy, which I tried not to give in to, but couldn't fight. As I drifted off, I heard the cabin door close and realized I was alone and realizing there had been no hesitation by these folks to provide assistance and no apparent concern of possible risk. Sometime later I woke and heard a voice. It was Wild Flower singing softly. The tune sounded like one of them church tunes, but I didn't understand none of the words. Church had never been much to me.

I felt my shoulder and was aware that it had been cleaned and dressed. It still hurt, but not as much. I wondered if the bullet had been removed. As I stirred I found myself faced by Wild Flower with another bowl of the same slurry I'd had before. In spite of the taste, I didn't fight it.

The next time I awakened must have been a whole day later. I tried to move. I was still too weak to even sit up. I wasn't sure if it had been my long exposure in the hot sun, wounded and without water or Wild Flower's drink that made me so weak. Jeb was back and sittin' at the table readin'. They spoke back and forth, sometimes in English, sometimes in what I realized was one of them Indian tongues. When Jeb saw that I was stirring he came over beside the bed.

"How you feeling, Pilgrim?"

"Better," I responded. "I really feel indebted to you for..."

Jeb cut me off and smiled. "Mercy triumphs over judgment," he said. "I believe I have some news for you."

"Oh?" I looked up wondering.

"Went into town yesterday for nails. The blacksmith was making some for me." He stroked his chin. "Seems they were about to hang a fella... a fella that looked a lot like you." He nodded slowly at what he'd just said and added, "It's a terrible thing to hang a man because he's killed someone. Not sure in such a situation just who is the murderer?"

"A hanging? Oh, no!" Was I jumpin' to conclusions? Anyway, I weren't in no hurry to go back and find out.

"Blacksmith said he was a fellow who had held up a stage and killed one of the drivers. Admitted it, even boasted about it. He didn't know much more about it than that. Does that fit your situation?"

"Yup! . . ." I stammered. "That's what they thought they nailed me for." I lay back, much relieved and thinking how unquestioning Jeb had been when he came to my assistance. "You . . . you just said something about 'mercy triumphs' . . . where does that come from, you a judge or somethin'? What's it mean?"

"James 2: 13. It comes from the Bible. It's a human failing. We all make judgments too quickly." He patted the side of the bed and looked away, almost a sad look I thought.

Wild Flower spoke to Jeb in her language before he went on. I looked in her direction. She had a beautiful warm smile. I already knew her hands were gentle. She was a good looker for an Indian gal. Having said that thought in my mind, I suddenly realized I'd just made what Jeb called a judgment. What did I know about these two kind strangers. They'd gone out of their way to help me.

"Time for some nourishment, "Jeb said. As he spoke, Wild Flower brought my clothing, all neatly washed and folded. She placed them at the foot of the bed and turned back to the meal she was preparing. Jeb went back to the table while I dressed, pleased that I had the strength and was no longer a fugitive. In spite of the effort, it felt good to stand up and move, even better to fill my stomach with a rich meat and vegetable stew. At the table I noticed what Jeb had been reading from was a big old tattered book. Jeb saw my look of surprise.

"This is my Bible," he said. "I was a circuit rider some years back."

"Was?" I asked. "Not now? What's a circuit rider, anyhow?" Jeb looked in the direction of Wild Flower, but didn't explain.

My lips formed the words" Wild Flower" and Jeb nodded imperceptibly. "James 2:13," It was all I said. He nodded again. The rest of the meal passed in silence. Lookin' 'round the cabin, it struck me that it was not only well built with a real wood floor and was nicely furnished; better'n any house I'd lived in. There was a hanging oil lamp in the kitchen area, a number of blue and white plates and bowls and a cast iron cooking stove. I could not help but wonder how all this had come about.

"You'll stay a few days longer before moving on?" Jeb asked.

"If I can return your kindness, I'd be mighty obliged. I ain't all that hurried to get back to town."

"There's always work to be done here," he said, smiling.

It was a couple of days later as we were notching the ends of some logs for a small outbuilding that I finally asked Jeb what happened to his circuit rider job. He didn't answer right off. He took a dipper full of water from a nearby leather pail and sat down. When he finished his drink he wiped his chin, then looked right at me.

"I'm not sure just how to begin or if you even want to hear. As you've already gathered, my marrying an Indian woman broke accepted relationships. It was down hill from that point on with the church hierarchy. I was a Chaplain in the military during the war and came west when the war ended. I rode the circuit for a few years and built up a number of small community church families. I also served as a missionary to some of the native people out here. I use the word people but not everyone out here does. During the course of my traveling and teaching I met Wild Flower. For whatever reason people wanted, I was suddenly not wanted. I lost my small church to another. It was a terrible blow to my pride as you might imagine."

"Ha! So you're a preacher man, that big Bible and all? So what do you do now?" I wasn't sure about what all he was saying, never having had no truck with the church where I'd been.

"I came to this spot, and remembering that Jesus was a carpenter, I built this small home and in the process found some answers for my situation. We're happy here."

Somehow his reply didn't answer my question. I just knew that fella' he spoke of was a good cuss word. So far I was still in the dark. I didn't want to offend the guy, so I pretended to understand.

"Well, what did you decide to do?"

"When I leave here and am gone for a few days at a time it is because I am in the land of Wild Flower's people. Mostly I teach, but I help in many ways. Yes, I'm a preacher. I have not found the native Americans of this land to be treated fairly. That in itself is another long story that I will spare you from."

"Preacher! Is that why the meat, squash and corn gets dumped at your door during the night?"

"So you've noticed? It is one way of saying 'thank you', yes." He handed me the dipper and changed his

Pollen in the Wind

line of thinkin'. "I noticed you were looking at my Bible again last evening."

"Yeah, I was. Biggest book I ever seen. Can't say I've ever read it. Not sure what . . . you know, your preacher business. "

"No, Henry. The book is far more than preaching, though it is full of lessons. Haven't you ever asked yourself questions . . . like, . . . what is the meaning of life? . . . where do I fit in? . . . how can I matter?" He propped himself up against a log and wiped his forehead. "How much of a question are you really asking?"

"I . . . I haven't any idea. Give it a shot, we'll see!"

So Jeb began. He explained that the Bible is really two parts, the first, an old part, Testament, he called it, which is full of history, laws of the Jewish people, some poetry or Psalms, as he called them, and some wise sayings. The other book is newer and deals with how people ought to live. Live together, as it was taught by that fella named Jesus. There was no question, Jeb must have been quite a preacher. I began to feel that he liked talkin' an' he spoke real good. I liked listening to 'im.

"Answer your questions?" he asked.

"With all that writing stowed in that book from what you call the beginning of time, why aren't we doing better than we are? Like those guys after me, they made a judgment . . . a wrong one!"

"Human nature gets in our way," he replied. He picked up the adze and brought its blade down hard on the side of the log. He really hit it hard, like he was mad at it. I was sure that weren't so. I've kicked the stable door a time or two, myself, and with no reason.

"Human nature? I repeated.

"Greed, bitterness . . .perhaps even self pity."

"Are you bitter that you ain't no longer a rider for

the Church?" I asked.

"I fight the feeling every day, fully aware that I should not be. But also fully aware that we are all the children of a single creator and no different, one from another. Whole nations struggle with the problem of bitterness. The north and south have just ended a devastating war and yet it will be ages before the south accepts the ending. Bitterness is the root of revenge . . . ah, sweet revenge, they say, but it's not. Revenge is a slow fire inside that eventually destroys a person."

He set the adze aside and sat down again apparently warming up to what he wanted to say next. "Who owned this land before we arrived and who before the Blackfoot, the Lakota, the Cheyenne? And what of them should they return to reclaim it or those that came even before? Where is there a spot on this earth not claimed by someone earlier than ourselves? Why need it be claimed by anyone as theirs when there is enough for all if considered fairly and with justice?

The Indian people do not really understand the concept of ownership of the land they live on. It belongs not to them but to its creator."

"Greed?" I asked, aware now that he had taught this lesson before and unlike the farmer who was going to feed his one cow what only the one needed, Jeb was about to dump a whole load.

"Let every man be swift to hear, slow to speak, slow to wrath. For the wrath of man worketh not the righteousness of God." He caught his breath and added,"What is faith without works?"

"Who said all that?" I asked hesitantly. He was way over my head.

"James, the brother of Jesus. It's all there in the New Testament."

"Who says it's all true?"

"The Bible is God's word, my son, filtered through the wants of mankind. It has been written, translated, rewritten and shaped to fit the wishes of the Church. Yes, ego and greed are there also. But its underlying wisdom is there for all. You have to dig for it."

Jeb continued to speak and I listened. He was a preacher alright! We worked some on the pile of logs he'd cut and when we rested he went on. Man, how he could talk. He talked about stuff I'd never given the time of day. I was beginning to be interested in what he had to say. I must have been blind to the world out there, but I s'pose if you don't know where you're headed, it don't matter what road you take.

As the light began to fade we gathered our tools and returned to the cabin. He quoted what he'd said was scripture the whole time we worked. I'd had an earful and a wagon load to think about. Seemed to make good sense; some of it anyways. I was tired, but somehow stirred-up to continue asking questions. They never taught nothin' like this in school.

Jeb didn't try to preach at me again but he did let me poke through his big Bible. I read bits and pieces from the Psalms and a guy named Isaiah. I had to ask for help when I didn't know or understand the words. After all, I'd only gone as far as sixth grade.

Finally, in another guy's story, a fella called Amos, I found a few lines I kind'a liked. It was Amos 7;7-9. I slowly started to read it aloud.

"Look, I am setting a plumb line among my people, Israel."

Jeb heard me read aloud and smiled. "Yes, siree! he said. "When we make decisions, it is important to realize that others are always trying to set standards for us to live by. We are free to decide what is right and what is wrong and so we too often get out of line or out of plumb with the will of our Creator." Jeb nodded again and smiled at Wild Flower. I suspect that Jeb felt I had accepted him as he was and as he had accepted me, and he felt good about it. I think he was pleased too, that I was asking big questions 'bout life. Perhaps it made him feel better 'bout his own.

This went on for a couple of weeks and by then I was fit as a fiddle. Lots of evenings we talked, stuff from his Bible book. If nothing, I was suddenly curious about a lot of things. Perhaps I could someday amount to somethin'. I felt different about myself, and it was because of Jeb, I'm certain. Wild Flower was a wonderful lady. I didn't blame Jeb for marrying her, or her caring for him.

Another week passed and finally the two of them considered me fully healed. Jeb asked if I was ready to return to town. I was and actually even felt better about myself. He rode me to the edge of Colstrip where I'd come from. As we rode I began to wonder some if back to town was where I wanted to go. Perhaps I'd work there long enough to pay my way back east or . . . maybe with more schoolin'? . . . I wasn't sure what. Somehow Jeb Hawley had me seein' more in life than lookin' at the back end of horses day in and out. I doubted if I could be the man he is, but I might could help somebody. He wasn't saying much himself along the trail as we rode, which was not like him. That was alright too.

Close to town he turned and looked right at me. I guess he'd been doin' some thinkin' too.

"You've been a big help to me, Pilgrim. I've enjoyed your company. When you feel you're ready, you ride back out this way, there's lots we could do together."

That sure made me feel good. I just nodded. I

thanked him for his and Wild Flower's help and his sharin' his preacher business. Only then did he speak about what we had shared.

"Pilgrim," he said, "be careful how your life lines up with your Creator's plumb line and you'll do just fine."

Yes, sir, Jeb was a real preacher and I for one remember him as well as that last one line sermon. "Amos," I said, "Chapter 7; 7-9," and he just smiled. With him, I guess it would always be a sermon. I think I knew then he was on to something and I'd be comin' back for another load.

Pulling Together

Snow! To me it was not a surprise. I'd heard the men talking about the sky yesterday evening as the wagons were rounded up into a circle. Even then the sky was gray and the wind had a cold sting to it. My little sister Emily would be delighted when she wiggled out of her snug quilt. I knew it was going to mean a lot more work for the men driving the wagons. I peeked out the back of the wagon where the flap was loose. My Dad and two other men were just a short distance away and I could hear them talking.

"Not going to make many miles today," said one of the men.

"Gotta keep pushin' on," Dad said. "We're more than a week behind schedule now. Weather will be closing in on us. We'd hoped to be in Oregon by the end of October." All three were blowing in their hands to warm them and their cheeks were red from the wind.

The tall man, I believe his name was Henry something or other, pulled his coat tighter and was stamping his feet. He was one of the men in the wagon behind ours that was being pulled by oxen. They sure are big powerful animals!

"Accordin' to the Colonel we'll be going through the notch up ahead. Snow sure ain't goin' ta help none."

I finished pulling on an extra pair of socks and scurried as quietly as I could to slide past Emily without waking her. Even at eight she was a real bother. I didn't like girls anyhow. Up front there was more activity and a fire that some of the women were working around. Ma was right there with the other women doin' her share. She was big on working together. I buttoned my jacket and climbed down. It was a soft wet snow and I nearly slipped on the wagon tongue before I reached the ground.

"Davey . . . get a hat on!" Mom saw me right off and yelled at me. Then she turned back to the pot of oatmeal that was steamin' away. By the time I got back, she handed me a bowl and a couple of pieces of bread and pointed out a dry place to sit. I didn't need to be yelled at for hot food, that's for sure.

As soon as I finished, I ducked off to see if Carley Dawson was up yet. A snow ball zipped by my head told me he was. Before I could bend down to pack one of my own, I got pasted by a good one from another direction.

"Hey! Where'd that come from?"

A loud laugh from across the circle at the Barner wagon answered my question.

"Come on, Carley! Hey, Adam, let's get 'im!" I shouted. But no such luck.

Mr. Barner, Bill's old man, came around from the back of their wagon and grabbed Billy. "You boys git yourselves over to that group of pines there by the creek and get some firewood. Make yourselves useful!"

"Aw, shucks," said Billy. "Can't we . . ." an arm and fingers pointing in the direction of the creek cut off debate.

"Let's go gang. The sooner we go, the quicker we're done," I said.

"Not for me," whined Adam as he headed in the direction of his wagon.

"It'll make more sense if we work together," said

Carley. "Come on, Adam."

He didn't join us, so it was Carley, Billy and me who went after the firewood. I'd done it before, breaking off the small lower branches of the pines and with a rope and a weight tied on the end, we could toss it up over higher branches and pull them down. It didn't take long, working together, to gather a couple of piles. By the time we got the wood back to the wagons, nearly everyone was up and out. On a better day, the sun would have just been peeking over the rolling country behind us. Other fires had been started and the men had come together with the Colonel to plan the day. When I reached our wagon, Ma had a pan with a cloth over it. When she saw me, I was to take it over to the Horton's wagon . . . Mrs. Horton wasn't well and they had three hungry men in their party to be fed.

The horses and other animals had been tethered during the night in the center of our circle, their breathing causing steam in the air that was freezing on their nostrils. It made them look like dragons, except it wasn't fire. The snow continued to fall, but seemed to be easing off some. By what I would guess to be seven o'clock, the order came to put out our fires and get ready to roll. There followed great activity as teams were put in place, cooking gear was stowed and people got themselves ready for another day on the trail. It had all become a well established routine since Fort Carson. The Colonel saw to that! I had my share of chores as did all the other kids, even Emily, who was now complaining about the wet sticky snow. Girls! She needn't worry, though. A few hours along the trail and a few thousand feet higher, it wouldn't be sticky at all. Finally, the order came from the Colonel to "Roll 'em!" and we started off.

Henry 'something's ' wagon, because of his oxen,

Pollen in the Wind

was moved to the head of the line, which made our progress somewhat slower. It did make things a lot easier for the rest of the wagons following in their tracks.

Billy came by riding their mare. He'd gone up to the head of the line and had learned that about noon we'd be starting up a very steep stretch of trail. It was a pass through the mountains, but he didn't know the name of it, if it had one. I asked Ma how we'd manage it and she didn't know. She usually said to ask Pa when she didn't know the answer.

"Well, son, it may take some extra teamwork, all pulling one wagon up through the pass one at a time."

"Will the Barner people help?" I asked. They been pretty independent much of the way so far, didn't want to help nor offered any. The Colonel had had to deal with them a time or two. Pa just laughed at my question.

"If they want to make it over, I believe they'll have to help some."

Sure enough, about noon, we all bunched up at the base of a long steep climb. Some men had been sent forward to prepare the way, cutting trees for levers and braces to put behind wagons so they wouldn't roll back The Colonel had made the trip before, usually not this late in the season. The snow added a few problems for all of us. Already higher up the mountain the snow was stinging cold in the wind as it whipped down through the pass. There was no question the next mile was going to be a difficult one, slipping and sliding.

The livestock and most of the women were led over the trail first. They were to get some hot coffee and soup ready for the men who would be working with the wagons. Pa insisted I go with Ma and Emily and help out where I could. That meant more firewood to be gathered. At fourteen , I felt I could help with the men, but Pa's word meant business.

"What about Indians, Pa?"

"In this weather?" he replied. His look suggested it was a foolish questions. I wasn't so sure.

Anyway, we staggered to the top and started down the far side toward a grove of trees the Colonel had picked out. The higher we got the thinner and more scraggly the trees seemed to be. I noticed right off, since I knew that firewood was a detail I'd be assigned to. Huge slabs of gray rock jutted up into the sky on each side of us, so we did have a spot that was out of the wind. Carley, Billy and me, we got started collecting wood. Billy carried the big pieces. He was almost as tall as my Pa and strong. Emily did help and carried some of the small stuff. I didn't see Adam or any of his party anywhere. By the time we finished, our mittens were soaked and our hands were freezing. The pine fires snapped and crackled as we got them going and the heat felt good. Billy's face was red as a beet and I supposed mine was too. Once we got warmed, he headed off to find his Pa's wagon, but not before sending a snowball in my direction. If I'd had my mittens on I'da sent one back. He missed me, anyway.

An hour later, a couple of the wagons had made it to the top and were starting down our side of the pass. It looked like it was going to be dangerous work. I sure wanted to see or be a part of it and hoped when I asked, that Ma wouldn't say no.

"Ma. Can Carley and me . . ." wrong approach, I suddenly realized. "Ma . . . is there anything more we need to do right now?"

Ma looked at the stack of firewood we'd gathered, then up the trail at the pass.

"Keep out of the men's way and be back here before dark." she answered. "Emily, you stay here and help me."

Can you imagine that? She read my mind like I'd written a big sign. So, Carley and me tried the same approach with his Ma and we took off.

Where wagons were coming down our side of the pass, there were men with ropes tied to the rear axles of the wagons holding them back. If they hadn't held firm the wagons would have careened forward out of control. At this point, only two had been brought down. The Harvey wagon was one of them, but the oxen were not with it. On the climb side of the pass, the two big oxen had been harnessed to another family's wagon and was slowly being hauled upward. Behind the wagon men used poles to brace against rolling back. There was a lot of grunting and quite a few words the men never used when the women were around. I'd heard most of them. Foot by foot each wagon was slowly moved up the slope. The men's breath in the air was like the snorting horses earlier in the morning, along with a lot of yelling. It was quite an undertaking.

"Man, that's work!" said Carley.

I replied, but was looking further down the line for the Barner wagon. We'd crossed a stream some days back and old man Barner had gotten his back up and wanted no help from anyone. "What's mine, I'll handle myself." he'd said. Actually he had done just what he said he would. I wondered about now. At the river it took us all a bit longer while we waited, which made the Colonel angry. With a team of four he'd not had trouble that time, but this situation didn't look so easy.

"You see the Barner wagon, Davey?" Carley asked.

"Yep, there behind the one with the brown canvas patch," I shouted back.

One by one over the afternoon the wagons were brought to the top, pushed, pulled and then lowered carefully down the far side. We stayed out of the way. If one of those wagons broke loose it would make a real smash bang mess and I sure wasn't going to get blamed for anything.

"Looks like the Barner wagon is next," Carley yelled at me.

"But they aren't going to use the oxen!" Do you think the four horses can do the job?"

"Beats me! Doesn't look like they want a hand. All the men are standing out of their way, "he shouted.

"Gotta do it themselves," I said, wondering.

There was the sound of old man Barner's whip and his team and four surged forward. Blamed if it didn't go fairly well for the first hundred or so feet . . . that is at first. The wagon slowed and came to a stop, Mr. Barner continuing to crack the whip and shouting at the horses as they pawed the ground trying to get their footing. Then they moved ahead again and the men left behind with the poles rushed up behind the wagon to prevent slippage. Barner yelled at them to stand off and inch by inch those poor horses struggled to the top. It would have been so much simpler had he let his neighbors help.

"Boy, is that ever hard on the horses," Carley said.

"Yeah, and they have the hard part ahead going down the other side."

The oxen were harnessed to another wagon down at the bottom and it started up, the men following along behind with their poles. The Colonel knew what he was doing.

"Let's get back to the top and watch the Barner

wagon.

Slipping and sliding up the rutted trail we headed up. The snow continued to fall but the flakes were getting smaller as the temperature dropped. The wind didn't let up one bit. It wouldn't be long before dark and the whole operation would have to wait till morning. I was glad to know our wagon had made it over. I'm sure everyone would be glad when this day was over. I had to agree that my question about Indians out in this kind of weather looked pretty foolish. Some of the men along the way as we worked our way to the top looked plum wore out. My Dad was one of 'em, along with Carley's and Billy's. They were all working together.

We got to the top in time to see the Barner wagon start down. They started off alright but in one very steep stretch even their four horses couldn't hold the wagon in line behind them. It looked like the wagon was going to run over the horses or even pass them. Old man Barner was yelling at the top of his voice. What happened was an awful sight. One horse lost its footing and went down, then the whole team and wagon tangled in the harnesses and pitched forward, then off to the side where it turned over. Old man Barner, his furniture and the whole works went flying. Mr. Barner broke his arm in the fall, two horses were lamed and had to be shot, furniture was smashed to smithereens with clothing scattered all over the snow. A lot of stuff was lost forever in the deeper snow. It was a real mess. Carley started to snicker but covered his mouth when he saw the look on my face.

Everybody rushed to help and Pa told us later at supper that Mr. Barner was going to be alright. A lot of their things were dug out of the snow, some things could be repaired and the wagon was turned upright. I felt badly for the two horses they lost. Mr. Barner apologized for being so pigheaded and the Colonel had a lot to say that even the firewood collectors in the wagon train already knew, and that includes my little sister as well.

Dance Hall Girls

Howard Horton is a handler at the local livery. He'd just finished grooming several horses in preparation of the arrival of the west bound stage. Until then he could sweep up a bit in the office or repair a few pieces of harness. He wasn't one to waste somebody else's time and he appreciated the job. Except for a brother in Denver he was alone in the world and had started west to join him but had run out of funds. Saving money to complete his trip was proving difficult. It wasn't that he wasted his earnings, he too often shared what he had. Just a week earlier he'd paid for a ball and bat for the kids that hung idly around the livery. Better they play a real game than get themselves into trouble. He was like that!

At five foot eight, slight of build, hardly handsome, Howard looked older than twenty-seven. This may have been caused by his years in service in the war between the States. He'd seen a lot during those years, perhaps too much and wondered when the world was going to return again to the world where he and his brother had grown up. He seldom smiled, or seemed to find reason to smile. Even his hair appeared to be graying early.

Howard lived alone in one of the back rooms of the local hotel, where he'd been given a modest rate in exchange for a few minor baggage-handling chores. That way he hoped to save enough to move on to Denver. When he wasn't working at the livery he read a lot, so was a quiet occupant, which the hotel folks appreciated. The Rattlesnake Saloon, down the street, already made more than enough noise for one small and growing town. The raucous activity there was something, along with the gambling and willing women that people talked about. He avoided all of it. Close to noon, one day, in a swirling cloud of dust and lusty shouting, the stage rolled up to the front of the hotel. Howard was there to assist the few arriving passengers with their baggage. Later he would ride down with the driver to make the change of horses for the next leg of the run.

He had just given an elderly man a hand down when a young woman waited her turn. In her late thirties, she was not pretty, but pleasant looking and nicely dressed in a pretty yellow bonnet over golden hair that hung half way down her back. He started to take a second look but was interrupted.

"Miss Connie's bag is that flowered one over there, Howard."

"Got it!" He picked it up, ready to accompany the young woman inside. As he turned toward her, she was looking right at him and smiling. It was a look that went right inside him, right through his granite gray eyes.

At the time Howard remembered mumbling some incoherent response to the driver and continuing about his business. But he didn't forget the incident or Connie's smile. In fact when he mounted the box with the driver to go on to the livery, he asked about her.

"Miss Connie Andersen, "the driver said, "old fashioned, but a lovely young woman."

Later, when he'd finished work, he stopped off at the desk and asked the clerk a few more questions.

"She'll be singing down at the Saloon, I understand," the clerk informed him.

"At the Rattlesnake?"

"It's what she came out here to do."

Howard thanked the man behind the desk and turned away. Could they have been talking about the same person? In his room he attended a few chores and finally buried himself in a book. But he didn't stay buried. By ten o'clock he got himself dressed and quietly went down the back stairs and to the street.

Standing in the street in front of the Rattlesnake, he watched the doors swing in and out as people came and went. They were all men, ranch hands, drifters, a few salesman. There were even a few wearing guns; a pretty rough looking crowd, though nothing he hadn't seen before. He could hear the piano and a banjo and when the doors were momentarily held open as someone went in or staggered out he could see a few tables and men holding cards. He knew this was all a part of the Rattlesnake but somehow its nature stirred vivid pictures of a different way of life. There were painted women in bright colored dresses leaning enticingly forward behind the players. He recalled his father's admonition about women letting their mammary glands hang out and had seen such when his regiment went on liberty. His father had called such activity pleasure without conscience.

Howard watched for several minutes wondering, and was about to turn away when he heard someone start to sing. He remembered what the clerk at the hotel had said and turned back. It was Connie, no question about it. She was dressed attractively in a long blue dress, hardly like the other girls at the tables. She had a sweet voice, a lot like his mother's voice when she sang in the church choir years before, but her voice was very nearly drowned out by the shouting men. Their encouragement evidently expected something different. Somehow she struggled through her number and escaped from the stage.

Howard felt sick.

It was several days later that Howard's path crossed Connie's on the boardwalk in front of the hotel. She smiled but her smile was not the same. There seemed to be a sadness in her eyes, or was he imagining? A week passed and Howard tried to put Connie out of his mind. It puzzled him; not that it was any of his business. Work at the livery stable continued much the same from one day to the next, perhaps even a little busier as more and more people poured into the town. It was the evenings in his room when he'd put his head back on his pillow that he'd see Connie in his mind, that first day when she got off the stage and smiled.

When Howard had served with the Union forces there had been occasional passes that allowed the men during training to go into town. Howard had gone, had enjoyed the comradeship and a few cool beers after a hot dusty day on the drill field. He'd made a number of friends but, as things turned out and they explored opportunities beyond sitting around drinking, joking and talking about girl friends and home, he found himself not attracted to the level of pleasure they pursued. So when you come right down to it, here in Hastings, Nebraska, was a young woman that with a friendly smile had touched something in Howard, yet was a participant in an unbecoming activity going on inside the Rattlesnake and perhaps even the rooms in back or on the floor above.

When things got out of hand there and gunfire followed with somebody hurt or killed, there was increased talk of what went on behind those swinging doors. Sometimes brawlers would come tumbling right out into the street. That's usually when the sheriff would have to intervene. Howard was irritated about the whole situation, but not sure if he wasn't really more angered at himself for even thinking about it. . . or about Connie.

One day, unexpectedly and quite by accident, he was in the apparel side of the general store and ran into Connie. He'd gone in to get himself a new shirt or two and evidently she'd wanted some sewing supplies.

"Morning, m'am," he said, "Miss Andersen," he added.

"Oh, hello, you know my name!" She smiled.

"Yes, "It was the same kind of smile and look he'd seen when he gave her a hand off the stage.

Perhaps it was just knowing her name that made the difference? He hardly knew what to say next. How could he speak his mind at such a chance encounter and him not on speaking terms beyond simple pleasantries.

He swallowed hard and studied the two shirts he was comparing. He liked both but one was all he felt he could afford just now. At the rate he was saving, it could be a long time before he managed to get further west to see his brother.

"If you want a button sewed on the shirt you're wearing . . ." She smiled, aware that she hadn't been asked, then added, "The bright blue one," she said, purposely bumping his elbow. "My favorite color and it goes with your nice tan."

"Oh, . . . oh? You think so?" Howard put aside the gray one. "Perhaps you're right, thank you." He looked at her again as he started to go. "I understand that you sing?"

"Well," she hesitated. She put her hand on Howard's arm. "I try," she said.

Howard paid for his shirt, the bright blue one, and

left Connie looking over threads and other sewing items. His mind was swirling. He could still feel the touch of her hand on his arm. He remembered years back when as a young boy and before he'd joined the Waterbury 26th Regiment that he'd had a girl friend. It had been his first love and when he thought about it he could for the longest time still feel the eager pressure of the girl's lips against his own; their first kiss. Returning home from service she had moved away, but he still remembered the feeling. Connie's touch had the same magic in it and now as he stumbled his way toward the livery, he was confused. How can Connie work in that place . . . with those other women? He shook his head; he had no answers.

"Howard, did you rub down that dust colored Roan that came in last evening?"

"Uh, no, Mr. Hawkins, I'll get right to it, sir." Which he did. And that was pretty much how the next few days passed. Mr. Hawkins even wondered if he was sick though he didn't suggest he take any time off. The town was growing so fast and with new people arriving the stable more than had its hands full to keep up. So, Howard was busy. That was, busy, on top of his personal confusion.

A few evenings later after work, Howard drifted, as if drawn by a magnet, down the street toward the Rattlesnake Saloon. He stood across the street and watched, occasionally getting glimpses of the activity and men going in and out. He hoped Connie would sing, but that didn't happen. What did happen was that the side door of the building opened spilling light into the narrow space between the saloon and the adjacent building. To his surprise it was the figure of a young woman that emerged. She was hurrying, nearly stumbling and as she reached the street she was sobbing. It was Connie!

"Connie?"

"Go away!"

"It's Howard, . . . you know . . . the livery stable?"

"Oh . . . oh, Howard, I've made a terrible mistake. I came with such hopes." She sobbed and held on to Howard's arm with both hands. For several minutes the two just stood there in the middle of the street - a young woman, sobbing uncontrollably and a serious and confused young man realizing that deep inside him he cared.

"I should never have come here! The newspaper ad had sounded so good and . . ." she sobbed again. She didn't go on just then but, by the time they had gotten back to the boarding house, Howard had the whole story, or at least enough of it. He asked if she was going to be all right, to which she assured him she was. Then he left and feeling very badly. They did see each other several times over the next week or so. Connie no longer went to the Rattlesnake. They were good days for both of them but her resources were running out. Howard guessed that they must be. As things turned out, Howard dipped into his savings and provided Connie with the means to return home. She resisted at first, of course, but finally agreed it was what she wanted just then; to return home. She said she'd write.

That was hardly the end however, because Connie came west again, not to sing or work in the dance hall but, realizing the kind of man Howard was and that she too, had in her better judgment, discovered her own feelings for him.

As their fourteen-year-old daughter and looking back, and having told you their story, I can say proudly that that was how my folks met sixteen or so years ago.

And you can bet your bottom dollar that I've learned some real lessons from my mom's experience. Real love is a matter of commitment, not simply an evening's pleasure."

Helping Hands

The sky to the west was dark. Amity Stevens thought it must be a lot later than it actually was, until she went past the tall clock in the sitting room. It was only three in the afternoon. Amity was alone with her two girls. Able Stevens had gone into town with their son Kenny for farm supplies, sacks to store their fall harvest of grain and a few other items needed at home. Town was a good day's trip over and back, so Amity was not expecting him anytime soon. One of the girls met Amity as she came into the kitchen. Beth and Polly had been making bread and this was one of their first major cooking ventures on their own. On a farm, everybody did their bit.

"Mom, it's getting dark early."

"I've noticed that and was just going to . . ." she didn't finish. She'd pulled aside the kitchen curtain and looked off in the distance. "Oh, my, it's dark all along the horizon. Oh, I hope it's not those pesky grasshoppers again. They just eat everything in sight. Oh, I hope not."

"Is there something wrong, Mom?" said Polly.

"I don't know."

"What should we do, Momma?" said Beth. She was the littlest and worried more than her eight year old sister.

Amity opened the back door and stepped out. The two girls were close behind her.

"The air is stuffy . . . like smoke," observed Polly.

"You're right! Oh, no. Can it be a fire?"

"Will that burn our house down, Momma?"

Amity didn't know and she didn't want to frighten her girls. Able was away. She was alone and wondering what to do. The men of the household wouldn't be home for hours. She looked at the house and the barn that Able had finished just the summer before. They'd been so lucky, from the first exciting day that they had raced away from the starting line in '62 to claim their homestead. Able had worked so hard. They had been fortunate to find property on the top of a rise that afforded view in every direction. From the back yard they could see for miles. Fire along the distant horizon was many miles away, but the cloud of smoke rose high in the afternoon sky, blotting out the sun. No wonder it had seemed later than it was. With the ever-present wind sweeping across the plains, it would not take long for a grass or crop fire to reach the Steven's.

"Polly, you go to the barn and get several empty feed sacks. Beth, you go with her and get a bucket, two if you can find two. Please don't linger, we have so much to do. Amity tried to speak quietly hoping to remain calm for the girls. Inside , her heart was already pounding and she was close to panic. How could she alone deal with what was approaching? If only Able and Kenny were here.

Just west of the barn was a section of their wheat crop, a plot of eight to ten acres. Able had said as the grain matured to a golden ripeness that this land would be their seed crop for the coming year. Could she possibly save it and the house? This was the year they had hoped to get ahead financially. But now?

Amity ran to the pump and worked the handle up and down, drawing clear cold water to the surface just as Beth and Polly returned from the barn.

Pollen in the Wind

"Beth, you fill the bucket . . . oh, you found two . . . good . . . .and Polly, you soak the feed bags in the buckets." Amity's mind was racing. If Able hadn't taken the wagon . . ."

"What are we going to do, Mom?"

"Please, you'll see. Just do as I say. Now Beth, you go to the kitchen and get some matches . . . now hurry."

"Matches?"

"On the shelf beside the kitchen stove, now go!"

"Yes, Momma," and off she ran. Polly began to cry.

Some time back Amity had heard some of the men talk about fire and hoped she understood what they had said. She had never expected to be alone in such a situation. There was no time to waste and so much to do. Her heart was pounding so hard. She ran toward the barn and brought out Kenny's pony, an iron rake and a section of rope. Able would have known what to do. Amity was frantically hoping she did. She helped Beth up onto the saddle, took the buckets, tied the ends of the rope to each bucket and hoisted them over the back of the horse, one on each side. Taking the halter and leading, the three started down the lane toward the west edge of the seed field. When they got there she set down the buckets and soaked the bags again. Amity lit a patch of dried grass and allowed it to burn a small spot. It spread quickly.

"Girls . . . each take a wet bag and follow after me." She took the rake and pulled the flaming grass back into the area burned and as the girls followed with the soaked bags dragging along the edge of the burning grass, they created an edge where they put out the fire. The side away from the house and the barn, they let burn.

"Try keep up with me, girls." Amity worked along in front of them. And soak the bags again so they don't burn."

"Momma, we're trying, but it's hot!"

"Yes, but we have no choice." She stopped to catch her breath and looked off to the west where the flaming grass and crops were now visible. That would be the Johnson place she thought. She doubled her efforts. The area of their back-burn was increasing in size. But would it be enough?

"The wind keeps blowing smoke in my eyes, Momma." Polly had stopped crying and was dipping the feed bags in the water as Amity had directed. Beth said she'd go for more water and headed toward the pump. The fire was spreading rapidly and the distant line of flames seemed to be racing closer and closer so quickly.

Amity was sobbing now as she frantically raked out the edges of flames along the crop line. Her effort seemed so small in contrast to the looming devastation speeding toward their home. "Oh, please, no . . . please!"

Small whirl wisps of wind lifted flaming grass upward and caused new flames to begin behind them that demanded attention. Beth spilled one bucket just as she arrived and began to cry along with her mother. Polly started to cry again. It looked hopeless. Amity looked back toward the house . . . so much hard work had gone into its building. Here were all the furnishings they had treasured and so carefully had brought west as they established their new home. All was now threatened. Her heart was praying as her blistered hands continued working. And if the fire enveloped them as they struggled, what then? Her mind struggled with the thoughts. She had to try!

Pollen in the Wind

In the glowing darkness Amity looked back once more toward the house. As she did she noticed small fires on each side of both the barn and house had ignited. Oh, Lord, already . . . but no! In the dim light she saw figures. The small fires had been set and were already growing.

"Able? Kenny?" She dared not stop to find out. "Polly, go tell your father where we are. Now hurry!"

She went and minutes later returned.

"It's Mr. Anderson and his hands," she said. "They've come to help."

Sobbing, choking, Amity fought back with every bit of energy she had left. It seemed like hours and her arms and shoulders ached with the exertion. Too quickly the raging grassland and wheat crop to the north burned wildly, the flames sweeping ever closer to where she worked. There were other fires to the north and south of the Steven's farm, some back-burn, some where other men beat at the flames with rakes and shovels. Hours passed and finally it ended, the last spirals of sparks lifting up into the night sky. Men gathered at the Stevens' well, drank deeply and splashed water on their sooty faces and hands. It had been the effort of them all that had done the job.

"You did just the right thing, Mrs. Stevens," said one of the Anderson's boys. When my father saw your line of fire, he felt we had a chance to cut off the fire. Sure sorry about your bigger fields."

"Thank you Rick," said an exhausted Amity, as she hugged Polly and Beth close to her. "We did save our home and the seed crop for next year. Able will be pleased." She paused. "How would such a thing get started?"

"Lightning, most likely," Rick replied. "It's been awfully dry lately and what should have been rain storms, only threatened. That's what my Dad said. He wasn't surprised."

Someone asked about Mr. Stevens and Amity explained. "Can you men come into the house? The girls have just baked some fresh bread, we'd like to share."

"Thank you Mam, we'd best be gettin' back to whatever problems we have at home.

There were no complaints by the girls about bathing that night and it took no time at all for them to get to sleep. It was well past midnight when Able and Kenny brought the buckboard into the yard. They were both smelly and covered with soot. They were glad to be home.

"At least we have the house and barn," he said as he washed and rolled into bed beside his wife. Too exhausted, Amity mumbled something and went back to sleep, moving close to the comforting body of her husband.

In the morning the Stevens' family dragged their sore and aching bodies to the kitchen door. With the sun high overhead already, the glow of the wheat crop beyond the barn was a striking contrast to the burned fields beyond.

"The seed crop!" he shouted. "You saved the seed crop!"

"We all saved the seed crop, Able, Mr. Anderson and his boys and a dozen others. Aren't good neighbors a blessing."

Able put his arm around his wife. "Would have been here if I could have."

"You were, dear. I saw yours and Kenny's clothes this morning. You were with us through our friends and neighbors.

A Thread of Truth

"Every once in a while I drink more than I should and wind up in jail. S'fact, the honest truth! It's for my own good, as some folks would say. I s'pose it is. At least I'm not a criminal like most of the fellas that land there. Well now, let me ease off'n that. Some of the fellas in the cell adjacent to the one with my name on it have some interesting stories, if you get 'em talkin'; which ain't always easy. I remember one in particular, if you'd like to hear."

"Try me, I've got time."

"Well, let's see. We was in adjacent cells, as was usual for me, a young kid and me. I tried to talk with him but he was just lookin' out the window at the mountains. You know how late in the afternoon they change color . . . the jagged peaks, from granite gray to deep blue. It happens when the sun starts to slide down behind the ridges. Shadows streak across the land between the foothills, creeping toward Tin Town here. Then all a'sudden they's gone. I used to watch the sunlight myself as it moved down my cell's wall just before it would make that final plunge off to the west in a blaze of color. Darkness would come swiftly and shortly the sky would change to a whole canopy of stars. As I say, when I go on a drinking binge that's where I used to wind up. I'm doing a lot better these days."

"Well, what about the kid in the next cell?"

"Oh, yeah! He was in for a serious crime. The whole thing done created quite a stir, people comin' from all 'round. He seemed like such a nice kid, too. As I say, I tried to talk with him. But he just wanted to lay on his rusty old cot and think about other things. I finally did get a few words out of him. Since this was to be his last day, he spoke about things he'd been thinkin' 'bout. Him and his family lived on a small ranch across the valley, not a big one by most standards, enough to raise fifty head or so. The ole man worked 'em hard, but was fair. I doubt life was any too easy. Of course the boys both learned to shoot.

"Oh,? So he has a brother?"

"Yep, had a brother, a brother named Cal. They used to ride together along the ridges, sometimes hunting and sometimes just watchin' the land around them. He was killed during the war between the States back in Richmond, toward the end of the war, it was. Father would give them each a couple of shells and off they'd go, a huntin' fresh meat. I guess they were both good with handguns and their Pa's Winchester. The old man pushed the boys to the limit expecting their best. He'd tell 'em he couldn't say how to live, but whatever, . . . live your life honestly. I agree, s'important! Their old man, he did care for them."

"How'd he get himself into trouble then?"

"Aw shucks, that ain't hard. Since the war ended this territory has been pretty hard hit with renegades, army remnants and too many that are servin' nobody but themselves. I think he said his Ma had passed on so it was only him and his father, but with him gettin' pretty big for his britches. You know, in a situation like that, home ain't never the same. He had a little gal that lived on the ranch across the creek from them; a little red-haired gal named Cynthia. He was smitten with her but her old man evidently didn't take to him. The kid said she had brown eyes and a smile sweeter than

Pollen in the Wind

his Ma's apple pies. Said he knew right from wrong just by the look in her eyes. His hangin' would just be the last straw for her . . . as well as for his Pa, when he heard."

"So they were going to hang him?"

"Sure 'nough! They claimed he'd robbed Tin Town's Bank and killed two tellers as he left.

"But you said he was innocent!'

"Well, that's what he said. How would I know any different?"

"What about his Pa? You said he cared."

"Yep, I did. One time the two boys was off in the mountains. They wasn't paying much attention to the weather and wound up in a mountain squall; a blindin' snow storm when they should have been home long past by then. Evidently the old man realized they must be in trouble and went after the two; tracked 'em down. He came riding right out of the swirling snow, tall in the saddle he rode. He gave 'em both Holy Hell, but then explained what they should have been noticing about the weather, the little signs nature shows us all. Yep, he cared, alright."

"So that was why he wanted to look off toward the mountains, just remembering?"

"That and thinkin' about his mother's apple pies. Said he could just imagine the smell of a fresh pie that had just come out of the oven and his hangin' 'round the kitchen hopin' for a slice to carry him on his way. His Ma usually obliged them both, then would hustle 'em off to finish their chores. Strange the things you think of when you're locked up all alone. Do it myself. Somewhere about then I drifted off to sleep and before you know it, it was mornin' and the deputy arrived. We each had a few minutes down the hall and a plate of beans and greasy bacon, . . . oh, and a cup of their coffee. That would have sobered me up fast if I'd had that the night before. The deputy and the kid was friends, but at this point, they sure didn't have much to say to each other. Guess neither one was strong on talk. He done what he had to and left. I asked him how they'd caught the kid."

"He said he'd been caught holding one of the Bank's canvas bags and his clothing fit the description of the robber as he was seen leaving the Bank."

"Pretty convincing!"

"They was even a few bills in the bag that added to the evidence. It was really the shootings that got everyone so riled up. The posse had picked up a trail in the foothills and rode right up on him as he held the bag. And him wearing a wide brim black hat, leather vest with red cloth backin' just like the description. Nothin' he could say would convince anybody and as you know the sheriff was up for re-election just then. They was all making a big thing out'a the hangin'. There was all kinds of activity, a fiddler, wagons arriving from all over the county, shouting, dogs barkin' "

"Sounds like they were sending the kid out in style. I suppose Doc Warren weighed him and all."

"Yeah! He felt pretty bad about it. The kid hadn't been much help around the ranch after his Ma had passed. I s'pose he felt sorry for him. Well, anyway, the hour finally came and a group of heavily armed deputies hustled the kid to the platform, arms tied behind his back. I'd been released by then so I got me a ringside seat where I could look out over the crowd. Sure enough, there was that little red-haired gal in the crowd, an looking mighty serious. The kid spotted her too, and with his lips he spoke to her. I couldn't see what, but I saw her lips shape an answer. I think it was

Pollen in the Wind

'I love you'. Yeah, I'm sure it was. Like his Pa, his word was true, she trusted him."

"Did she stay to watch?"

"No, she didn't. Evidently she'd learned what she wanted and slipped off. Her old man stayed though, lookin' triumphant. Doc had asked the same question and he'd said he was innocent. Doc started to put the hood on the lad, but he evidently preferred to look off toward the mountains. So the Sheriff nudged Doc out of the way and slipped the noose over his head. The crowd hushed as the Sheriff reached for the release that would open the platform's trap door . . . there was a sudden hush . . . and in that very moment we all heard the crack of a Winchester rifle. A dozen eyes turned toward a rider coming into town, riding tall in the saddle and with another man in tow behind him. I knew right off it had to be the kid's dad, the way he'd described him. He pushed right through the crowd right up to the platform. He paid no heed at all to them guns suddenly pointed at him. I pushed closer to the platform myself so I could hear what was being said. He asked the Sheriff straight out, "Did the boy say he done it? "

The Sheriff looked over the crowd, rubbed a gnarled fist over his chin and grinned.

"What did he say?"

"They all say they're innocent," the Sheriff said. "We goin' to hang 'im. "He obviously felt sure of the support all around him. But that kid's old man held that Winchester right to the Sheriff's belly. And he spoke so soft I could barely hear him."

"Well, what did he say?"

"He said,"You got a man who says he didn't do it. His word is good and I believe him."

"The sheriff looked out over the crowd and

smirked. There must have been twenty guns pointed at the kid's Pa. He didn't stand a chance, but he sat his horse and pushed the muzzle of the Winchester harder against the Sheriff's belly. The crowd was silent as death. Doc Warren, he quietly stepped over to the kid and removed the noose from his neck. As he did, the rope parted at the top, apparently shot through, except for a few thin threads. The old man just looked up and smiled. He knew he hadn't missed. "The boy said he didn't do it and I got a man here who bragged he was gettin' away with it. And sure enough , the fella behind him was wearing a wide brim black hat and a leather vest with red cloth backing.

"Oh, wow!

"Wait, there's more to the story. He was released of course and though I've not seen him, I do know the kid did marry the red-headed gal . . . Cynthia. That was quite a while back now. They've since had kids of their own and I can tell you, from what I hear, they insist that their kids tell the truth, no matter how thin a thread it hangs on."

Old Hands at Poker

Old Pete sat on the rickety Deacon's bench in front of Crawford's hardware store. Pete had been a prospector during Silver City's heyday, but not like so many who spent their fortunes as fast as they dug them out of the earth. Pete Hardesty had tucked a good percentage of his diggings in the local bank where he hoped it was safe.

Back then he knew he wouldn't be able to maintain his youthful pace forever and now at ninety-three, he enjoys the warm sun, sitting, chatting and observing as Silver City moves into the next century.

"Town's kinda quiet this morning, eh, Pete?"

"Yup, usually so on Tuesdays 'bout this time. Bank across the street's had only one customer."

Mr. Crawford smiled as he put a few display items on the boardwalk that was the front part of his store. "You just sittin' there watching your money?"

Pete's sitting on Mr. Crawford's bench had become something of a friendly joke, but his wisdom to save something out of his earlier efforts had not. If you wanted to know what was going on in town, you could very nearly learn whatever you wanted from Old Pete.

"Yup, somebody's got to!" He spat a mouthful of juice at a passing fly.

Mr. Crawford went on about his business and left Pete just as his long time friend Zeke Horton tied his mule to the hitching rail and headed for a spot on the Deacon's bench.

"Ain't like you to be in town on a Tuesday, Zeke."

"Nope, but I got me some business down to the assayer's office, then up to the bank." He grinned, showing a mouthful of crooked and broken teeth.

"You finally come to your senses, eh?"

"Took sixty odd years , but I have to admit you done the right thing."

"Then you better git on down there and git your business over with afore you change your mind. I take it you hit a good run of yellow."

"Shush! He motioned to keep Pete from broadcasting the fact, then leaned over close to him and whispered in a hoarse whisper that anyone could hear, "a good bit, and this time," he scratched the back of his shaggy gray head, "I'm going to bank it . . . well . . . most of it. I'll keep out some for a new suit, a cool beer and some carrots for the animal. Each time I've come to town I see you sittin' here and had the envy of you."

Zeke went back to his donkey and fished out a sizeable pouch from the saddle bag. "Dolly, you been a reliable friend." He swatted the rear end of the donkey raising a small cloud of dust. "Say, Pete, whose strawberry dun is that tied down the street between the miller's and the restaurant? Sure good lookin' horse flesh."

"Saw it once a couple of days ago, myself, same place. Too good to be a cowhand's horse. Don't know whose. So it's back, eh?"

"Yup, he's a dandy." Zeke started to return to the bench, but changed his mind and headed down to the assayer's office. "Save me a seat. This time I've earned one." He held the pouch over his head, kicked his heels together, nearly losing his balance in the process, and walked on.

"Old fool," Pete said half aloud.

Mr. Crawford brought out a long handled butter

churn and added it to the hardware on display. He overheard Pete's comment about his friend. "You two been friends a long time, haven't you?"

"Yup, you might say." Pete looked off into the distance and put a gnarled fist against the wrinkled stubble of his face. "Our trails been together or crossin' over a good many years, seen fortunes made and wasted, played some mighty good poker, seen gold madness, shoot-outs . . . and seen this town grow from a cluster of tents to the two story buildings on both sides of the street that we have now . . . a good many years and we've both managed to keep our scalps. Though I don't know how Zeke ever managed such a feat."

If Mr. Crawford had had the time he would have waited for a tale of some Rocky Mountain adventure, fighting Indians, or one of the two saving the other's life.

"A man don't even have to pack a gun no more," Pete added.

"Things are better, yes, but too much is still done from behind a gun." With more to do, Mr. Crawford went back inside.

Alone, Pete let his mind drift back over the years. He had carried a .44 when he was a youngster, defended himself in the high ranges from both claim jumpers and Indians. He survived mountain storms, hunger, thirst and even walked with a limp from the bite of a rattler, where alone he'd cut off the blood flow to his leg and cut out the poisoned flesh. Isolated in the mountains he taught himself to read and could quote unaided whole chapters from his tattered King James Bible. Only a few years back he'd set aside the lonely drudgery of his prospecting to allow his worn out body to soak up the sunshine in leisure. He smiled again at his friend's decision to quit the hard life and join him as he watched the world roll by.

"Move it over friend."

"You're back, been to the bank yet?"

"Not sure I want to play my whole hand just yet."

"Oh? And what kind of cards are you holding that makes you say that? What do you know that the rest of us citizens don't?"

"Walked part way with Sam from the telegraph office. He was lookin' for Deputy Dobson. Seems that Marshall Carlson was wired to go over to Leadville to identify a prisoner Sheriff Henry was holding."

"So what was wrong with that?"

"Sam didn't think of it at the time, but the telegram didn't spell the Marshall's name right . . . made him wonder if the request had actually come from Sheriff Henry. They been friends and worked together for a good many years."

"He didn't know that Dobson had gone over to the Bar Six Ranch to busy himself around Miss Sally-Ann?" I saw him leave hours ago. Durn show-off."

"Can't say just why, but somehow I'm reminded of the stories of the Hardin boys over in the Springs a few years back. They sent the law off on a wild goose chase and then waltzed right into the bank and cleaned 'em out, slick as a whistle."

"And you think that strawberry dun ties into it."

"Just a gut feelin' . . . too fine a horse for anyone we know of. So I ain't going to put my cash in the bank just yet. Besides, I like the feel of it here in my pocket."

"Ya durn fool, that bank is where my money is. Do you think we can just sit here and let someone walk off with it?"

"How do you expect to stop it? You don't carry no gun anymore and all I have is my shotgun there on

Pollen in the Wind

Dolly."

"I could draw my money out," he made a face as though he knew when he said it, it wasn't a good idea. "Too many other people have their money in there too. We gotta do something better."

The two old prospectors stared at each other wondering.

"And even if the young deputy was here, what could he do? He ain't hardly dry behind the ears?"

"Well, my money's in that bank and we've got to come up with something." Again the old timers puzzled. After several minutes Pete stood up.

"Take the end of the bench, we're going across the street to do our sittin'."

"To the bank? We can watch the hold up just fine from here. You have one of your durn fool idees?"

"Yup, now take the end of the bench, then come back and get your shotgun."

"An hour ago I accepted your better judgment, but now you've gone just plumb loco."

Although Zeke complained, he took his end of the bench and together pushing and pulling across the ruts, they dragged it across the street and placed it beside the front door to the bank. Zeke muttered negatively through the whole effort.

"Think we should tell 'em inside?"

"Nope. If we're wrong, we'd both look like fools. Don't want anyone to get excited over the possibilities. We'll play this hand out ourselves. Now . . . you get your shotgun and bring a blanket from your bedroll . . . and I'll just borrow the handle from the butter churn."

"You're aiming to get the pair of us killed, damn you!"

"If we wind up broke when the bank is robbed, what is life going to be worth to us? With the Marshall out of town, we're on our own."

"It's your money in there. Not mine! I sure ain't no hero."

"Not yet, you ain't. We been in worse situations than this, so just play it my way."

"Stoppin' a robbery has never been one of 'em."

Minutes later and still muttering under his breath, Zeke took his place beside Pete on the Deacon's bench.

"And none too soon, I'd say. You see what I see down the street? The rider of that horse was just scoutin' the situation. "

As he spoke, three mounted riders, riding abreast, cautiously eased up the street toward the bank. As they rode they watched the doors and windows of the stores they passed. The street was still empty. Sure enough, there was that beautiful strawberry dun. In all likelihood, the riders had been noticed from behind closed doors and windows, but this didn't look like their business. And typical of Tuesdays, there were no shoppers in sight and the law was safely out of town. Pete nudged Zeke with his elbow and whispered. "Let me do the bidding."

Sitting perfectly still, the riders seemed not to notice the two old prospectors seated on the Deacon's bench, a blanket spread across their laps. The rider in the center pulled up short right in front of them before he noticed.

"You old men there . . . get yourselves off the street."

"Not a chance! You three aimin' to hold up the bank? Well, not today, you ain't!"

"You heard me old man, move!"

Though his knees were shaking under the blanket, Pete cleared his throat and spoke. "My advice to you, sir, is to loosen your gun belts, drop down off your

Pollen in the Wind

horses and walk back the way you came." As he spoke, Zeke revealed his shotgun. The shape under the blanket where Pete sat suggested a second weapon.

For a whole minute the three riders looked down at the old men, considering their odds. Here sat two old men with shotguns aimed at their bellies at ten foot distance. Would they stand a chance against their fast draw on two old men? It is even quite possible that the riders considered jumping their horses right into the old timers, but the relocation of the bank's rain barrel to a position in front of the bench had anticipated that possibility. To have lived into their nineties, there were few tricks these old men hadn't learned or heard about.

The men looked at each other. One rubbed his chin, puzzled.

"I'm callin' the play and it'll cost ya," said Pete.

Slowly, carefully, the three mounted men loosened their gun belts and let them fall to the ground with a thud..

"Now the horses," said Pete.

The three hesitated, again weighing the odds. Finally, the three slowly slid to the ground.

"Damn you, old man! Satisfied?"

"Now, one at a time, turn and start walkin' outa town the way you came."

Under his whiskers, Zeke was grinning at his gutsy friend and the fact that they had faced them down and the three were practically running. Minutes later the street was empty again.

"Can you pick up their weapons, I don't think I can stand up just yet."

"You do it, I'm going in and deposit my money now."

Mr. Crawford rushed across the street and other shop keepers along the street who had seen the confrontation from their security, rushed forward to express their praise. Later in the afternoon, Marshall Carlson returned, pieced together the events during his absence and sought out the whereabouts of his two surprise stand-ins.

"Appreciated what you did today, Pete, Zeke." He warmly shook their hands. "You saved our bank and I understand you had all your resources there." He shook his head in amazed approval. "Thanks! Did you really expect to pull it off with an old shotgun and a stick under a blanket?"

"It was a bluff, we admit."

"Well!" The Marshall smiled, "You played your cards just right. But, what if you'd had to shoot at them?"

"Shoot? Couldn't have," responded Zeke, flicking some imaginary dust from his new shirt. "My shotgun ain't been loaded for months. We wouldn't have had a chance."

"Did you know that, Pete?"

"Nope . . . we just done what we thought was right. But then I guess in cards or whatever, that's what a bluff is all about. You play in life what yer dealt!"

Discovery

A burning ball of fire crept slowly across an airless July sky, its heat bearing down relentlessly on the semi-arid land around me. A black raven pranced back and forth from where I lay, raucously scolding me for invading its private domain. Overhead, its mate soared gracefully in the still air. A turquoise and gold collared lizard skittered towards me, inspecting my presence, posing briefly before disappearing between some rocks. It had not been my intention to be thrown painfully from my horse to so abruptly enter their world. I'd tried to negotiate the rugged slope of the mesa ahead of me when my mare lost her footing, catapulting us both against the rocks. With her foreleg twisted and broken I would have no alternative but to put her out of her misery. The thought was appalling to me, so I put it off for the moment.

Until this time, my week in the canyon area north of Durango had gone fairly well. But now to be injured and isolated so far from help, I realized for a greenhorn such an adventure alone had been a foolish idea. Books and intellectual pursuits more suited my nature. Already four days out from my host's ranch I knew the little food and water I packed would not see me safely all the way back. I had assured them that if my return was later, search would not be necessary. I was now in doubt. Other than a bruised arm, a swollen and a possibly broken ankle and other minor scratches, I was physically able to move, even though painfully. So, I lay panting in the partial shade of a twisted old sagebrush collecting my thoughts, wondering where to go from here and how to get there.

It had been photographs by the pioneer photographer William Henry Jackson that had sufficiently peaked my curiosity about some ancient dwellings in one or more of the canyon areas some distance outside of Mancos, Colorado that had challenged me. At the age of twenty five, my imaginative mind soared with the thrilling expectation of potential discovery of a lost civilization. As an archeological student of ancient middle eastern ruins, the challenge, refused at this point in time by the Smithsonian Institution due to lack of funds, was to me an overwhelming opportunity. Alone however, it was proving to be naive judgment on my part.

Crawling slowly over broken chunks of sandstone I worked my way toward my suffering equine friend. Several times she tried to rise, her eyes bulging with a terror she did not understand, her nostrils flaring and snorting. The Winchester in the saddle boot was on the far side, her weight holding it firmly under her body. Somehow I would have to stand and pull the reins forward to shift her weight in an effort to help her rise. Hopefully she would then fall to the opposite side freeing the butt of the rifle sufficiently to be retrieved. Following a number of frustrating and agonizing attempts, I did manage to free the rifle only to reward my suffering mare with a bullet to her head; an act I dreaded. I tried not to think about what I was doing, but knew it had to be. That done, having been frustratingly unable to encourage the mare to rise, caused me to slump where I stood, exhausted and drenched in perspiration. Even now her dead eyes seemed to follow me in condemnation. For a moment the world around me began to swirl and fade. The pain of my ankle and my exertions was taking a toll. I fought to remain conscious and began gradually to crawl back toward the small area of shade where I had fallen. As I inched my way forward the warning hiss of a slowly coiling snake caused me to freeze where I was. My activity had disturbed what ever it had been doing and now coiled and hissing, wanted me away. We two, eyed each other suspiciously. Given a moment to observe carefully I recognized from earlier description that the snake was not a fearsome rattler but rather a large and angry bull snake, non-poisonous and most likely abroad hunting mice or other small critters. Thank goodness for that! None-the-less, I was not assured of increased confidence in my well-being.

In time I was able to cautiously back away, communicating unintended harmful intent on my part to which the snake obliged me by doing the same.

Pulling my pack within reach with a stick I dug around for the small compass I'd brought but so far hadn't wisely used. When I found it I also found the glass broken and the needle missing. In my fall it had struck a rock. With the sun so nearly directly overhead it was difficult for the moment to orient myself. I sank back wondering, beginning to struggle against the fear rising within me. I had to force myself to remain calm. At least, I thought my head was beginning to clear.

Looking around me I could see a long canyon stretching out ahead of me. There was little question that the rough vegetation in the canyon bottom, tangles of greasewood, sagebrush and varieties of prickly cactus would make traveling on foot difficult. Once into the canyon, access to the top of the mesa in my condition would be precarious. Off to what I presumed to be north, the sides of the canyon appeared to be even steeper. Alone, injured, uncertain as to my location and distances, real panic began to creep into my thinking. Previous study of what little was known of the area seemed to offer limited consolation. Food, water and rest seemed for the moment my first concern; certainly water. Walking or limping my way back to civilization would take longer than three days, a human limitation I'd learned from my host back in Mancos. One thing instinct told me was not to let panic overtake good thinking. Gathering strength I decided to attend my injured ankle first.

With my knife I hacked off a portion of the twisted old sagebrush beside me to provide a crude splint. I used the reins from the mare to bind it all together. Then I cut a larger piece that would serve as a crutch. Neither effort proved easy so by the time I was ready to travel, daylight was beginning to fade and I was physically and emotionally drained. I decided to stay where I was and rest for the night. Finding a level spot nearby and away from my dead mare I began to prepare for over night. There was no telling what attraction the dead mare would be to night animals. Looking around me the shaggy juniper bark of trees nearby appeared to offer a suitable bedding material. Hobbling back and forth I created an adequate sleeping area in front of a large overhanging rock that would provide protection behind my spot. From the body of my mare I retrieved a blanket, other leather harness pieces and the cinch buckle; anything I thought might prove useful. Then I began to gather a supply of firewood. I knew there would be coyotes, possibly even larger animals that would be attracted to the body of my horse. How to start a fire without matches was beyond my pioneering skills. I realized very quickly there was more to simply rubbing two sticks together. Scared as I was, my ankle swollen and throbbing, I decided to save what food I had till morning. As the daylight began to fade, I huddled in my makeshift nest and began to nod and drift off.

It was the sound of something moving in the low growth nearby that startled me into frightened consciousness. I reached for the Winchester not knowing what to anticipate. In the dim light of early evening a big burly man appeared. Behind him followed a pack mule. He saw me immediately and asked with surprising politeness if he could approach closer. What was this I was seeing so far from any known settlement? I lowered my weapon and responded. As I've said, my visitor was a big burly fellow with a bushy head and full beard, dressed almost entirely in skins. He carried a rifle, but it was covered by a soft leather sheaf and he'd made no effort to cause alarm. At his waist he wore a huge knife, also encased in a fringed leather sheath. My fears began to give way to questions.

"Got a problem, traveler?" he asked. His voice was soft spoken and not demanding.

I explained what had occurred and my predicament, then asked how he'd found me.

"Vultures circling overhead gave your dead horse away. When I crossed your trail a ways back and followed, it lead me right to you."

"My trail?"

The big man grinned. "Yup, broken twigs, scratched rocks, a few hoof prints of a shod horse . . . knew it wasn't Indian."

Amazing, I thought, and acknowledged his sharp eyes as well as his coming. He looked at my ankle and grunted.

"Broke," he said. "We'll stay put the night."

With that he pushed aside my collected firewood, scooped out a little hollow in the earth, added some dried grass and twigs and with flint and steel, in minutes, started a fire. He let it burn for a few minutes building up a few coals, but even then kept it small. I offered larger sticks which he refused, shaking his shaggy head.

"It don't need to burn bigger'n our need. Smoke from a big fire can be smelled from a distance."

"Indians?" I asked, startled that there was a danger of that kind.

"Utes, Navajos or Apaches, it is their land."

"Oh!" was all I could manage.

From his mule he pulled a pack of his own from which he took a coffee pot and a slab of bacon. He hardly wasted a motion and quickly had a pot of coffee heating at the edge of his fire. From a small pouch he poured out a handful of bluish-gray juniper berries and motioned my sharing.

"Name's Woodford," he said, holding out a big gnarled fist of a hand with a grip that would pale the strength of a vise.

"Uh, my name's Alexander, Cameron . . . I'm called 'Cam' for short."

Again I expressed my appreciation of his arrival and wondered at the same time what had brought him to this remote area and where he was really going. Where had he come from and why? He offered no information about himself.

Following our simple supper he momentarily left camp, disappearing into the brush, returning shortly with a few pads from a prickly pear. He set them in the bed of hot coals of our dying fire to roast. Minutes later he pulled them out, carefully, but easily, he removed their sharp spines and held one out for me to sample. Behind the protective bristles, now removed, was a sweet gelatinous fruit that topped off our simple meal.

Pollen in the Wind

I admired the man's capacity to live off the land as he obviously was doing and I began to feel a bit easier. Still wondering why Woodford was traveling in this area I finally asked. Conjecture was not good enough. He replied.

"That clay mug you just drank from, came from here. It was made by people who once lived here." He paused. "Perhaps the same reason you're here."

"Then you know of dwellings nearby?"

"Yup! Lots of questions, not many answers."

"An ancient civilization?"

"Most likely." He didn't go on. I inquired as to what might have happened to it.

"Number of things possible." Woodford settled down, making himself comfortable. "Tree rings provide us with some ideas. Good years, they're wide, dry years, they're thin. An old stump shows too long a dry spell. Hard on crops. People moved away."

"But . . . "

"Enemies possibly," he continued. "Reason they built into the sides of the canyon walls."

"Think we'll ever know?" I asked.

"Nope. Humankind don't take to obvious answers." He didn't elaborate. Surprisingly he let the fire die out, covered the hollow with the sandy soil he'd removed. From his pack he took out a small book which he carefully opened and read to himself. I wondered how he could see with so little daylight and he said he knew all the lines anyhow. I could not see what the book was, but guessed at what it might be. I learned later it was not a Bible, but instead an Oxford book of English verse. He had noticed my attention and stopped. "John Donne" was all he said. At the time however, it made me wonder all the more about him, why he'd left the civilized world behind him to take up such a lonely wilderness life here in the Nation's southwest. Days later as we traveled he softly, to himself, spoke a few sad lines.

"Stay, O sweet and do not rise!
The light that shines comes from thine eyes;
The day breaks not: it is my heart,
Because that you and I must part."
"Donne? I asked. He nodded. I knew his work.

Was he escaping from something or someone . . . or to someplace? In either case he was a self reliant man at peace with himself and where he was, confident in what he was about. What went on inside him remained a mystery. Buried sadness, or sadness being buried, I concluded.

When he finished reading that first evening, or perhaps reciting, he pulled a gray and tattered Confederate blanket over himself and his broad-brimmed hat down over his face. For Woodford the day was over, and he was ready for sleep. A rasping snore soon followed.

The next morning, well before the sun made its warming appearance, we shared coffee and what food I had left in my pack. Then he checked my ankle and nodded his head with approval that the swelling had diminished. In fact over the next two days we moved slowly along the sides of the canyon observing sandstone walls, strange pits Woodford called kivas and several structures of more than two stories in height. I made sketches in a note pad and asked a lot of questions. He replied where he had reasonable answers but really didn't talk a lot. He acknowledged his silence simply by saying that "words are only important if you have something to say." In my mind I added, 'or wanted to say'. He was a remarkable person, almost more interesting than the ancient ruins we were seeing.

Pollen in the Wind

He pointed out the carefully chipped and shaped stones of some of the walls, the obvious thought that had gone into their construction . . . the stone slabs or pieces of wood for lintels over doorways as they had been set into surrounding sandstone blocks . . . surfaces skillfully chipped and shaped by pecking, creating a dimpled surface effect . . . and notches where timbers, most likely mountain pine, had once been placed to provide roof structures over the round pits or kivas. There were shell beads as well as a few bracelets in more than one structure, suggesting sources for the turquoise in them to have come from other areas through commerce. There were potsherds lying about that I would have wished to carry back with me but he discouraged it.

"Someday we'll learn more if we leave be."

He was right of course. Analysis of pottery and other artifacts can tell a lot to a person who knows how to view them. Just the simple pinched surfaces or corrugations in the pottery suggested a change from the smoother black-on-white pieces that lay around their fire pits. I made more sketches.

With secure homes in the sides of the cliffs, safe from enemies, protected from the extremes of weather, the question of their abandonment bothered me. Perhaps it had not occurred all at once but over time as the population exceeded the capacity of the area to support more people or perhaps even the wish of great numbers to migrate southward to easier living, more fertile land, new opportunity. It struck me that it was not unlike our own move westward as the U.S. grew. Lincoln had suggested of the Civil War that it was about a "new birth of freedom." Bits of Woodford's clothing suggested the possibility of his participation in the struggle between the States. His sadness certainly suggested deep felt loss.

Further to the north there was less tree cover, more service berry, cliff fendlerbush and grasses, the possible consequences of forest fires that destroyed tree cover and the same plant material as further south. As we traveled we saw a small herd of elk, a gray fox and signs of big horn sheep. Woodford knew them all and pointed out their tracks as he identified them. He also knew how to find small sources of water. Who was this big man? Were his gentle ways deceiving me? Each day I worried less as I saw more completely into this unique person.

My opinions about Woodford were, of course, all conjecture on my part. For several days we had seen where an earlier civilization had lived and had vanished, their disappearance a mystery; a whole civilization gone, wiped out by the natural environment or by conflicts within itself. Mankind has a way of doing such things to itself.

As we moved closer day by day toward our own civilization, I was increasingly amazed by the quiet wisdom of this big rough-shod man who had come to my rescue. Each day my ankle improved, and I could walk now unaided and without the crutch. A week had passed by the time we came in sight of a settlement. It was at the edge of the town we parted, once again Woodford holding out his big ham of a fist, a lonely sadness in his brown eyes.

"They say the soul knows how to re-provision itself . . . if we let it." was all he said as he turned and left. Hardly moments later when I looked back for one last look, he was nowhere to be seen . . . like the ancient civilization that had prevailed so long before us he was nowhere in sight. I had in my twelve day adventure learned far more than I'd ever hoped, realizing that as

Woodford had shown me, our own small worlds are not all there is to be seen and that our real strengths come from within ourselves, though sometimes through a lonely healing struggle.

The Trunk

She was a beautiful woman, full figured and easy to look at. She had a confident air about her that was most appealing. Confidence, as you must know, is something that grows out of experience and she'd had plenty of that. Her name was Lillie Lovegood, a singer and entertainer at the Gold Strike Saloon in a small Colorado mining town. Few travelers west would recognize the name of the town, but her name was widely identified and remembered.

She was a high alto when she sang and the heart of many a miner melted at the sight and sound of Lillie when she performed. She had some good moves. She also had other selective talents that further extended her reputation.

Evenings at the Gold Strike were noisy, crowded with boisterous cowhands, miners and card sharks; not always friendly with each other. It was a hard life for all of them, but no less difficult for a beautiful woman in a slam-bang shanty town in the late '60's. Although Lillie herself was a major attraction at the Gold Strike, it was not only her presence that attracted work weary and throat dry clientele. Behind the long imported mahogany bar hung an eight-foot long painting of Lillie wearing not one stitch of clothing. Stretched out for the world to see, she lay unblushing and relaxed, leaving absolutely nothing to anyone's imagination. It would be impossible to estimate the number of jaws that dropped and eyes that glazed over as they stared during the course of a single evening.

Pollen in the Wind

It was on into the early morning hours sometime last year in the quiet privacy of her dressing room that I learned the story behind why she was willing to so totally expose herself long enough to be captured on canvas by a painter's brush. Lillie, at first, without speaking, simply pointed to what once must have been a handsome arched top and cowhide covered trunk that sat in the corner of her crowded and colorful quarters. It seemed totally out of place. It was battered and worn, hardly an item of tasteful selection. She raised her eyebrows in an unspoken suggestion that implied there was a story beyond her reaction to my question. Her brown eyes danced mischievously. It took time to benefit her fuller response. Although her story of the trunk and uniquely its relation to the audacious painting over the bar was concluded here at the Gold Strike, it actually began in New Orleans where Lillie had visited briefly before traveling west and ultimately to Colorado. She had seen a red velvet dress; actually tried it on, but discovered the cost was way beyond her means at the time. She didn't forget the dress however when she moved on west.

At the time she talked with the owner of the Gold Strike about working as an entertainer, the dress was not a part of her limited wardrobe. Somehow the dress became an issue. Discussion of the red velvet dress became a part of her agreement. The owner, a calculating, perhaps even devious, businessman with a roving eye and a fanciful notion of his own, wanted a picture of Lillie to be painted and hung over the bar. With such a vision to wet the appetite and entice his customers, her live presence would be a sure-fire draw. Handsomely clothed in such a beautiful and exciting low-cut dress, just as she had described it, completely captured and stimulated his active male imagination. Lillie was hired and as agreed, ordered the dress to be sent. She would wear it and a painting would be made. In time she received word that the dress order had been received and it would be shipped. It would be coming on an Overland Stage with an anticipated arrival date which suitably coincided with the owner's lavish completion of a stage and related curtains and special lighting.

An itinerant artist was retained and kept sufficiently sober to undertake the large canvas assignment. Work on the painting began, the composition developed, the background advanced and Lillie's head and shoulders exquisitely painted. It was at this point that a problem became evident. The problem was with the painter. Without the dress the artist refused to proceed on sketchy verbal descriptions alone to complete the painting. Lillie was confident the necessary dress would arrive any day, certainly in time. There seemed no great cause for concern.

In New Orleans, the dress was carefully wrapped and packed in a small arched top trunk, locked and routed for shipment. It was a handsomely made little trunk, well built and carefully studded with decorative brass tacks in its cowhide covering. It was placed on the platform ready for shipment. At this point arrangements fell apart. A fire broke out in the warehouse, schedules for some unexplained reason became lost or confused and the trunk was determined to belong aboard a freight shipment to the Arizona territory. In Flagstaff, the trunk, unprotected, sat for weeks like a homeless orphan. It suffered several rainstorms and a small dust storm with all identifying tags and labeling gradually obliterated. So it sat! It was a young new-timer's curiosity about the small hidebound trunk that initiated steps toward recovery.

Meanwhile the owner of the Gold Strike was daily claiming anxiety that his blow-out stage show was nearing completion and his beautiful centerpiece star would be unable to fulfill her part of the bargain to make that all important first night opening the success he had bargained for. The painting simply had to be completed. Lillie assured him, positively, that of course, things would work out. He just smiled. In fact, she was so positive she was willing to wager on its timely arrival.

The young man in Flagstaff, unaware of urgency, but curious, pried open the hasp lock on the weary little trunk and carefully inspected the contents. Perhaps there would be a clue as to its intended destination. The handsome velvet dress he found carefully protected inside was unlike anything he had ever seen. He recognized immediately that such a costly dress was far beyond the demands of an ordinary person. He didn't stop there. He brought the matter of the little misdirected trunk and its very special contents to the attention of his superior. Together they accepted the challenge. By a series of telegraph communications and searches, the original routing was re-established and the trunk was hastily reshipped to Colorado. It was shipped to the care of a Miss Lillie Lovegood, but also included in the shipping instructions, the name of the owner of the Gold Strike; a curious bit of added information.

The trunk arrived, battered and weather stained on the outside. The special dress, carefully wrapped and protected inside, was happily received in good condition. However, the major opening date had passed and an alternative event had had to be hastily improvised. Without the dress, the owner insisted that is how she would be painted. The artist naturally and most willingly fulfilled his commission under the owner's revised direction.

Since their grand opening there is no question the Gold Strike had become the most popular watering hole in Colorado. And there in the corner of Lillie's dressing room Lillie keeps the little trunk. As part of her lavish decor, it hardly fits. That doesn't matter at all to her. Since their grand opening, the owner of the Gold Strike has been smugly smiling all the way to the bank. And in the privacy of her dressing room, Lillie smiles quietly to herself and sometimes wonders why the trunk's return included the name of the Gold Strike's owner. She had made and certainly fulfilled her wager. For Lillie, the little trunk sits forlornly in the corner of her dressing room, an ever present and silent reminder of the risky consequences of a woman's overconfidence with a calculating male entrepreneur.

Hallowed Ground

The reality of family loss is a burden too difficult to imagine. Kathleen Wheeler, at thirty-eight, was a widow. She and her husband Andrew had grown up as friends in Woodbury, a small town in New England. Grade school, high school and quite a few years of oversight had gradually given way to a mutual and deeper discovery of each other. Their love was a bond forever. To them, love, family and home were more than simple words.

They had married in '43 and together started and operated a small farm that made a sufficient livelihood to raise a family of three husky boys. Six cows, a yard full of chickens, fruit trees and a large vegetable garden kept them busy. The soil was rocky, as testified by the line of stone walls along their property lines, the stones all painfully removed from the garden area. Theirs was little different than many in Woodbury and the surrounding countryside. They were a close knit and caring family and all shared in the chores of working the farm. Of the three, Robert, James and Noel, Noel was their inquisitive youngster, his dark mischievous eyes and ready grin too easily capturing the affection of those around him. James was the oldest, a leader. All three were good boys and had grown into fine young men by the time the nation had become involved in the conflict over the secession of seven and ultimately eleven states from the Union in 1860.

For so many years loyalty to one's State had taken precedence over loyalty to the Union. Such had been a voluntary understanding since the beginning of the Union, although New England at one point had itself considered secession following the war of 1812. The difference in the patterns of living between the north and the south were at the roots of the ultimate conflict. As the nation had grown following the Louisiana Purchase and then the Mexican War, there developed an increasingly bitter struggle over whether new states would be recognized as free or as slave states. In 1818, brief compromise was accomplished when Missouri and Maine joined the Union, with one slave and one free. In 1850 Texas, New Mexico, Arizona and California were brought into the Union. When Kansas and Nebraska joined as white settlements with the repeal of the Missouri Compromise in 1854 sectional differences intensified. Harriet Beecher Stowe's indictment of slavery in Uncle Tom's Cabin further increased partisan feelings. One issue after another gradually brought the issue of slavery into more intense public debate. The die was ultimately cast after the Dred Scott Case and followed by the Lincoln-Douglas debates with the Republican strength of the north leading to Lincoln's election in 1860. Both Kathleen and Andrew had agreed that slavery was a political, social and moral wrong, but to go to war over it had never been in their thinking. The early hours and demands of the farm offered little time for serious understanding of the politics and the debates going on in public life. They had not taken the time.

Shortly after April 12, in 1861, when southern batteries opened fire on Fort Sumter, Andrew Wheeler felt compelled as his patriotic duty to volunteer to serve the Union. He accepted it as an obligation that would be quickly settled. He had argued that the industry, railroads and economy of the North would be an overwhelming advantage against the rural agricultural states below latitude thirty six degrees, thirty minutes. That was about the politically determined latitude at that time that separated slave and non slave states. He was to have been a one year volunteer, as was his option in response to the May call for men. Neither had considered the possible impact of his not returning. He served only a few months, only to be killed in the first disastrous Battle of Bull Run.

Upon receipt of the news from the War Department regarding her husband's death, Kathleen was unbelieving. This could not be. She would not believe it and for days simply denied the reality of the news. The letter she had received had been a mistake. Yes, of course there had been some error. Not her Andrew, no! Andrew was a man who had difficulty killing the holiday turkey or an occasional chicken for the Wheeler dinner table. She would not accept the information and inquired. Yes, it was so! Then as others around her, over the months that followed, also began to receive letters from the War Department, the reality of her loss began to sink in. Alone - the thought terrified her. How could she live without her partner; only half a life? The battle the newspapers had reported indicated that although superior for northern forces, it had turned it into panic and disaster. The new Confederacy had won. Over the following months, little news was good. Capable generals seemed unable to bring the superior strength of the northern armies to victory. Anger set in. Kathleen was furious that for no reason of his own making, she'd lost her husband. She missed Andrew more than words could describe. Their love had been so strong. The war didn't make sense. No war made sense. Any woman who brought life into the world would agree.

Sharing Kathleen's anger and resentment, the three boys felt impelled to join the military, intending to deal with the situation in their own way. Kathleen was unable to persuade them otherwise, too distraught to argue effectively and feeling very much alone in her grief. So, together, the boys signed on. She couldn't stop them. As for the farm chores, friends helped and the hours and routine of daily milking, garden and housework consumed each day. She purposely filled every day, every minute, with things that simply had to be done, or so she thought. Though exhausted at the end of day, real sleep came only with restless difficulty. Of course, without Andrew and now the boys, friends gathered round seeking to provide comfort. She found sympathy and real understanding to be far apart.

Kathleen, though now alone, had not been left destitute, as together, she and Andrew had planned well. She was good with numbers and Andrew had deferred all the record keeping to her. She had saved where she was able, a New England trait. They owned their small acreage and house and with added help until the boys returned home, time and the pressure of work might gradually allow some degree of acceptance and recognition of the loss in her life. Being alone was the hardest, particularly when the day's work was done and she'd slip into bed unable to reach out to touch her Andrew and feel secure. Tears would too slowly be followed by sleep.

Letters began to come from the boys and these helped. They were alright and following their basic training, they were assigned to an artillery unit, filling out a group from Illinois that needed three replacements. They wrote that they would be going west. They would be together. Their letters mentioned a lot of marching, boredom and food unlike what they had shared at home. Small actions seemed to occur nearly every day and one time Noel, somewhere in Ohio took a prisoner in a brief and indecisive encounter. He didn't explain further. The southern lad was a volunteer and no older than himself, poorly clothed and without shoes. He was from a "hollar" somewhere in Tennessee and the two of them, after their initial confrontation, found some humor in the way each of them talked; how they pronounced different words of their common language. Under other circumstances Noel suggested they might have become friends. The lad, Billy Joe, was sent to the rear the following day along with other men taken prisoner during the day. Noel never mentioned him again, but the experience had made him wonder about what they were all doing. All three boys, in their letters, spoke of the size of the country, its beauty, always the continual marching and the huge numbers of men that it took to make up an army. It seemed that the men moved day in and day out, and slept on the ground at night wherever they were. The boys felt lucky much of the time to ride on the caissons of their field guns. One thing their letters made no mention of was the number of casualties, how forces stood hardly more than three hundred yards from each other and facing each other fired point blank. There was no mention of medical attention, nor the likelihood that even the simplest of wounds by infection alone was proving fatal or certainly incapacitating. They shared none of the horror of what they were about and Kathleen could never have possibly imagined. Disease alone took so many lives. Robert said he was keeping a dairy that he would share when they came home.

    Weeks dragged into months and the year '61 and '62 dragged into '63. Kathleen was aware of the battles that were taking place along the east coast states and the Union's recent defeat at Fair Oaks, and other places with unknown names. There was also growing public discontent with the overall progress of the war. Yet, hate it as she did, she felt captive to each piece of news. Robert took an interest in where they were going and the military objectives and tried to explain something about an Anaconda cutting the south in two and like the snake, squeezing it to death. Kathleen wasn't sure she understood, but it sounded important. All the marching, advancing and retreating didn't mean much either until she began to look at a map locating places like Paducah, Kentucky, Belmont, Missouri; and others along the Ohio River where it flows into the Mississippi. She began to see that the river was a critical part of what Robert, her student of the three, called the western campaign under the command of a Brigadier General named Grant. Robert also pointed out that the area of the river and its tributaries made up the largest system of waterways in the world; a water basin larger than all of western Europe. With its black loamy soils where they traveled, so different from New England, there were huge plantations of cotton. There was no wonder to him why New Orleans was one of the world's busiest ports and militarily important. He expressed quite an interest in the size of farms; farms which were referred to as plantations. Robert's letters came alive with descriptions of places and people; the stubby, stoop-shouldered man in the rumpled uniform who was their leader, looking more like a refugee from some shanty town than their commanding officer. And there were others.

Robert did write of the capture of Fort Henry on February 6, followed by Fort Donelson where Mr. Grant's insistence on an "immediate and unconditional surrender" was even written up in the local newspapers at home. There were, of course, from many envious sources, rumors of political infighting for command, unauthorized independent actions, so claimed by a Major General Halleck who aspired to taking over command of the western campaigns. As if the fighting itself wasn't burden enough for the nation. Too cryptic for real understanding, Kathleen took solace in the boy's safety and receipt of the letters themselves. Most recent letters spoke of the funny looking gunboats, "turtles" as they called them, as naval forces began to blast their way down along the Mississippi in April. Then followed Shiloh where great gray clouds of smoke from burning cotton fields and stacked bales of cotton covered the land like a pall of doom. Robert anticipated that their forces, numbering in the thousands, would soon be moving toward Fort Pillow and Corinth. The latter was one of the principle east-west rail junctions of the Western Confederacy. But campaigning toward Corinth was not what happened to her boys.

Six field guns of the 1st Illinois Light Artillery, on April 17 and under the command of a Colonel Benjamin Grierson, a tall gangling cavalryman, who with a 1700 man force, was assigned a diversionary campaign of its own. The boys had been assigned to his brigade but had no idea what it meant or where they would be heading. Typically, cavalry moved quite rapidly and field pieces would slow them down. From that date until well into May there were no letters.

Kathleen, without an occasional letter was desperate and empty, more alone than ever. She thought the worst, anticipating any day she would receive one or more communications from the War Department. The silence wore heavily. She began to lose weight, slept even more restlessly and dreaded each purposeless day. April dragged into May and beyond without word.

Even with President Lincoln's repeated urging, for whatever reason, General McClellan failed to move forward toward capture of Richmond. The news along the eastern seaboard subsequently reported yet another defeat of Federal forces in what papers called the Jackson Valley Campaign. People were growing increasingly weary of the war and its draining consequences.

Finally, in early July, Kathleen received a fat letter. It came from the Federal headquarters in Baton Rouge. All three boys, now young men, were safe, tremendously weary from what Robert described as an unbelievable 600 mile campaign from La Grange, Tennessee to Baton Rouge, Mississippi, an adventure he assured her he would plan to write when he could. Their Colonel Grierson had proven himself a clever and creative leader. They had fooled the enemy, tricked the local population and avoided both capture and losses. They had destroyed immense quantities of military supplies, rail centers and miles of tracks and most important of all, had adequately confused Confederate forces to draw sufficient numbers into fruitless pursuit. Their activity made more readily possible General Grant's capture of that key city on the bluffs - Vicksburg. All of Baton Rouge had turned out to welcome their brigade. Over the whole sixteen day adventure, Colonel Grierson had lost only twenty-six of his men. "And to think, Mom," Robert wrote, "before the war Colonel Grierson had been a composer, pianist and music teacher who disliked horses." Kathleen was jubilant with her news, yet in her joy she also had begun to think painfully of the losses of human life that the nation was experiencing, both Union and Confederate.

Back in September of '62 Antietam had been reported as the bloodiest one-day battle in all of U.S. history, taking the lives of some 23,000 men, a costly triumph for nobody. There followed others including Fredericksburg early in December of '63, another sickening defeat, men squandered in foolhardy efforts. The loss of Union troops counted in the thousands. In November 1863 President Lincoln spoke in a political debate at Gettysburg saying, ". . . It is for the living, to be dedicated here to the unfinished work which they who fought here have thus far so nobly advanced . . . that these dead shall not have died in vain." Kathleen wondered, when the war would end, if ever it would, how many lives on both sides would never be the same? From the beginning of time men had fought each other and in thousands of years to what end? Somehow the world would go on. And yes, General Grant would receive more stars as he moved up the advancement ladder. There would be more battles, the loss of more lives. Kathleen often cried, not so much from what the boys wrote, but too frequently from sheer loneliness without her family. Or often she cried from what she could imagine of the incommunicable experiences and passion of the battlefield; fields littered with the dead and dying, her boys seeing and being a part of it, perhaps lying there themselves.

The boys continued to write, increasingly mentioning the rich lands they had traveled through in the west. "What a privilege it would be to farm such land, perhaps when the war ended." They were good letters, filled with support, love of home and family and understanding.

For a long time Kathleen thought of the President's words . . ." that these dead shall not have died in vain." She repeated them over and over realizing that here was a good man; a politician, yes, but a caring man with deep feelings. More weeks slipped by. General Grant was brought from the west and put in command in place of McClellan. He was still the man in the rumpled uniform, either smoking or drinking, but he was respected and knew the job he had to do. For too long efforts to take Richmond, the Confederate capital, had fallen short.

In November, as the leaves turned color, Confederate General Lee, with a similar idea in mind, moved north along the Shenandoah Valley. They came as far north as the small Pennsylvania town of Gettysburg. Washington was just within reach. In the three day battle that followed, had he not rested his weary troops and pushed on, he might have carried the day. He didn't and in the gamble the south lost a third of his forces and retreat was his only option. Kathleen felt no great relief or joy in the Union victory or the southern loss at Fredericksburg that followed.

Letters stopped coming from the boys again. Kathleen wondered what to expect. She marked another month off her calendar. Two days later three smiling young men jarred the entry bell at the front of the store. They were home! Robert had a beard and looked so much older than his years. Noel held his mother close and sobbed with relief. James quietly waited his turn, his lips tight, saying nothing. They had all grown, filled out into manhood. Minutes later the "closed" sign was hung at the front door and the small family went home. Home, home, Noel sobbed. As tired as the young men were from their round-about trip home, they sat together in the oil light of the parlor, talking, staring at each other and at times too choked up to

Pollen in the Wind

express their thoughts and feelings.

Days passed and in time each of her boys shared bits and pieces of their story. There was much they didn't share and very likely never would. And Kathleen didn't press them. Quietly she knew. They had done their job. The most difficult day of their visit was the morning they wore their uniforms to the breakfast table. There was little comment, mostly assurances, expressions of love. They would be returning to their brigade.

Amazingly, the war did go on, the boys were transferred to Federal forces in the east. Kathleen learned the names of Chancellorville, Chicamaugua, Cold Harbor, Spotsylvania Court House and too many others, some victories, some defeats, but all involving the lives of the nation's young men. Grant, now in command of the Federal forces in the east following McClellan's inability to advantageously bring down Confederate General Lee, seemed to be making some progress. His goal was to move toward and capture Richmond, the Confederate capital. Hopes rose and withered, as the Federal Government hovered close to financial bankruptcy. There was even the thought of a negotiated and humiliating end to the war. It was at this low emotional level that Kathleen received a communication from the War Department; James had been killed by a sniper's bullet while in the lines before Petersburg. Two days later she received a similar envelope. Noel was listed as missing in action. Kathleen was stunned. For so long she had dreaded the possibility of such communications. She treasured the short time of their recent visit. Now the lives of three of her family had been taken from her. Two and possibly three had given their lives over four years of bitter fighting, and still no end in sight. And if and when the formal war ended, would there ever be an end to the probable resentment, bitterness and debate? It was a dear neighbor who again helped her over the hollow days that followed.

Finally, at a place called Appomattox Court House, it all ended. Two gentlemen came together to humbly end the effusion of blood of the Nation's war weary manhood. General Grant had finally brought the Northern Army of Virginia under General Robert E. Lee to its knees. It was a generous peace, simply accepted, and over the months that followed, men both north and south began to return to the homes they'd left behind. Robert included. Joy was mixed with tears as his diminished family spoke quietly and thankfully, cried, and held each other close. They had been terrible years for them as well as for the nation.

Somehow over the ensuing months Robert, even though glad to be home, proved restless and ill at ease. It was difficult to set aside the experiences and tensions of daily rituals, expectations and consequences. Somewhere in the back of his mind had grown an itch to see again the rich loamy western lands where his early travels had taken him. The three boys together had been fortunate over so many years, until the last. Like his mother the "holes" in their family were deeply felt. He spoke of the places they had been and of some of their experiences together. He did try to write of some of their experiences, but the painful battlefield images made the process too painful. As they talked of these things Kathleen questioned and expressed a wish that she might walk the now empty battlefields where her family had been brutally diminished. At first Robert did not fully understand, nor understand why his mother would want to venture to such places, but he would listen. Gradually he saw meaning to his mother's wish . . . to walk the same consecrated ground where her Andrew had given his life and where also two of her sons had lost their lives; his sons. Yes, he would go with her. Together they explored what such a journey might mean, along with other possibilities.

Kathleen recalled that months before the war had started, a series of laws had been passed and in a pre-election declaration had been acted on in '62. As a veteran, a citizen could acquire a tract of land in the public domain not exceeding 160 acres. There were limitations as to where land was available that excluded the original thirteen and six other states. Robert inquired and found that people had been moving west in small but increasing numbers and this series of laws had been enacted as an incentive for the settlement of the west. To a large extent the opportunity had appealed to prospectors, miners, venturesome immigrants and even outlaws. None-the-less, the idea appealed to both of them. Kathleen saw in her son his needs. He was a young man, anxious not only to bury a terrible chapter in his life but to stretch, reach out and fulfill the potential within him. He needed a wife and the opportunity of a family of his own, not the burden of an aging mother. They realized they could each help the other. Together they gathered the kind of information they might need. They learned their obligations required them to settle for not less than five years. They inquired about some of the trails people had traveled, the Sante Fe Trail, the Oregon Trail and others. Scandinavian Americans had been moving to Montana for several years. Wagon trains had blazed trails all the way across the country. The more they talked, the more excited the two became. Without Andrew in Woodbury, there was nothing to hold them to a rocky New England farm.

Part of their venture would include, as they had finally decided, to walk the silent battlefields, to stand in the awesome silence, to hear in their minds the roar of cannon, the low moans of the wounded, the voices calling for help that seemed always to be asking "why?" So, hand in hand they walked and wept. Together, they did these things. Kathleen, with tears streaming down her cheeks, stood with eyes closed, listening intently, hearing in her mind the moans and cries of the dead and dying, waiting. Then she knelt, continuing to sob. Robert gently put his strong arm around her. Holding her close he suggested that perhaps it had been a mistake to come and it was best to go. It was while traveling back to Woodbury and their small farm, Kathleen, who had been quiet most all the way, lost in her own thoughts, suggested it was time to look forward in their lives, and join the hundreds of people moving westward, starting new lives, filling the great expanse of the growing nation.

It was shortly after that the farm was sold and connections were made with agents. There were many others who like themselves had sold out comfortable homes to start life anew; new opportunities. They were unlike the gold seekers who only years earlier in the '40's had trailed west hoping to strike it 'rich'. Traveling to Omaha they completed their final arrangements and in a big wagon called a prairie schooner, they became just one of the many. From there they traveled westward, through great expanses of open country, some wild and beautiful, some barren, rocky and spectacular, a few small towns. They traveled west along the Platte River and in North Platte, where the trail divided, they decided to follow the North Platte. They were told that the south trail crossed whole stretches of alkalye wasteland, sand and clay and poisonous water. They were also told by travelers returning along the trail who "had seen the elephant" (had made it out west) not to take any cut-offs. They were learning slowly, uncomplaining in spite of the hardships. Somewhere beyond Scots Bluff they moved into Wyoming territory and on up toward Fort Laramie and Douglas. This was beautiful country, though said to be Shawnee and only questionably safe. Even so, Robert would often ride off into the countryside along their route. One day he returned all excited and out of breath; he had found a place. It was a place he said he could in time call home. It was a parcel with a stream, aspen and tall pine as well as open meadows. It was the kind of place he'd dreamed about. Initiating inquiry, Robert found the land to be Federal and as public land was available. That very evening they settled matters with their wagon master and parted company. Two other families felt good about the area they had traveled into and became neighbors just as soon as land claims and titles could be arranged. They were pleased that a small town, a row of wooden store fronts, a church, a one room school, and a hardware store, all huddled together in a valley, would not be far away.

    Working together with their new neighbors they built small cabins. The first year was difficult, the winter worse than anything New England had ever dealt. But they held firm. They both spoke of what they'd had, what they'd left and the good memories experienced. These gave them strength to look forward. Kathleen recalled so clearly the efforts she and her Andrew had made on the stone covered New England hills. They had done it together. Once again, each day was a challenge. Yet, as the days and months passed she quietly found a new strength, in and beyond herself and in the land. She was quietly glad they had traveled the battlefields before starting west. She had walked where Andrew had last been; where he had given his life. Yes, the memories she cherished were of Andrew when they had begun their lives together building on their small farm. They had been so much in love, a privilege for which she was ever mindful. Now the demands of her new life carried a different feeling, an affinity beyond herself that brought her closer to her Andrew. She gradually found a new peace within herself.

It was no surprise to Kathleen when Robert, at the end of one working day, put on a clean shirt and rode over to one of their new neighbors. Nor was it later a surprise to her that the following year he married a little red-headed girl from one of the wagons that had traveled west with them and settled nearby.

A room was added that Kathleen might remain an active part of her son's new family. It was there until her death in her early sixties that she shared in the work and good times of a growing family. Robert and his Mary had two sons and a daughter, Cameron, Jeffrey and Geena. During those years, as she was able, Kathleen would walk to a small rise that looked out toward their house and the valley below and when a sudden breeze would touch her gently on the cheek she would smile and know finally that in spite of all that had happened over the years, and though she missed her dear Andrew's presence, she had never really been alone. Life does go on. God had taken her heart in his healing hands and would safely see her where again she and her dear Andrew would be one.

She loved the spirituality of the land and that God was in every rock and blade of grass. And she knew in her heart that her Andrew was nearby, even in that gentle breeze, and that without hurrying, in time she would hold his hand and they would be together once again for ever.

The Iron Horse

"Is that really your picture on the piano, Grampa?"

"Yes, Ruthie, dat is your old Grampa, long ago." Abraham Menin had been an accountant for the Union Pacific Company back in the days of its major expansion westward. He was retired now and living quietly alone in an eastern city. His wife had played the piano when she was living, but Abe, as all his friends called him, wanted to keep the piano after she'd passed. Music had always been a part of his life and Eva had played so beautifully. It was one part of his past that he treasured, and it was also a good place to put the pictures of his family.

"Are you the one in the background here?" Ruthie had climbed up on the piano stool to point out what she remembered he had once before pointed out to her.

"Dat is me. Of course I vas much younger in those days." He smiled at the two little girls who had come to visit their Grampa.

"I can't see, Ruthie, let me see too."

So, the picture was taken off the piano and brought down to the level of the two little girls. What the picture showed was the meeting of the Central Pacific with the Union Pacific rail lines at Promontory, Utah, May 10, 1869. There were a good many people gathered around as the last spike was being driven to complete the cross country tracks. That last spike was called a "Golden Spike" and well might it have been, considering the great sums of money that had made it possible.

Pollen in the Wind

"Which one are you, Grampa? said little Esther.

"Oh, I'm the one here in the back of the picture. All the important people are standing here up front. Ya, dot's me, right here." He pointed to himself off to the side of the larger group.

"You should have been right up front, Grampa."

"Oh, no, dot vas for the important people, like I say. I vas only in the business of keeping books.

Abe had been born in Austria, and as a young man had emigrated to America, met Eva at Ellis Island and in time married. He struggled to learn English and while going to night school had gained his citizenship. Life had not been easy, but he'd lived it with personal integrity.

"What does it mean to keep books?" asked Ruthie.

"Vell, it's a long story. You see, to build a big railroad all the vay across our country vas not an easy job. It took lots of money, money to pay the men, money for all the materials and so on. Keeping the books provided a record of all the dollars spent."

"Money to buy the land too?"

"Vell, our government helped a lot there with Federal Land Grants." He stopped there, thinking how best to explain to two five and eight year old grandchildren how the government could give away 130 million acres of land without expecting to receive something in return. It had been Senator Stephen A. Douglas and a William King who had sponsored the first grants. That was only the beginning. This had happened before he'd gone to work as an accountant, but he had a pretty good idea who beyond the railroads benefited.

"Ya, it took lots of money and vun of my jobs vas to write it all down in a book. Dat's vat an accountant does, dat vas my job." Ya, I kept the numbers . . . dat vas . . ." He didn't finish; he knew there was more to it. Abe was proud of the education he'd had and the means to earn a solid living. It was not a job he talked about at home or anywhere, but inside his mind he was proud of his skill.

"Tell us about the railroads, Grampa."

With one little girl seated on each side of him Grampa Menin began to tell a story, but before he did, he went to the closet and pulled down an old and tattered photograph album. Here he could show some of the work that had to be done to accomplish such a major undertaking. There he had collected pictures and post cards of train cars and even some of the workmen laying down ties and spiking the sections of steel rail to them. Carefully, he explained what a trestle was and all the timbers that had to be used to create it; a bridge across a wide stream or deep canyon in the mountains. There was one picture he had of the trestle at Devil's Gate in Utah where the engineers had run three engines and two cabooses out in the middle of it, just to test its strength.

"Those engines are big. What makes them go?"

"Oh, my yes. They burn wood and the heat of the wood makes the water in this part here form steam." He pointed to the back of the engine, the place where the engineer stood and the fireman, the big boiler in front, and how the pistons connected to the wheels.

"It is the steam that powers the vheels to make them go. It took a lot of trees to keep them going. Nowadays vee don't use wood. Vee use coal and when it burns, it causes the water to make the steam."

"Oh!" It was the girls' only comment. The mechanics of it all didn't seem to matter to the little girls as they both looked toward other pictures.

"Why do they call it an Iron Horse, Grampa?"

"You are a funny one, Esther. Vhy do you tink they might name it an Iron Horse?"

"Because it does the work of a horse," volunteered Ruthie. "And because it's made of iron, silly."

"Right you are! Trains can haul huge amounts of freight. Some years ago they carried thousands of soldiers and the supplies they needed. Ya, dey can carry many things. The cars go over the tracks with a click, click, clickity click, the engine up front chugging away as it pulls a dozen or more cars. The cars that carry people can be pretty fancy, with comfortable seats and even fixed up for serving food. They even have cars that you can sleep in. They call them Pullman cars."

"Was that the kind of car you rode in?"

"Not one of the fanciest, Ruthie." Abe turned the page looking for another picture that might be of interest. He was really enjoying his company. They came so infrequently.

"Oh, what is this one Grampa?"

"Vell, let me see," he scratched his head. "Dat vas a town called Bear River City." He began to chuckle. "It is no longer dere. You see, while they were building the railroad, many workmen had to have places to live. And when they finished the work laying the tracks, the people moved on to another place to live. Some of the towns were only tents, some where little more than shacks."

"But, there are stores here and . . . and places to eat. . ." said Ruthie.

"Many were not good towns, Ruthie. The men who worked on laying the tracks and doing all the hard physical work were a rough lot, too quick to do bad things. There were no police there, so personal protection and justice vas done by fists and guns . . .

not good towns." To explain the saloons and houses of prostitution and what went on when the men came to town to spend their hard earned dollars was another side of the story that needn't be shared.

"No, Ruthie they were not real towns, because they vanished when the work was done and the men moved on."

"But there are towns and cities in the west now?"

"Cheyenne is one that comes to mind, yes. There are many others today. When there are big ranches and herds of cattle that need to be brought to market, the cowpunchers bring their herds to be shipped east from the railhead cities. This is still done. Railroad trains can carry huge loads of freight and do. Cheyenne is one city that managed to survive and prosper after the work of the railroad was completed. There are others, of course, as I say."

"You know a lot, don't you, Grampa?"

It was a naive question of course. Grampa did know a great deal about the expansion and business practices of the railroads. Little grandchildren didn't need to know of the graft and corruption that prevailed in the letting of contracts; the over-pricing of building materials; rate discrimination between one customer and another; rebates, inflated costs that created great wealth for the Ames brothers, Oakes and Oliver, Thomas C. Durant and Sidney Dillon. Oh, there were other names too, both good and bad, and company names like The Credit Mobilier, a false front construction company, one of many.

With the railroads growing at such a rapid rate they had become near monopolies and rates for traffic could change without warning, sometimes even weekly. No, it was not a time of high public and private morality. Grampa, as an accountant was aware

Pollen in the Wind

of what was going on, he saw so many of the numbers and the contracts. They were not pleasant years for him, knowing what he did.

"Yes, I do know a lot about the expansion of our railroads. After the problems between the north and south were settled at a place called Appomattox, rail lines grew seven times over. In fact rail construction moved vell ahead of what was then called the frontier. Hundreds of miles of new rail lines" he added.

"How did they get the trains over the big mountains?" asked Esther.

"Here's a picture that shows a steep incline along the side of a mountain where they cut away enough earth for the tracks. And this one is of a snow shed that protected the tracks from the heavy snow drifts that would occur in winter. All this took a lot of work and a lot of men to build. It vas not easy work."

"Where did all the men come from who worked for you?" Ruthie was asking good questions and Abe enjoyed their visits. He saw too little of them and wanted to make the most of each brief time.

"Men came from all over," he said "Some were brought all the way to America from China, just to do some of the hard work. A good many of them still live on our west coast. Men came from all over, good men and bad men."

"Bad men?" asked Esther.

"Not all the men came to work. Once in a while there would be a hold-up and bad men would try to rob a train. You see, with many men working, they had to be paid which meant that there had to be money on the trains to pay the workers. It takes a lot of money for a country to grow."

"Did they ever catch the bad men?" Esther went on.

"Ya, groups of men would get together and ride after them. They caught a lot of them. Robbing trains vas not a good business to be in."

"Were there Indians?" Esther seemed to like the adventure side of Abe's story.

"I believe there were. You see the Indian people lived on the lands that the rail lines were crossing, and they hunted the buffalo that also lived there. They used the meat for food and the hides for trading with each other. The trains were not a good thing for the Indian people. Hunters killed a lot of buffalo just for the sport of it as vell as for the hides which they sold."

Grampa turned a few pages, obviously looking for something. "I don't have a picture of a buffalo. Hunters killed so many."

"We saw a picture of one at school, Grampa; big furry animals like the one on the coin."

Grampa laughed. "That may be the only one you'll ever see. They killed that many. Vhat the buffalo meant to the Indians is another story. You see, it vas their land dat vee were taking away from them. When you are older I vill try to explain." For years Abe had struggled with questions of how business was being done and had rationalized that he didn't arrange the terms, only wrote down the numbers. Grampa knew the aspects of doing business without moral concerns was an abstract concept that two little girls would hardly understand. He never told Eve. She would have been furious.

"You didn't tell us why you were in that picture on the piano, Grampa," said Ruthie, coming back to her earlier question.

"Vell, no." Grampa rubbed the back of his head wondering if he could answer Ruthie's question in a way they would understand. "My being there vas . . .

vas a kind of opportunity that they felt I deserved. It made me more a part of what they had been doing with the numbers. It vas after that I retired, your Gramma and me."

"For all the work on the books you did for them, Grampa?"

"Ya, I vould say dat. For many years I had worked in a little office in Chicago, then in Council Bluffs, as the lines expanded westward; a good many years. Ya, I vould say dat I was given the trip west to see the driving of the last spike. I knew too much of the business behind the building of it all. A lot of business with numbers, ya. I vould say dat vas so."

The Conquistadors

Wade Freeman stood in the open doorway looking out across the open grassland of the Freeman ranch, a ranch of several thousand acres south of Santa Rosa, New Mexico. His father, a rugged barrel-chested and graying man sat in a big chair across the room behind him, staring at his eighteen year old son. He rested his chin in a gnarled and sun colored fist as he pondered their situation. Without faith in something, solution to his problem appeared bleak!

"We only have eight weeks left, son. I see no way we can meet our contract deadline. It's getting late in the season to be searching for wild horses. Too soon the weather will close us out."

"You've always been able to complete your Army contracts, Dad." With hands on his hips the tall young man turned to face his crippled father. "We can still search. Between Tim and the hands we can make one more sweep of the northwest section. It's mesa country and I'm sure there are wild horses out there. I just believe there has to be."

"We're more than thirty short and it's a long way to Abilene, son. If these old legs of mine . . ." He stopped short. Wade Freeman senior was not one to seek pity or forward excuses. Over fifty years in this part of the country, he'd traveled a good many trails; fights with Mexico, the Apache, rustlers and the extremes of weather. Already widowed by eight years, the loss of three sons and the hard life of the southwest, his fire was nearly out. "I've made my last drive up the trail, son."

"But, Dad . . . we'll find more. I . . ."

"You still have that wild notion about the mestenos, don't you son?"

It was the myth of the Spanish conquistadors, Hernan Cortez, Francisco Vasquez de Coronado, Juan de Grijalva, and the search for the Seven Cities of Cibola. They were a small army of gold seekers, gold seekers who had brought their spotted horses to the New World and vanished. The young man was positive a whole herd of mustangs roamed free somewhere on the mesas to the north. From the time he'd learned to ride he hoped some day to find them. It would be now or never!

"Dad, hear me out." He came over by his Dad's big chair and unfolded a pocket-worn map of the Sonona and lands along the Chisholm trail north through Indian territory. "We haven't looked in this area for months." He had circled an area to the northwest. He put his hand affectionately on his Dad's shoulder.

The older man looked up at his son. The lad was strong, hardened by the physically demanding work of the ranch and full of the same fire he had himself brought west as a younger man. He'd been disciplined by the whole process of introducing wild horses to human contact and driving them north to meet Army contracts. With periodic Indian uprisings in the territories farther north, the pursuit of Geronimo and scattered bands of Crow and Blackfoot, the U.S. Calvary yearly needed horses for their mounted men. And Wade Freeman had annually sent hundreds of horses north to fill the need. He shook his head at the boy's blind faith in a story where there had been no proof. They were only stories told around campfires, repeated over and over. He took the map from his son and looked at it carefully.

"This area here, Dad." His son pointed. "Look, I see it this way. Tim can take some of the hands and start north along the Pecos. There's a water hole about here. If he can set up a camp there with the lot we've already gathered and wait there."

"Wait for what, boy?" It was his frustration surfacing.

"Give me four hands and ten days. Dad. We'll join Tim there and either take north the contract number or whatever we've rounded up. We'll get at least a few more. I just feel we'll . . ."

His Dad broke in again. "It's a long shot, son . . . a long shot . . . no, it's more than that, it's blind faith."

"Dad, please! Allow me the chance. So is marriage an act of faith . . . religion is all based on faith. You just have to believe. Let me try." This was a debate they'd had many times before, but his Dad wasn't crippled then and limited to a chair.

Wade senior closed his eyes. Minutes passed. He sighed heavily and put his big hand on top of his son's. "Yes, your mother and I came out here as an act of faith in our potential. We had a good many fine years." He nodded his head slowly. "I guess I can't deny you this."

So it was that the hands were called from the bunk house to the big main room. That evening, a varied collection of cowhands that had been with the Freeman spread for years, had endured all the same hardship of trail drives north, scraps with Mexican bandits and the tedium of the day to day efforts of working with horses in all kinds of weather, joined Mr. Freeman in the big room.

Young Wade outlined what he had in mind. He let

Pollen in the Wind

his younger brother Tim pick his men, making sure he drew at least a couple of the older hands himself.

"We'll need a corral about here, near the water hole," he began. "Most of you have been there before and know what is available. If and when we find what I hope to find, we'll drive east to meet you. By joining forces here," he pointed to a place on his map, "we'll cut off nearly a week or more along the trail by my group's not having to come all the way back to the ranch. Any questions?"

"Only one, Mr. Freeman," said one of the hands, "and that one's been around for a long time. We all know the myth." There was a murmur of agreement that it could be a wasted effort, but . . . if it was what they were called to do, they would all do their best. There was genuine respect for the Freemans.

"Tim, you'll need a few days to be ready to roll north, chuck wagon, weapons, gear and tools to put together an enclosure. Tex, you work along with Tim."

"Got it!" Tex was one of the best trail men and the hands would follow him anywhere.

"Bill. Juan, Slade and Hank, you'll be with me. Juan, you're one of our best with wild horses."

Juan nodded and grinned, showing one gold tooth in front. Juan was a tall wiry Mexican who had been on the Freeman payroll for years; hard working, quiet, capable. The others knew him as a quiet man of faith. He also believed the stories of the band of Spanish gold seekers who had brought spotted horses to this part of the southwest and had never again been seen. There were few men who believed them to still be wandering somewhere in the lands to the north. But Juan believed.

"Gracias, Senor Wade. Juan like go."

"You think I'm crazy?

"No crazy. I know story. My blood is Spanish. Is

true story!"

"I'd like to leave by noon tomorrow. We'll split up what we need to do, food, extra horses, you know the routine."

Wade Freeman senior's voice was a bit husky when he put his arm around his son after the others had left. "You're like your Ma, Wade. She never doubted for a minute we'd make it here. You know I'll be with you every mile."

As planned, the four hands and Wade saddled their horses, secured the last cinch and rode north. It was a peaceful ride, each man thinking his own thoughts. Hank rode point. Bill trailed with the spare horses. Slade volunteered to pack the food, he said only because he liked to eat regular, and Juan rode along with young Wade.

"You think I'm crazy?" Wade asked the man beside him.

"No crazy, Senor Wade. I say again . . . is more than story!" He nodded, thinking before he again spoke.

The story was of men who had come from the Extremadura, the hot dry lands of northern Spain and not at all familiar with western weather. 1699 had proven to be a very bad winter and these men were believed to have become lost; never finding their way back to the coast.

"Si, Senor Wade. 400 years 'go. It was late in year, as today. Bad winter! Si," he nodded his head with conviction. "Good story. They still wander."

"And their horses? "asked Wade. "It's more than a myth to you?"

"Mestenos! That is Spanish word for "strayed" senor. The myth is that these . . .these conquistadoras still search their way. Si, and their spotted horses, they still exist."

"Today the story is claimed to be a myth! So you too believe?"

"Si. There are tales of sightings, but no proof Senor Wade."

"Are we being foolish, Juan? As you say, it is already late in the season."

"Guizas, senor, perhaps. We give it a week . . . eh? We should be able to add a dozen or more horses even if we no find the Spanish mestenos. Horses are social animal, they hold together in groups. Should be easy to spot."

"I'm glad you're with me, Juan."

"Gracias, Senor Wade." Juan was an older man, had been with his dad almost from the start. He knew his business, he knew horses. "If we spot the leader, we'll have them all." He pulled a small bag from his shirt pocket and bit off a piece of tobacco that he tucked into his cheek. "We find," he added. He looked to the sky and pointed. "Sky say, we may see early snow ahead."

"I guess," Wade replied. He took his compass from his pocket and checked their location, referring to his tattered map. He did this several times as they traveled north and west, winding their way amongst the big cactus and abundant plant life, surrounded by the sandstone shapes of a long past era when so much of this New Mexico land had been under water. They were wild wind eroded towers that jutted upward into the sky, colorful and picturesque. It was a rugged land. The small group trailed along the edge of a gully, slowly climbing higher across the rocky terrain. They stopped briefly, walked their mounts for a mile or more and by late afternoon determined they had covered close to twenty miles. With a chilly wind sweeping out of the northwest they hunkered down for the night below a protective tilted outcrop.

The men tethered their mounts, built a small fire and jokingly looked to Slade for grub and hot coffee. That was the duty he'd drawn, and he'd gone about it with enthusiasm. He surprised them all with a cake he'd gotten from Chan, the cook in the kitchen, before they'd left the ranch.

"Now don't count on chow like this from here on, guys."

For two days they trailed further onto the higher ground of the mesas without a sign of anything, not a single track to follow. In spite of their skills, without shoes wild horses would be more difficult to track.

Once or twice Juan anxiously looked to the sky for clues as to what the weather was doing. Camp was made each night and Slade produced other small surprises that Chan, back at the ranch, had also made available. For all the uncertainty of their venture they were all in good spirits. Every added horse would add to their pay at the end of the drive. With the kitchen chores completed, five weary men rolled into their blankets.

Morning surprised them all with a light dusting of snow. Breaking camp took little time and they continued the sweep of the land before them. With field glasses they surveyed the open land further out beyond them. The terrain was increasingly rocky with sandstone piers jutting dramatically into the sky; beautiful, desolate, silent. Before the day was out, the temperature moderated and slowly a dense fog reduced their search horizon to a few hundred yards. Darkness came early under those conditions and they welcomed a warm fire and camp. Slade quickly had a pot of coffee underway. To these men, that always came first. Horses were, as before, tethered head to tail, a short distance from their fire and travel gear.

Talk around the fire dealt with the task ahead should they be so fortunate as to encounter any horses at all, or the potential of the old myth.

"When we see these mustangs, we'll have to surround 'em in order to catch them . . . no small task in weather like this, eh fellows?" said Hank. He spit off to the side and pulled his sheepskin close around his neck. If anyone doubted, it was Hank. ". . . in weather like this," he grumbled aloud.

"Si, mi amigo," said Juan, laughing. "One step at a time. If we see them, we corner them against the cliff of the mesa. They not try to escape down. But first we find them, eh?"

"You really think we'll find them, Juan?"

"Si, I think."

Wade knew these men; good men. Juan had perhaps the most experience in breaking a horse to the weight and will of a rider. Whatever their leader does, the highly developed social ranking and behavior of the group would hold them together.

"The real trick will be to pick their leader, the wildest of the group, then prove we intend no harm," said Hank, continuing to express his doubts.

"Paciencia, Senor Hank, Patience. We have all done this before."

"You look at me with one eye, Juan."

"Si, I am like the horse, suspicious, careful. I hear what you say with one eye." It was not annoyance, but doubt that bothered Hank. "When horse look at you with both eyes," continued Juan, "the fear turns to curiosity. Only then, he yield to rope. You must have faith, amigo."

So went their friendly chatter.

The fog continued to thicken and by the time the group settled down for the night one could hardly see thirty feet. A few more sticks were added to the fire as it slowly died. The cold damp forced the men to pull their blankets up close around their heads. Sleep followed and was welcome.

It must have been in the earliest hours of morning when a snort and nicker from the area of the tethered horses awakened Wade. He pulled himself upright, reached for his Winchester and started in the direction of the horses. The last dying embers of the fire cast an unworldly reflection against the inclosing fog. He shivered.

He had hardly gone more than ten feet, when before him, a short distance away, at the edge of their camp, shrouded by the fog, stood a small group of men. They were bronze colored men, like Juan. They were wearing strange metal armor that glistened in the eery light. Their hair was long and gray and by their sides hung great swords. Wade was startled and leveled his Winchester, but then looking closely, he saw there was no substance to these men he faced.

They faced each other in silence. Some words were spoken in Spanish, but he did not fully understand. There was no threat in the voices he heard. His mind tried to shake him free of sleep. Could these armor clad travelers be the men of the ancient myth? If direction was what they sought he did know the word, "donde' and "por favor". Hesitantly, Wade pointed in the direction of the Pecos River, off to the east. It would lead them south and toward Mexico. Slowly he motioned with his arm. "Rio Pecos" he said and pointed again. Someone spoke the word "gracias, amigo," and as mysteriously as these men had appeared they were quietly swallowed up by the swirling fog. They were nowhere in sight!

Wade stood silent, dumbfounded, staring intently into the surrounding empty fog. He shook his head to clear his mind of the brief and unexpected encounter. His mind was still on the men he'd seen, or what he thought he'd seen. He nearly tripped as he went on to check the sound from the tethered horses that had awakened him. What he found was that all the horses were securely tied but his own. His mare was gone! "Gone!" he stammered. Slowly he returned to his blanket.

Juan mumbled something to him as he lay down again, but he did not hear. Confused, Wade pulled his blanket up around him. He was shaking, but it was not from the cold. Until morning there was nothing that he could do but wait. Could it be that his mare had smelled the scent of a stallion and had broken loose? Could she have been taken by the night visitors? Sleep came with difficulty and proved a restless, disturbing sleep. By morning, it was Hank who had to awaken him.

"During the night . . ." Wade began, "my horse got loose. She's not with the others." Then too, how could he also explain what only he had seen?

Having returned from the direction of the horses, Slade agreed. "Your mare must have worked loose during the night. I heard a noise and saw you were already up." He rubbed his hands together for warmth. "She won't be far off." He turned away to busy himself with breakfast.

Breakfast passed quietly. Evidently Juan had been awake, too, but no one spoke of any visitors. Wade dismissed his encounter as something he'd dreamed, though throughout the day he could not convince himself that what he had seen had not been so. And too, there was the disappearance of his mare that puzzled him.

"Today we find horses," said Juan. "Juan certain now!"

With gear packed, the group buried the coals of their morning fire and left camp. By mid-morning the fog had entirely dissipated leaving a beautiful clear but chilly day. Each step of the way Wade carefully observed the surrounding terrain. At one point Slade was sent off to explore what appeared to be a small canyon. When he reported back he had good news.

"Box canyon, Wade. Now all we need is something to put in it."

"We will," assured Juan, grinning broadly. He seemed as optimistic as Wade. In fact, he seemed convinced.

Close to noon, it was Bill, riding point that saw them first. "Forty, fifty, no sixty . . .and Wade," he called back," your mare is with them."

"She knew ."exclaimed Wade, as he rode up beside Bill. "She got the scent," he said, relieved.

So the work began. Sticks with small flags were made to be used to encourage, but not frighten, the running herd in the direction of the cliff along the edge of the mesa. By noon they were gathered, stopped by the steep drop-off and the line of riders who had guided them this way. These were strong powerful mustangs that had roamed free and now stood nervously watching their captors, snorting and pawing the ground. They pranced and moved restlessly watching the riders. The confrontation lasted for over an hour, each watching the other. Finally Juan spoke.

"The prancing one with the spotted neck. He is wild one they will follow. I will let him know my smell." Dropping to the ground he very slowly approached.

"Good, Juan, but ease over to my mare first. She will know you and remember. We can show we intend no harm when she allows approach."

"Si, I will do, senor."

Little by little, Juan approached Wade's mare who let him approach and rub her neck. Then he slowly eased toward the wild one with the brown and white spotting on his neck. He watched the stallion's ears. He did not want to startle him, to see the ears lay back against his head. Gradually the stallion's fear turned to curiosity and Juan was able to get close enough to touch the wild one's sides and tail. As the stallion turned and looked at him, Juan winked, a big grinning wink, at the ranch hands standing off ready to pursue if the herd panicked and bolted. All the time he talked to him in gentle terms, mostly Spanish, soft, soothing, assuring words.

Hours later, he yielded to Juan's rope and lunge line. He was one step closer to convincing each horse he would be a trustworthy leader. It was a slow process.

"Enough for today, Juan," called Wade. We need to move them back along the trail to that box canyon. We'll work with them there until they feel more comfortable with us."

"Si, Senor Wade. They know our smell and touch now. Is halter and weight of a man that will be difficult."

"We have time yet," said Wade. He was more than pleased. He was excited. If all went well, they would meet his father's Army contract. For the moment he almost forgot his strange visitors.

Carefully, the men guided the herd back along the edge of the mesa and down to where Slade had found the box canyon. With their encampment and horses tethered at the entrance they could breath easy for the night. In spite of the chill in the air, the mood was jubilant. With their round-up they had carried the myth of the lost or strayed horses to its conclusion. The numbers made them happy. Juan spent hours in amongst the mustangs, touching, rubbing down, talking to them. He continued speaking in Spanish; gentle, comforting words. He carried a water bucket to them and slowly discerned the ranking of each horse within the group. He was up early the next morning and with a broad grin announced that the stallion had briefly allowed his weight upon its back.

Each man then began to follow Juan's example and all day they worked in amongst the herd. It would take time to teach each the pressures and movements of a rider's body for them to follow, but it would be done. Pressure on the right flank would move them to the left and so on. The halter and bit was another day and the men had come prepared.

Checking his compass Wade decided it was time to move the herd again, down off the mesa and east to the water hole where they would meet his brother, Ben, and the rest of the hands.

"Slade, would you and Bill ride back along the east side of the mesa to find a route down. I don't need to remind you that these horses can handle a rougher trail than our mounts."

Slade laughed. "Right! That crazy group could quickly outrun us all and leave us starting all over."

Hours later, Slade did find a route they could manage and the herd was guardedly moved down and on to the east toward the Pecos. Each evening the men worked in and amongst the horses, preparing them for what was ahead. Wade thoughtfully watched their skill

Pollen in the Wind

and patience at work. He also wondered if the mysterious night visitors had traveled in this direction. There was no sign of them. He must have been dreaming.

Three days later the herd reached the waterhole. They were moved into the enclosure Tim and the hands had prepared. The work of training continued for several days as a new social structure amongst the horses developed. Soon, with the expanded crew of seasoned riders, Wade felt they were ready to move along the trail north to Abilene. Wade was again more than pleased and shared his feelings with the men. He knew his Dad would be proud of what they all had accomplished and he shared his appreciation.

They were all pleased that they could meet the terms of the contract with the Army. Yes, of course it meant more money in their pockets, too.

It was only when Wade went to personally thank Juan for his particular efforts that he spoke of the night that his mare had broken free; thoughts that had not actually been far from his mind.

"Slade and I saw you get up that night, Senor Wade."

"But you never mentioned it, Juan."

"No reason, Senor. Slade not see what we two saw and only you and I heard. It was you and I, Senor Wade, who had the faith. You are like your father, Senor. Only you and I who saw. To see what others do not even believe, Senor Wade, is that not what faith is all about?" Juan grinned, his gold tooth shining behind an expanding smile.

Doc Who?

Doc Parker was not really a doctor, at least not from any medical school. Some years back, someone had called him Doc and he liked the title and all its connotations and it stuck. He's been called Doc ever since. For a chap who came west, it was certainly not to work in medicine, or really to work seriously at all. I can make that statement with the utmost confidence. Work was not his style, although everywhere one turned in the 1860's, there was abundant opportunity.

The incident that earned him the chevron of "Doc" occurred purely by chance. He had been aboard a stage running from Denver to Pueblo that was carrying a cash box. Bandits had intercepted and halted the stage at the crest of a hill and stated their characteristic demands. The stage driver had heroically reached for a weapon and succeeded only in causing his unanticipated wound. In pain, he toppled off the coach breaking his arm as he struck the ground. Then, as if to add more trouble to the situation, one of the passengers also attempted the role of hero. He was shot as well. So, here we had a coach with four terrified passengers and one of the drivers lying on the ground writhing in sheer agony.

Enter Elmer Parker, passenger, dressed like a city banker and full of talk. Yes, one might say he could talk the bark off a tree. Well, with copious expurgatory defamations he stripped the bandits verbally into submission and retreat, leaving the overland conveyance and its desperate wayfarers to fend for themselves. In that moment of weakened judgment an element of admiration was in the making. Yes, one might forward the impression that here was a man who could not only forcefully expound on almost any subject, but offered yet potentially other untapped capabilities. I hasten to amend that thought, for so long as there was no party present in his audience who might actually know more about what was being said, at least then, he exhibited sufficient sagacity to keep his mouth shut.

In his life such exception was hardly the rule.

Well, let me tell you, Elmer Parker does have a gift of gab that would make a lawyer think twice. I heard him forward an argument one time sufficiently to win his point that he'd been present in the Ford Theater when John Wilkes Booth shot President Abraham Lincoln. When a call went out for medical attention, he was subsequently notified and immediately asked to come to the man's assistance, a request he deferred due to his other party allegiance; a conflict of interest, he stated. Later he was confronted with some fairly basic truths regarding his whereabouts at that precise time which he adroitly shrugged off as inconsequential to his earlier argument, which he had won at the time.

So here at the stagecoach hold-up, he typically accepted the collective accolades and stepped forward, as the chief of surgery at one of the larger eastern medical practices, to offer his modest skills in behalf of the beleaguered victims. He did help set the driver's broken arm by cleverly responding to the subtle admonishments and clues offered by a lady passenger whose son had at one time experienced a similar difficulty. Fortunately, the bullet in the driver's shoulder had passed clean through so a splash of whiskey and a piece of petticoat from the same lady passenger solved that medical challenge. For the other unfortunate passenger, he was fully capable of identifying a dead man.

Naturally, when the stage arrived at its next immediate destination he was heralded by the passengers by the unprecedented title of Doctor Elmer Parker, a recognition he hardly refuted, but later trimmed to the more modest Doc Parker and has since never relinquished.

Oh, there have been a few situations here in Dodge where after a gunfight someone has called for medical response and Doc's name was forwarded. In more circumstances than one it was found that he was too busy to break away from what he was doing to respond to some foolish gunfighter's lamentations.

Of course, well after the fact, he would expound on the time he nursed Billy the Kid back from the brink of death or patched up Butch Cassidy. Frequently complimented for his substantial and copious vocabulary, he would gently remind you that Webster had sought his assistance on numerous occasions where some subtle elucidation was beyond the man's comprehension.

Town Meetings, where all the rural folks would ride their wagons, coaches and equine transportation into town to participate in the matters of local government, were affairs he wouldn't miss. As a consultant to numerous former presidents, he, without hesitation and with total equanimity would respond in exhaustive detail how democracy was meant to work. If real work and some personal risk were not involved in his allowing his candidacy to be advanced politically, he could easily have propelled himself into public office. There is no telling how far verbal diarrhea might politically have propelled him into the public arena.

Pollen in the Wind

Talking his way out of such a situation, had he been foolish enough to succumb to the transient accolades of his partisans, on more than one instance severely tested his verbal dexterity.

"So why am I sharing these few idiosyncrasies and perhaps suggesting some degree of concern about Doc Parker?"

Doc used to play Black Jack and Poker at the Silverado Saloon. He played a sufficiently propitious game as to provide an adequate revenue stream toward offsetting his whiskey bills and attendance to other more basic fiscal obligations. After all, in cards, he'd made himself available to the authors of Gore's Game of Better Bridge and other renowned texts on poker and other assorted card games. I will say he had a fantastic memory for all kinds of abstruse trivia as well as an imagination that could create any missing details for any subject one might consider.

It was there at the Silverado that he met one of the lady 'entertainers.' Her education hadn't gone beyond the seventh grade before she'd come west and it certainly made her vulnerable to Doc's verbal fluency and his gentlemanly manner. His physical appearance was not unlike my own in height, looks and mannerisms. That alone would prove to me to be a sufficient compliment. However, in a joint moment of romantic weakness he proposed to the panting light of his life and she accepted. Not only that, but she held him to it, at least suggesting one trait I'd consider desirable. The relationship added to their mutual resources and significantly to Doc's personal wardrobe. That's why when you see him, he looks the part of a distinguished statesman. Of course, if asked about any noteworthy diplomatic challenges he'd ever experienced, he will feign a momentary memory loss and hesitatingly recall and speak to the peace treaty his expertise had afforded toward a solution to the Boer Wars in South Africa. Time and language prove no barrier to his fertile imagination and willingness to expose his ostensible wisdom.

His wife, and I must add, my mother, lost her life accidentally from a wild bullet in a shoot out at the Silverado. Hers was one wound that would have stripped him of his nickname had he arrived on the scene hours earlier when he just might possibly have been of some help.

But, enough idle chatter. Having now shared my birth and parentage, in response to your question, "Doc Who?", I can readily understand why you might also be inclined to wonder about me. Someday we'll discover the pattern inside our parents that pass along their traits. There are some we'd surely be better off without. I've been told more than a few times, more often than I appreciate, I'm perhaps too much like my father, another Doc Parker."

"Waicu"

Sooner or later, most small and expanding towns in the growing west added a weekly newspaper or in some cases one that offered special editions or extras. To start a small town paper was venture capitalism at its riskiest. These were rough and tumble towns and with less regard for what was right than simply raw news events.

Henry McNeil had been a typesetter and eventually a newsman and editor in Pittsburgh before he and his wife moved west. He'd always wanted to run his own paper and believed that in one of the new towns he could make a go of it. It was an opportunity he accepted and with only mild protestations from his wife Emma they had in 1854, headed for the Black Hills.

So it was that Henry McNeil relocated all the way to Montana. In 1860 there had been a gold strike nearby and even though most of the soldiers in that area had been withdrawn to the demands of the Civil War, by the time the war ended in '66 the government had again sent troops and an expedition to open the Bozeman Trail into Montana. The trail represented a trespass into and across the last hunting grounds of the Lakota Indians.

As a cub reporter, having received a journalism background at one of the big eastern colleges and now working for McNeil's Weekly Gazette, Roger Davidson was enthusiastically following a lead regarding Chief Red Cloud. It was the latter's sign or signature on the

Fort Laramie Treaty that was now being violated by the United States Government and he wanted to cover the events currently taking place. He was fascinated by the names he was learning . . . Bull Bear, Spotted Tail, Crazy Horse, Sitting Bull, Hunkpapa, Two Kettle and others. He was not in agreement with what was going on, and openly wrote and spoke his opinions.

"But, sir, that treaty signed by Red Cloud at Fort Laramie assured the Oglala 'absolute' and undisturbed use of the Great Sioux Reservation. It's bad enough that we've rounded up these people and forced them onto patches of land where they formerly roamed free."

"That clause in the treaty denying 'passage over, settlement or residence in that territory without consent' was ten years ago." Mr. McNeil didn't go on.

"I see real trouble brewing, sir. We should be on top of it. It's right that our editorials should express opinion!"

Again McNeil didn't respond leaving Roger wondering.

Roger returned to his desk stewing, as his boss walked away, not wanting to discuss the issue further. Roger simply did not agree with anything that was taking place regarding the Indians. It was perhaps with good reason. He leaned back in his chair remembering. He glanced at the big print calendar on the wall of the printing room and noticed the date. An experience just a year ago, almost to the day, had influenced his opinion of the Indian people. Hardly 'wild beasts', he thought recalling. The local problem today was 'gold'.

Traveling west, he'd had a mishap. Startled, for whatever reason he didn't know, his horse had unexpectedly reared, tossing him violently to the ground. His head hit a rock and he lay unconscious on the ground. He lay there for quite a time. It was his horse that actually saved him as well as having nearly killed him.

A small party of Indians, traveling in nearly the same direction, saw Roger's horse, untied, reins dragging and the horse just grazing. Out of curiosity they investigated and very quickly, not far from the rider-less horse, they found Roger. They looked him over finding him breathing, a mean looking gash on his head, but otherwise alive. They washed his wound and very shortly brought him round. At first Roger was terrified by the sun colored men around him. Then he realized they were helping him. One brought his horse over beside him and when Roger stood up, feeling slightly better, they evidently thought he could ride again. They helped him mount his horse and actually rode with him for a distance before they turned off the trail to go their own way.

Unable to converse with them, Roger did look very closely at them, particularly the tall proud one who seemed to be giving directions to the others. He hoped if he ever saw him again he could return the courtesy.

Interrupting his thoughts, Mr. McNeil had come back by Roger's desk.

"Son, we report the news, the events as they happen, not what we think is going to happen nor what we would like to see happen. I know how you feel."

"Mr. McNeil, it was Commissioner of Indian Affairs, Francis Walker, who just this year made the statement that our handling of the Indians was 'not a question of national dignity in the treatment of savages by a civilized power'."

"Roger, put it aside!"

"But the whole purpose of the reservations was . . . and these are his words too . . . 'to reduce the wild beasts to the condition of supplicants for charity.' Those are cruel words. Gold in the Black Hills is the root cause of this."

"Agreed! Our love for possessions is a disease with us, but curing it is beyond our capacity as a weekly publication."

"With the Union Pacific Railroad already crossing the country to the south, in another few years when the Northern Pacific Railroad is completed up here, their hunting grounds will be no more. The once great Sioux nation will be boxed in, at least totally dependent on our Indian Agents to provide for them."

"Not our business," said McNeil, trying not to show his growing irritation with Roger. He liked the lad. He'd never had a family of his own. Roger had been home to dinner numerous times and Emma liked him too.

"But business is at the bottom of all this," insisted Roger.

McNeil nodded.

"Waicu!" said Roger, almost under his breath.

"What does that mean?" said McNeil.

"It means 'he-who-takes-the-fat', in other words, the greedy ones. That's what the influx of our people into this area and south have done to the buffalo herds, decimated, no, exterminated them, a unique animal the Indians have revered and relied on for centuries."

"President Grant has sent a message to Red Cloud that the Hills would be respected by law and by treaty."

"Sure, until the law is changed!"

"Enough, Roger! I don't want to continue this discussion for now. Can we do that? Let's close up and go home for supper. Emma is expecting both of us." He put his hand affectionately on Roger's shoulder, then took off his green visor cap and moved toward the coat tree in the front office. There was no question he enjoyed his young journalist's enthusiasm, but their business was reporting news. Expressing opinion was for the editorial page and that could have its effect on circulation. He had a lot at stake.

Supper was shepherd's pie, with beef, naturally. Who-ever heard of meat other than beef in this part of the country. Office talk was prohibited at the table. Emma thought that kind of talk not only excluded her but was simply an extension of the office. She enjoyed other subjects. Henry enjoyed the relief as well. He didn't like to argue with Roger over matters he knew cut so close to Washington's politics. He knew that politics without principle only led to difficulties further down the road. He'd been on a big paper staff long enough to know there were limits if the paper was to survive. After dinner the three invited a neighbor and they played three card Loo for pennies. Henry lost fifteen cents before the evening was over.

At his rented room Roger prepared for bed and eventually lay back against his pillow, thinking. He freely acknowledged, as Henry had more than once told him, he was like a dog with an old bone. He was more inclined to chew on it than bury it.

As he relaxed, he tried to put himself in their place, to better understand the Indian position. How difficult it must be for the natives of this great land to be rounded up and parked on reservations. Then to have the reservations themselves taken from them through legal deceit when something of value on the land is discovered. It was a process that seemed to be repeated over and over. The sacred earth of the Paha Sapa was literally being stripped of its gold and minerals. Sitting Bull had warned the whites who crowded the streets of Cheyenne waiting for their supplies, that the land was his and he would fight. Crazy Horse had said he would not sell the land on which his people walked. It was well past midnight when Roger finally drifted off.

The following week was a busy one. Roger interviewed quite a number of the gold-hungry miners who had followed Custer's route into the Black Hills and had wantingly killed off the game, clouded the streams and burned timber. They were a boisterous, hard drinking lot, and those who came did not hesitate to use their weapons against the Indians.

By the spring of '76 the situation had grown no better and Roger continued to debate Indian problems. Argue was what Henry called it. Henry was glad to grant Roger's request that he accompany Major Marcu Reno on a reconnaissance into the area of the Greasy Grass Creek.

As the column of blue coated soldiers rode out, Roger rode along and before long was able to approach the Major. "Sir? Is the great sun dance at Medicine Rocks still going on?"

"Well, son, no." replied Reno. The latest information we have learned from our Shoshone scouts is that a raid was made against General Crook which was a defeat for our people. But, I assure you that will not happen again."

Roger thought about that for quite a few miles. "The Indians were strong enough and sufficiently well led to defeat the United States Army?" The following morning he again approached Major Reno.

"How could this happen, sir? Why?"

"A chief called Crazy Horse," was all he said.

"So we are doing more than a reconnaissance expedition?"

Pollen in the Wind

The Major smiled. "We have our orders, son. Now I suggest you return to the rear of our column. We'll be making contact before the day is out."

Roger did that, sickened at heart and also beginning to experience fear rising within him. He had very mixed feelings. When the column stopped and they walked to rest their horses or just halted entirely, Roger made notes in a small pad that he had started. For him, it was the beginnings of a journal of the events taking place around him since the breaking of the Laramie Treaty.

It wasn't many days after that that the column rode over a ridge just east of Greasy Grass Creek when seemingly out of the sky a hundred arrows rained down on the column, much in the manner of field artillery being directed from some advanced lookout. There was no telling where they were coming from. The effect was bloody. The troops were ordered to take what they believed to be a defensive position just as a second flight of arrows fell upon them, again from out of sight, and decimating the column. From forward, a mounted body of Crazy Horse's braves swept toward the disorganized Blue Coats. For the moment, the attack was turned back. Major Reno knew they would reorganize and attack again. It would be only a matter of time. Hasty withdrawal was necessary before they could be surrounded. He ordered the bugler to sound their retreat. For Roger, it was terrifying.

Shortly after, Colonel Custer, who had been leading a second column and reportedly eager to add to his war record, was surrounded and was to a man wiped out. When Reno's column arrived at the place, not a man was left alive. Roger heard the place was called Little Big Horn. He was glad when the column turned back and finally to town. He returned safely to the office of the Weekly Gazette. The experience was not one he wanted to repeat or talk about. Writing about it would be even more difficult.

In the meantime, during his absence, Henry had received word by telegraph through a New York newspaper that the claims of the Sioux to any of the land in the Black Hills was to be denied to all Indians. A policy of confinement and extermination was to follow. He knew now that Roger's expressed fears had called the shots correctly. Hunting rights by Indians were terminated and all food and supplies, already difficult to come by without concessions, would hence forth be distributed from Missouri. He felt badly and for Roger in particular. What would he tell Roger when he returned to work in the morning?

"Now dear," said Emma, "they can be educated and civilized, even converted to Christianity and everything will turn out alright."

"No, no, Emma, you don't understand all that is involved in this whole business. It is the people in Washington who have allowed this to happen. The pressure of hundreds of people pushing into the Black Hills has put pressure on the military to protect them, which they haven't been entirely able to do. There are bad policies at work here with gold a major part of the problem. Political cost is also at stake for the politicians. The Indians are a communal people, they do not fit or want to fit into our traditional means of existence. Poor Roger. I don't know what he'll do."

"Now, dear, we won't let the Indians starve, you know that."

Roger did not return the next day. He was exhausted, more from what he struggled to deal with inwardly, than physical hardship. Henry tried to bring him up to date with events, but the situation seemed to be rapidly going from bad to worse. By the end of '76 Sitting Bull had gone to Canada and Crazy Horse was being pursued by General Miles. Red Cloud and Spotted Tail traveled to Washington to hear the words of the Great White Father, leaving Crazy Horse to stand alone. In the end they had all signed treaties with the white man and in the end in all of them, the white man had broken his solemn council.

"Economics without morality," shouted Roger. From then on for days at a time, he sat at his desk, sometimes scribbling notes, sometimes just sitting. He saw these people through different eyes. He could not believe what was taking place. He began to lose weight and his eyes became like lifeless holes in a snow bank. He refused invitations to have dinner with the McNeils, play Loo or even spend an evening. For a time he wrote critical letters to Washington, then letters to his own Weekly Gazette under a variety of assumed names. Nothing changed.

In the fall of '77 Crazy Horse was enticed to go to Fort Robinson. Henry sent Roger to cover the story. Was this to be a beneficial meeting or a trick? He hoped it would ease Roger's mind some to experience a first hand meeting between the Indians and authorities as well as get him involved again in the newspaper business. He hoped it was not a trick simply to catch him. It was not a large gathering, mostly Blue Coat officers, a couple of officials and several invited Indians, one of whom was, of course, Crazy Horse. Crazy Horse appeared nervous, but stood proud and tall with the others, causing Roger to recall something familiar about him. Yes, he was the man who had helped him years earlier, and now, as Crazy Horse looked around the cluster of people, he recognized Roger. He looked right through him, straightened himself taller and purposely turned his back to him. What he thought nobody would ever know, because too soon after the brief meeting and under circumstances that nobody could make clear, Crazy Horse was fatally stabbed. One after another, laws had been passed and were being passed to justify the government's position and safeguard white interests. The Black Hills Act, Dawes Act, the General Allotment Act, the Major Crimes Act and the Homestead Act were all designed by Congress to support the settlement and exploitation of the west and in the process somehow supposedly assist the redman into the mainstream of the white man's ways. Indian chiefs were turned against each other and in turn each was subsequently deceived by the inhumanity of the white man. Roger's journal contained a long litany of the sad events, thinking that he would in time publish the shameful record.

"Roger, the Gazette would be closed down or even destroyed by vigilantes if we were to include your opinions in the paper. We can't afford the risk. Yet, I can't disagree with your opinion."

The record speaks for itself, sir."

"I know. Perhaps someday. As you have said so often, principle suffers under the weight of politics. Powerful interests, I'm afraid." That ended further discussion and nearly their friendship.

Roger, one cold wintry day, decided to travel to Cheyenne to talk with the Indian Agent. There had to be some give somewhere. In his run down condition, it was a foolish venture and Henry could not talk him out of going. The weather proved bitter cold and his meeting proved to be a wasted effort. Discouraged and bone tired he came down with pneumonia riding into a bitter wind as he headed home. His death followed shortly there after. Emma and Henry had lost their 'son'.

Henry and Emma took care of funeral arrangements which were brief and simple. There were a few people that joined the gathering, but not really many real friends. Roger had taken on too great a personal burden and turned away too many by his obsession. Such had been the situation when years back the great Cherokee nation had been moved to new lands. Politicians and money would always be a problem. Emma shared her thoughts with the preacher and also one of the last entries in Roger's journal. It was actually a paragraph taken from Red Cloud's farewell address to the Lakota people.

"Shadows are long and dark before me. I shall soon lie down to rise no more. While my spirit is with my body, the smoke of my breath shall be towards the Sun, for he knows all things and knows that I am still true to him."

Shortly after, the weekly Gazette closed its doors. Henry knew in his heart that greed and politics was a bad combination and would have an impact on the growth of the nation and perhaps even far beyond in times to come. Perhaps a newspaper should represent both news events as well as editorially share a responsibility to express an honest judgment as well. Roger had called it 'back-bone', right or wrong, it's where a paper should stand, otherwise it will put up with anything and stand for nothing."

The Measure of a Man

A tall thin rider eased a weary mountain pony toward the livery just beyond the Goldtown Saloon. He spoke quietly to his mount as he removed the saddle and blanket roll, saw his horse fed and bedded down. He slapped the trail dust from a faded Army shirt and wiped his hands on the seat of neatly patched denims. He pushed a wide brimmed hat back on his head and ran a hand through sun bleached curly hair. His cheek bones were red from one more blazing hot day of Colorado sun. Another wooden town, he thought, just like so many others since Lincoln. With a relaxed stride, silver spurs jingling, he headed for the saloon and approached the bar.

The room was nearly empty except for a noisy group at the bar. The last rays of daylight slanted across the room through two windows, spilling across empty tables. Even inside the room was warm. The bartender moved to meet him.

"Whiskey."

The bartender filled a shot glass and picked up the waiting silver dollar. He dropped it into a metal cash box on the back bar and in the mirror studied the weather toughened features of the tall man. No one to mess with, he thought.

"Can you recommend a room with a tub?"

"Clean rooms across the street . . . tub is extra," he said, without turning.

"Thanks." With his drink in his hand the tall man moved a few steps away from the others. The bartender straightened some half empty bottles on the back bar and continued to watch him in the gold framed mirror above.

So did a big burly drinker further down along the bar. He was one of the noisiest, certainly the loudest. The fellow, too heavy for twenty, shifted his weight and with a haughty sneer appraised the newcomer.

"Don't like our company, stranger? What's your name?"

"Just ridin' through. Only want to wet my whistle." He noted the loud mouth's Colt was holstered low and tied down. His friends beyond him moved away from the bar.

"So, 'Mr. Ridin', we're not good enough to drink with, huh?" He winked at the bartender who also eased out of the way. He'd seen this one gun down strangers just for the sport. So had 'Ridin'' seen others like him. So many small towns had at least one overconfident braggart who built a reputation adding wooden crosses to the hill beyond town.

'Ridin' emptied his glass. "Not looking for trouble," he said patiently. It had already been a long day. He'd found the challenges of raising a young family more meaningful than fighting and raising hell. At twenty-six and a veteran of the Mexican Wars, he was through with that life. Now as foreman completing a cattle drive from El Paso, he was anxious to get home to his wife and little ones. With cautious blue eyes, he measured the big man, the way he stood and how he planted his feet. He wiped a strong suntanned hand across parched lips and quietly hoped the big man would back off. It was the man's drink that was doing the talking.

"I asked you a question, 'Mr. Ridin'. Or ain't you man enough to answer? It takes a man to wear a gun, or are you pretending ?" His voice was getting louder. He glanced over at his friends who snickered. He wasn't backing off at all.

The bartender backed away from the bar, glancing at the big gold framed mirror, not the first he'd had shipped from back east.

'Ridin' didn't want to answer. Every bully with a gun feels he's got an edge. This one was, with all the self assurance of ignorance, no different.

"Hey, you!" The voice was demanding.

'Ridin' slowly set his glass on the bar and took a step toward the loud mouth. Ramrodding a crew of thirty-odd trail riders, you see and deal with all kinds. He saw no way to put off the inevitable. He'd decided he might as well meet him head on.

"You fat, loud mouthed slob, if you had a brain in your head you'd back off while you still could."

The gunfighter's face was livid, he snarled, his nostrils flaring. His hand dropped to his gun and he drew. But his gun never cleared leather.

A silver flash, the jingle of a silver spur and the big man crumpled to the floor gasping and holding his groin.

"Dam fool!" said 'Ridin'." He put down another silver dollar on the bar.

The bar room was silent. The loud mouth's friend stood mute; his mouth open wide. There was only the pained groan of the would-be gun fighter as he lay gasping on the floor. A dog barked somewhere down the street. The bartender, hand shaking, filled the tall man's glass. He leaned over and spoke in a voice only for him.

"Don't turn your back on that one. You should have killed him."

"I've seen my fill of that," said 'Ridin'. Thanks."

He threw his head back emptying his glass and walked out. The jingle of spurs could be heard as long strides took him along the connected porches of the adjacent wooden buildings. He made a stop at an office that took about an hour, then returned to rent a room for the night. The bartender was right, it was clean, the tub was extra. The tall man lay stretched out on the big brass bed that came with the room and closed his eyes. He thought for a while about his earlier experience at the bar. He wondered if man truly chose his fate or whether it was all in greater hands. Fatigue weighed more heavily than conjecture and putting thoughts aside, he slept.

Awake before sunlight, 'Ridin' dressed and crossed the street to order some breakfast. A young round faced Mexican girl took his order for eggs, a slice of ham, coffee and pan-fried potatoes, which she very quickly set on the table before him. It would be another long day in the saddle and the first day's meal was the important one. She spoke little English and he obliged with the little he knew of her own language. She smiled appreciatively as she turned to attend other customers.

Outside, activity was increasing and it was time to be on his way. 'Ridin' paid his young waitress and said "Good day." She smiled and replied.

"Si Dios quiere."

'Ridin' nodded and stepped out into the morning. Yes, 'if God wills', he translated to himself, reminded of the bar tender's warning of last evening.

At the livery his horse had been well treated and an old man with a scrub brush mustache and a cheek full of tobacco had him saddled and ready as requested for morning. 'Ridin' mounted, touched his hat and headed west.

The street diminished to a trail that wound its way through a narrow pass, then down along the side of a mountain to a lower plateau. By nature, his eyes studied the ridges and clumps of aspen along the trail. A quail burst out of a thicket off ahead of him, too far ahead for it to have been disturbed by his presence. He eased the leather loop that secured his colt and stretched his fingers. No telling what might have disturbed that bird. He considered the situation that he might be about to face, but put worry aside.

The trail turned and crossed a stream where the water widened and moved more slowly. It would not be too long before his route leveled out to cross through scrub growth of a drier terrain. Before he crossed, he dismounted to let his horse drink and to fill his own canteen. As he screwed the cap back on his canteen he heard a metallic click; the hammer of a gun being cocked. It was behind him.

"So you thought you'd sneak off, huh?"

He recognized the loud voice and without turning tried to picture from just where behind him it had come. He finished capping his canteen and brought a handful up to his lips, then dropped his left hand to the little sandy spot at his feet. He moved as naturally as he could, pretending that the voice he'd heard, he had imagined. The barrel of a rifle was jabbed painfully in his back below his ribs. He already knew he hadn't imagined company.

"Back up now slow and easy-like," the voice said impatiently. "We just decided we goin' to have a hangin'. Now turn around with your hands out wide."

'Ridin' did just that, with arms out wide, he turned slowly. His eyes quickly noted the loud mouth's "we" in fact meant four. The big man backed a few feet away from him. Two others were leading horses from

Pollen in the Wind

where they'd been hiding. One had a coil of rope in his hand. A third was standing with a foolish, excited grin, off to the left. He had his pistol drawn and cocked. He'd been the one who snickered. Crazy eyes, thought 'Ridin'. He pegged him as unpredictable and dangerous.

"I'd say you learn rather slow, fella. You know I could have killed you yesterday." He watched each man's reactions carefully. He was stalling.

"You wasted your chance 'Mr. Ridin'. I don't cotton to strangers in my town."

"Your town? Aren't you presuming something? I thought Marshall Tom Allen was the law in that town?" He spoke slowly, patiently trying to gain time. He had reason. "At least that's what I learned yesterday when I left the saloon. I understand Tom would be glad to lock you up."

The big man forced laughter, "Ha, ha. He knows I've outdrawn the others . . . all legal-like. And we ain't in town now so we just goin' to hang you, ain't we boys?" He turned slightly to benefit the agreement of his back-up.

It was all that 'Ridin' needed and too late for the big man to correct his mistake. 'Ridin' stepped to the right to put the big man between himself and the one who snickered. With his left hand he hurled the fist full of sand he'd scooped up while drinking, full in the face of the big man as he turned back. The rifle in his hands went off but he'd been momentarily blinded by the sand. 'Ridin' fired, his shot smashing hard into the butt of the rifle, sending it spinning out of the big man's hands. He didn't want to kill him if he could avoid it.

Behind the big man, 'Crazy eyes' fired twice, one bullet going wild. The second thumped into the big man's back. Death came without understanding. He fell forward, clearing the line of fire. 'Crazy eyes' fired wildly again. Given no alternative, 'Ridin' returned fire. 'Crazy eyes' stood facing 'Ridin', a curious look on his face. A small red spot between his eyes became larger, as the back of his head erupted. He fell backwards into the brush.

Up the trail from the direction of town could be heard the sound of a horse, traveling fast. The two men holding the hanging party's horses faced 'Ridin's' gun and didn't dare move. The odds had been too quickly narrowed.

As the rider rounded the bend he reined in and stopped. He saw at a glance that the fight was over.

"Sorry I'm late Bill," he addressed the tall man. "But, it doesn't look like you needed my help after all. He glanced at the bodies. "I guess some people can't seem to learn it's not the gun, but the man behind it that counts."

"Nope, and some get killed learning it."

Together, the two, Marshall Tom Allen and Bill, hoisted the two bodies over their saddled horses and Tom, with the two would-be hangmen, headed back toward town. En route, one of the two in custody ventured to ask how he'd known the man called Bill. "Why, hell, only a damned fool wouldn't recognize the likes of Bill Hickock."

"Teach"

Miss Abbey is remembered as more than an old maid school teacher. Over her forty years of teaching, mostly back east in a small New England village is where she'd come from. Here, she'd become a fixture in our community of Cedar Rock. She'd been here long enough now to have taught at least a few parents across the valley how to read and write. I'd guess she's taught more then one generation that moved west. But, what made her special to folks and even to us kids was that she taught a lot more than the basics of numbers, reading and writing. She taught us how to live in a changing world. She shared a personal philosophy, not just in the classroom but by the way she lived. Yes, sir, her philosophy on how to conduct one's self was so simple it could be summed up in one sentence. In fact, years back, she'd done just that on a cardboard strip she'd tacked to the wall above the chalkboard.

"The measure of a person is what he or she would do in a situation where they knew nobody would ever find out about it."

Graying, her long hair coiled up in a bun and held in place with a long toothed comb, Miss Abbey was somewhat bent over. The wrinkles in her face were friendly ones and her eyes were full of the wonder and sparkle of a youngster. I can't say in the years I attended her one room school or the few years since that I ever heard anyone speak a bad word about her.

When she spoke, she spoke with a sincere humility, yet I have to add, it was also with considerable authority. She wasn't one to give you the last word on something, only the latest as she knew it. As kids we may not have at the time recognized it, but today most all of us do recognize what education is all about or at least what education could be.

Affectionately and only behind her back, then and even now, we know her as "Teach." Yes, she taught her students how to think, not just answers to questions that would be test answers.

"I remember late one afternoon, school was out for the day and a number of us had come into town for one reason or another and we were chewin' the fat just outside Mr. Hitchcock's general store. "Teach," Miss Abbey, that is, was coming along the boardwalk and durned if she didn't nearly trip on the edge of a board that had warped out of shape. Charlie Dawson caught her arm and prevented her from falling. She surely would have broken something at her age. As it was, the papers she'd been looking at as she walked, went flying all over the place. We all pitched in and gathered them up for her. They were an odd looking bunch of papers, all kinds of little pictures, Indian signs and I suppose words.

We asked what they were. She first thanked Charlie and then began to explain. "Yes, I was putting together the language of the Algonquian people, specifically the Blackfoot tribe that lives just east of the Rockies. I'm looking forward to visiting some friends in Montana later this year. It's just a little homework on my part."

"Are they Indians?" we asked.

"Mr. Appleton isn't, but his wife is Indian, and it is Indian territory."

We didn't quite know what to say.

"Mr. Appleton is an Indian Agent, lived here a

Pollen in the Wind

few years back before he took the job with the government. He was before your time in school."

"Oh, but . . .?"

"Married to an Indian . . .?" we stammered.

We'd heard of mountain men who took a 'squaw' over the winter months. This was different!

Miss Abbey cut off our questions. She frowned, evidently trying to recall some bit of information, some bit of knowledge from her deep well of experience by way of response to our questioning looks. "Isn't a lake fed by many different springs and streams? Aren't our lives fed and enriched in much the same way? It is the whole of everything we have touched or has touched us that makes us what we are."

It almost seemed like the sun came out as she smiled up at us.

"So you're learning the Indian language?" we asked. "Wow!"

"You're Carl Johnson, aren't you? How you've grown, tall and strong. Did you ever marry that little red-headed girl who sat in front of you . . . red-headed before you dipped her pigtails in your ink well?" She chuckled, recalling.

We all laughed. That was quite a while back for us. There wasn't much that went on in her classroom that she wasn't aware of. She knew us all, inside and out, seldom forgetting a face. I suppose her personal interest in each one of us made our response to her as a teacher a positive one and made the whole learning process more worth while.

"Yes, I am Carl Johnson and yes, I'm still chasing Sally Benson. Knowing her, you'd never guess she was handicapped. Somehow she doesn't seem to be when we are together. Perhaps soon . . ." the start of my reply was cut off by an elbow in my ribs and more laughter.

"So because of your visit to Montana, you're learning about the Blackfoot?"

"Yes. I leave, why actually next week, on the Overland Stage. It'll be too bumpy a ride I hear to do much by way of study, so I don't have a lot of time left."

"You can't learn a whole language in just a few days," we all responded.

"No, you're right, but I can learn some of the important words."

"Important words?"

"Of course, you know them and I'm sure you use them. They are 'please' and 'thank you', and even 'how can I help you?' Or, 'it's nice to be with you'. None are very big words but they all carry valuable messages when they are sincere."

Not much more was said just then, but it gave us something to think about. We agreed, Miss Abbey was still teaching.

It wasn't until almost a month later that two of us ran into Miss Abbey in the hardware store. Since I'd been working for Mr. Hale in the building business, I'd gone in for a few pounds of nails. Miss Abbey was there for a hook to hang a picture or something. She picked up a small hook and asked if it would support very much.

"What kind of surface are you going to be putting it into?"

"Wood, the wall over my stove in the parlor. I brought home a small treasure, a drawing."

"From your trip?" asked Charlie Dawson.

"Yes, you remembered I was going out to Bozeman to visit a friend. How nice of you to remember."

"The fellow who married the Indian lady?"

"Yes, "she replied. "Squaw may be the term many

Pollen in the Wind

of us use but the word to me seems to suggest a rather plump and perhaps uneducated person. 'Singing Bird' would hardly fit such a description. She was tall as you are Carl, straight and slender, long dark hair and beautiful dark eyes. She was shy at first which I anticipated, but just a lovely young woman as I got to know her, or rather as we got to know each other."

"So you had a good time?"

"Oh, my yes, an adventure from the very start. The stage ride out was a bit more excitement than expected. We traveled in the company of a cavalry escort. It seems there were some mining men that had a squabble with some of the area people out there . . . I'm told they cheated them."

"Indians?" we both asked, interrupting.

"Yes, but keep in mind that they are people, too. They have rights just like you and me. Anyway," she paused, evidently getting her thoughts in order, "these mining men took advantage of several Indians and when they realized how they had been cheated, if that is what it was, they decided to get even. That's never a good approach to solving a problem . . . but even we learn that lesson the hard way at times. We've simply taken from them what we've wanted."

As Miss Abbey spoke I wanted to hear all she had to say but knew, too, I was not being paid wages for standing around the hardware store. Charlie made a slight motion with his head and eyes that didn't go unnoticed, so that pretty well wrapped up part of her story. It wasn't until a rainy afternoon that I saw her again and with the excuse of helping her across the street . . . you know how muddy and churned up our street gets when it rains all day. Well, we stood under the cover in front of Mr. Crawford's store waiting for a break . . . which reminded me how we'd met the last time, in Mr. Crawford's I mean. So, I asked.

"Did you get your gift or whatever it was hung over the stove in your parlor?"

She laughed and nodded. "It worked out beautifully and I thank you for your advice."

"You know, you never finished telling Charlie and me about the rest of your visit to Bozeman. I think that's where you said you were off to."

"Oh, I realized you boys had obligations. No, I guess we didn't finish." She pulled her shawl around her shoulders and dodged a trickle of rain that was leaking through Mr. Crawford's tin roof.

"I'm not workin' today, ma'am. I've wondered how it all turned out; your trip and all."

"Well, let's see. The cavalry lads rode with us nearly the whole way." She paused. "Most of them are nice fellows, a few tough old timers that had actually experienced fighting against Indians, Geronimo, or one of his . . . his group. I suppose they carried out their orders as they came down the line. I felt sorry the orders haven't all made a lot of sense at times. I feel sure if we made more effort to keep our word . . ." she shook her head and looked off down the empty street. "Anyway, we had no trouble over the trip. I had a few black and blue spots from the ride however." She patted her hip where she'd evidently bounced around some.

"And what about the Indian lady?"

"A lovely person and I did use a few words out of the studying I'd done. Actually, 'Singing Bird' spoke quite good English and is even reading some . . . . a lovely person," she repeated. "Mr. Appleton has helped her in so many ways with patience and understanding."

"I guess we have jumped to too many conclusions

Pollen in the Wind

and have done a lot of bad things in dealing with the Indians."

Mr. Crawford came to the door of the store just then. Evidently he'd heard us talking. He poked his head out, looked down the muddy street, nodded to the two of us and went back inside.

Miss Abbey adjusted her shawl around her shoulders. She wasn't one to leave you with the fringes of an issue. She wasn't bashful about telling you where she stood on things. I knew I was going to go away with something more to think about.

"You realize, Carl, that our United States is a melting pot of peoples from all over the world. The Irish in New England, the Spanish in some of our southern states and California. Then there are the Chinese who have been brought in to work on the railroads being built south of us here. All have come for reasons of their own and somehow are melting into the fabric of this great nation. We'll see it happen someday."

"But is there a difference with the Indian people? We seem to have rounded a good many of them into reservations as though they had done something wrong." I knew when I said that, she would have more to say. There had to be more to it.

"A philosophical difference, Carl. One that is perhaps at the root of much of our mutual problem. It is in how we differ in the area of land ownership. We carve out little pieces of property, claim them as ours, buy them and sell them as you would a pound of nails. They believe the earth belongs to everyone, white man as well as Indian. The earth was provided for our use by the earth's creator, and they don't understand how we can buy and sell it. The attraction of a few beads and trinkets in no way diminishes their belief that we all own it and they are giving up nothing since they don't recognize ownership in the first place."

"But they do sell land. Didn't we trade for land in New England and haven't we done similar things here in the west?"

"As you know, I came from a small New England town. I'm aware of many properties in that town that have been bought but still the deeds reserve all the hunting and fishing rights for a local tribe in perpetuity. That means forever. Chief Eskimonk in the Pomperaug Valley has such a right as it is written into one of the deeds I know about. It was a neighbor's property."

I listened, unable to answer. She went on.

"How do you change a philosophy of ownership that has prevailed since the beginning of time? Our discovery of this great land is not a matter of nobody knowing that it was here. It has been here all the while. We've come here as the newcomers."

"Guess I've never thought of it that way," I said.

"The government's policies have been shaped to serve our interests, not always theirs. Mr. Appleton can tell you a thing or two about that."

"You mean we've lacked moral principle in how we've dealt with them?"

"My friend, who is the Indian agent, is trying to improve things. We had some good discussions. It is not a simple problem and not without fault on both sides . . . but so different than with other people who have settled here. These people were all here before any of us came. I fear it will be many years before the problem is resolved. We have to work at it."

Miss Abbey's face showed her concern and as I looked at this frail little woman I wished there were more like her in the world. She was one of a kind. It is too bad that wisdom often only comes with older age.

As I looked at her I recalled a class one day when she'd shared some of her wisdom of a man who said not to judge another until you've walked in his footsteps. I repeated the line as I'd remembered it at the time.

She looked up at me and changed 'footsteps' to 'moccasins'. She beamed.

"You're right, Carl. That man's name was Seneca, a member of a tribe of Iroquoian people who lived back east in the area of the Genesee River. He was a very wise Indian; well ahead of his time."

I don't know why I did it, but I put my arms around 'Teach' . . . Miss Abbey, I mean, and hugged her." I remembered so clearly how we had visited that day.

Carl sat back, thinking over past events. It was a whole minute before he returned his attention to the rest of the committee members gathered together in the town offices.

"Enough story telling . . . what I've told you about Miss Abbey was a few years ago now. As some of you know, Miss Abbey left us shortly after that. As you may also know, I am married to Cynthia, and . . . and sadly as a nation, we've come nowhere near to solving our problems on how to live with each other."

A Wise Choice of Words

When the cards were dealt, I picked mine up from the table. I couldn't believe my eyes; a straight flush. Was this possible or was I being encouraged to risk everything? I'd been losin' more pots than I cared to and needed to win; a big win. With this hand it was all I could do to keep a serious face. Was luck involved?

As each man picked up his cards and glanced at them, he looked around the table to take note of any expression that might reveal what another man had. The tall thin cowpoke to my right hadn't done too well. I noticed he shook his head ever so slightly at what he held in his hand. The big man across the table drew deeply on the stub of a cigar. He'd played a lot of poker and his expression revealed nothing. After a week on my own doin' odd jobs around town I'd heard he had a reputation as a bad loser. I'd been warned about playing cards with strangers and he'd been mentioned. He'd filled in when another man had dropped out so I was kind of stuck with the situation.

The fellow in the red checkered shirt to my left had a crooked eye and seemed to scratch the back of his neck a lot. I figured he hadn't played poker much more than I had.

But, here I was, left home, going on seventeen and wantin' to sow a few wild oats, as they say. Pa and me hadn't been gettin' along too well for some time. We'd had words. Ma took time to listen to me and she tried to see things through my eyes much of the time, but not Pa. From his actions I had the feelin' he didn't

Pollen in the Wind

really care. Ma cried when I left, though lookin' back, I think it was more because of Pa and me than my leaving. Here in town I'd taken a cheap room in the hotel. I scrubbed pots and pans in the kitchen and was available for other odd jobs to pay my own way. I wasn't doing all that well with money. With the cards I held in my hand now, things were going to change. I sure hoped I wasn't being suckered.

The play began. Each of the others tossed in a card or two hopin' to improve his hand. I stood firm.

"You open, kid," the big man said.

I pretended to puzzle over my initial bid and finally put a silver dollar in the pot. I didn't have more than a few left, wages Pa had insisted I take when I left the ranch.

"You got it coming to you, boy," he'd insisted. "Don't consider it a gift. You earned it."

If Pa could only see the hand I now held.

The cowpoke antied up and raised. The bidding went around a few times, me laboring over each raise, the big man puffin' out a cloud of stinkin' smoke at each turn. Both the cowpoke and the crooked eye man finally dropped out. Then it was between me and the big man across the table. I began to wonder about the stories people had told about him. He had hard eyes, a cruel look about him. His cigar had gone out, but he continued to chew on the end of it. There were gravy stains on the front of his shirt. Not once did his expression change. When he glanced at me, it was a mean look. I noticed a few idlers in the big room began to gather around our table to watch. They knew the big man's reputation. I noticed too that, like most of us, he carried a gun, but his was tied down, like a gun fighter. The day hadn't started hot but, of a sudden, it sure had gotten hot over the last hour.

Gradually my money wound up at the center of the table and all I had left was Granddad's gold watch. It was a beauty, but so was the hand I held. I put the watch on the table. The big man nodded approval with no change of expression.

"Unless you have a Royal Flush, kid, you're out of luck."

The big man finally called and placed his cards on the table, but he put them face down. He started to rake the pile of silver dollars and Granddad's watch to his side of the table.

"You goin' to turn your cards face up, mister?"

"You doubt me, kid?"

I wished he wouldn't call me kid. It reminded me of Pa callin' me 'boy'. I bit my lip and answered, trying to keep my voice steadier than my knees. "I'd like to see them, sir."

"Calling me a liar, eh?" He pushed his chair back from the table and loosened the leather thong on his Colt. Behind me, onlookers moved aside. I really began to sweat. Then he leaned over and began to turn his cards over . . . Ace, King, Queen of spades. Shall I spare you the rest?"

My heart sank. I realized I was being taken.

The big man laughed and raked the pot closer to his side of the table. I noticed his right hand was held free above his pistol. That's when people really moved clear.

I was wearing a gun, but never intended its use in a situation like this. My brother and me used to play fast draw out on the range and killing a rattler or varmint was about the limit. Pa had told us never to draw a gun on a person except in self defense. But I needed that pot and seein' Granddad's watch being picked up by that big greasy fellow was more than I could stand. I wanted to know if I'd lost the hand fair and square. I just couldn't believe what I was seein'.

"Not a liar at all, sir . . . just interested in seein' the rest of your cards."

He turned over the next card, a Jack of Spades. "That convince you, kid? Now you either walk out of here or draw. I don't like being called a liar."

"There's one more card, sir," I said, and reached to turn it over. The room was quiet as death itself.

The big man's left hand crashed down on mine scattering the pot and splitting the table. With his free hand he drew his gun and fired.

Pulled to the right by the force of the big man's fist, his shot went wild somewhere off to my left. As he fired, I drew and fired in self defense. I hadn't wanted to kill the man. It all happened so quickly. Just the same, a red spot right between the big man's eyes told the story. His gun sagged and clattered to the floor just seconds before he pitched forward and fell. I turned over his last card; a red four. He'd been bluffing all along and now was dead. It could have been me.

For a moment I was terrified, alone in a room full of strangers and standin' over a man I'd just killed.

"Kid, you were fast!"

"I never seen such shootin'."

I started to say I'd been lucky, but the spoken praise and sudden attention made me feel important.

"Drinks on the house!" called out the bartender and suddenly I found myself being moved to the bar.

There seemed to be nothing but admiration in the faces of the men pushing and shoving along beside me. Was I a little taller, more of a man? I sure felt different. Mine had been a good shot, fast, as they were now saying.

"Whiskey," I said.

I drank one, two, three, then lost track. I couldn't keep up with the toasts. The big man didn't seem to have had many friends. My head swam with the praise and I bought a round or two of drinks myself.

Next thing I knew, it was mornin'. I was in bed. I didn't feel too good. Lying beside me was another person, a woman I'd never seen before. My head felt awful.

"Who are you?" I pushed the hip of the woman beside me. She awakened and squinted in my direction. She sure wasn't wearin' much . . . but neither was I.

"Huh?" She yawned a stale smelling yawn and smiled. "How's my lover boy today?"

"What are you doin' here?" I asked.

She smiled again and pursed her lips. "You're quite the local hot shot . . . and I don't mean with a six shooter only."

Clothes were scattered around the small room between the door and the bed. A tattered shade filtered the sunlight through dirty window panes. It wasn't my room. I slipped out of bed and put on some clothes and my boots. From a pitcher on a broken-down dresser, I poured some water into a basin and washed my face. I felt sick and dirty. I looked at the woman in bed, perhaps thirty, flabby and with more color than was her own. I couldn't help comparing her to the golden haired girl on the ranch next to ours. I swallowed hard.

"You called me 'lover boy'? What you mean to say we . . . ?"

"Well sugar, you really passed out, but for the same money, I won't tell a soul."

Relieved, I told her, "Don't do no braggin' on my account." I started to add something else, but a gentle knock on the door interrupted. I opened the door and faced a broad shouldered man with a handlebar mustache and a silver star.

"A number of us have talked a bit about last evening and it's our feeling you'd best move on. This town doesn't need gunfighters and you've just made yourself a prime target."

The man spoke plain and to the point and with a firmness that could hardly be denied; the same tone of voice Pa used when I'd not followed instructions. Once in a while I could get around Pa, but something told me there was no gettin' around this man.

"Uh . . . the man was cheatin' me. I shot fair an' square . . . what?"

I could see from his eyes he wasn't going to accept debate. I stepped back out of the way to let the sheriff come in. Only his eyes looked beyond me and with a jerk of his thumb he motioned the woman in bed to clear out.

"Pay her and be gone, young fellow."

Things seemed to be happening too fast for the condition my head was in. I stumbled into the rest of my clothes and a few minutes later I was on my way to the livery stable. Down stairs they allowed me coffee and that was all. It was hot! It did help some, the cobwebs in my head, I mean. I reached into my pockets. Most of my money was gone including Granddad's gold watch. I had only a dollar left to pay for the care of my horse; not very much after winning the big pot. The loss of the watch bothered me most. I should have picked it up right off. Pa never had much patience with the words 'should have'. There wasn't much more I could do, so I started down the street, my eyes adjusting to the bright sun.

Just short of the livery stable I saw my watch. It was hangin' on a low sign and there were several fellows pretending they were making fast draws with Granddad's watch as the target. Evidently one of them had been watching the card game and recognized that the watch was important to me. I walked right over to the watch and reached to retrieve it. Someone fired and the cord suspending the watch was cut clean. The watch fell into the dirt at my feet.

Again I reached for it, but another shot kicked up dust inches from my hand. I straightened up and looked toward the group of fellows a few yards away watchin' me. There were four of them. Our ages were not all that far apart.

One was standing separated from the others, a stupid grin on his face, his gun hand free and expectant. This was not a game I wanted to play and the sheriff's words were becoming fact faster than I could have imagined.

What's a stinkin' cattleman need a watch like that for?"

"Because it belongs to him should be reason enough," I answered, now fully awake, all my senses sharp and me a touch angered.

"Well, then why don't you pick it up? Or are you too big a man to bend that far?" He looked toward the other fellows with a smug taunting look of self confidence.

I didn't have a quick answer. Somehow I saw something of myself in his look and didn't like what I was seeing. I looked over the group, now spread out from each other. They all had their guns tied down and none looked too bright. For a moment I wished they were all out on some ranch working, or better still, that I was. But, here I was, surely too big for my britches, all on my own and gettin' deeper into trouble by the minute.

Pollen in the Wind

Carefully, I turned my left side toward the group and slowly lowered myself to one knee to pick up my watch. The expectant one suddenly drew and fired. As I dove to the side I drew my gun and returned fire from my hip under my body. My bullet smashed him in the wrist of his gun hand and he screamed in pain. A second fellow drew, but didn't fire. The sheriff had appeared from around the corner of the livery stable, his gun drawn. I held my fire but felt certain I could have taken the next contender.

"Clear out, all of you and consider yourself lucky that this kid's shot missed your gut." Then he turned to me.

I heard the word 'missed' and knew that I hadn't missed. I'd hit just what I aimed at . . . his gun hand. I could have killed the fellow. My one such experience had already been more than I'd bargained for. I said nothing, deciding not to argue his point, though I sure wanted to.

"Missed his gut by a mile, I'd say," repeated the sheriff. "Kid," he looked straight at me. "You're broad shouldered and bright looking. If I'm any judge of young men, you have the makings of a fine man, just green from the neck up. I suggest you think about what I've just said. Now leave town!" He holstered his gun and followed the would-be gunfighters up the street.

The wounded fellow was holding his hand, whimperin', his face contorted with pain. He'd never hold a gun in that hand again. His former admirers had already wandered off in separate directions. Then, too, my fast-draw reputation by the sheriff's choice of words was over. I slowly began to realize he'd done me a favor. For once, I'd kept my mouth shut when reprimanded by an elder. When I rode in, Pa looked at me for a minute, rubbed his chin in a knowin' way and never asked a single question.

"There's young ones out on the south range that need branding, son. We can ride together."

Riding out, I asked myself a lot of questions. We don't brag about the stupid things we do in life, and Pa had a slight smile on his face that suggested to me he had a pretty good idea what I'd been up to. I had a feelin' that Pa and I were more alike than I'd sure realized. My own stubbornness and youthful pride had prevented me from giving him half a chance.

Sure, there's more to life than luck . . . I knew I hadn't missed my shot, but I also realized the sheriff had chosen his words with a purpose.

Perspective

It had been a long dry spell in Montana, but finally Butte was on the receiving end of a good rainstorm and already the main street was rutted and muddy. There would surely be a break when Henry Marston could get across the street to finish his errands and get his horse. It hadn't started to rain when he had gone into McRae's Hardware, so now as he stood under the roof on the boardwalk in front, he just waited. The front door of the store banged open and two young lads pushed each other out.

"What colors did you get, David?"

"Mostly red ones," responded his brother. They had evidently each been given a penny to window shop McRae's small candy corner and had carefully made selections.

"Whoops! Excuse me mister," said James as he bumped into Henry Marston. "Hey, ain't you the new school teacher come to town? Mr. McRae said you just been in."

"I am," said Henry. "And are you to be two of my students when school starts?"

The boys made a face at each other and nodded their heads. David, looking down, noticed Henry's boots. His face lit up.

"Hey! Are those Army boots?"

Henry, self-consciously looked at his feet. "They are. It is taking a long time to wear them out. I'm glad I have them today."

"You were in the Army?"

Henry nodded. "A few years back now . . . a difficult time for our country. You fellows might not have even been born yet."

"I'm seven," said David. James was a baby when Pa came home. He's ten. We came out here from Georgia to make a new start. That's what Pa says, anyhow."

"What are your names?"

"I'm David, this is James. What did you do in the war? Did you shoot any Yankees?"

"Glad to meet you David and James. I'm Henry Marston, Mr. Marston to you fellows."

He didn't answer their questions. He'd seen and experienced enough during those years that the war was something he preferred to put behind him.

"Were you a soldier?" David persisted. At his age, shooting and chasing bandits or Indians was his kind of sport.

"Yes," said Henry. "I was a private in the Army. I spent a lot of time in a balloon, looking out over enemy lines. From up in the air you could get a good idea what was going on far below over quite a large area. And, no, I didn't shoot any Yankees, I didn't shoot anybody."

"Aw, shucks!" said David, his face showing disappointment. My Pa . . ."

"What you talkin' to a Yankee fer?" interrupted a big burly fellow slamming the door behind him. He'd heard just enough to put a label on him.

"Mr. Marston's our new teacher, Pa," said James. "We was just makin' friends."

Henry held out his hand and said, "Henry Marston, sir. You have a fine pair of young . . ." but he was cut off by an angry glare from the boy's father who made no effort to respond to Henry's extended hand.

"Boys, you go back in the store with your Ma. I'm going fer the wagon." With that, he plunged into the muddy street in the direction of his team and flatbed.

Both boys looked at Henry and dutifully turned toward the door. As they did, the door opened and an attractive young woman stood there. She smiled at Henry and spoke to the boys.

"David, I need your feet in here if we're going to get shoes for those growing feet of yours."

"Ma, this is Mr. Marston, our new school teacher."

"Oh, howdy do. I'm Mrs. Butler. You must have met my husband just a moment ago."

"Well, yes and no," Henry said haltingly.

"Pa called him a Yankee!"

"Hush, David, that's not nice. That's history and it's over. I'm sorry, Mr. Marston. Those years were hard on my husband."

"I'm sure they were, Mam. They were hard years for the whole nation. Unfortunately, it is our children who are the victims of their parents' wars."

Mrs. Butler paused and looked at Henry. "What is it that you teach, Mr. Marston?" She put her arm around David, though her look was friendly.

"Fourth, fifth and sixth grades, Mam. This will be my first experience. Last spring I finished my schooling in Ohio."

"I'll be in your class," said James. "I'm going into fifth grade."

"Good for you, James. I'll look forward to having you in my class."

"Now boys," said Mrs. Butler, "What was it your father told you to do?"

"Oh, yeah! Let's go, James," he said, pushing his little brother toward the door.

For a moment Henry and Mrs. Butler stood quietly, looking at the muddy street, the rain, and both, and in their minds, asking themselves questions. "I'd never thought of it that way, Mr. Marston, about the war, but I do suppose you're right about the children, I mean . . ."

"What? Oh, yes! I'm afraid the seeds of every new war are sown in the last one. Sad," he added softly.

"But you don't think . . .you don't think we'll have it all over again, do you?"

Mrs. Butler was in her late twenties. She'd had older brothers take up arms when the call came and possibly even her father had been involved. Sherman's march through Georgia had left a trail of death, destruction and the ruin of many farms and families. With the end finally at Appomattox Court House, the rush of Yankee carpetbaggers had taken every opportunity to take advantage of the failed economy. George Butler had come home in one piece, but a bitter man. Moving west had been their hope toward starting over.

"No, Mrs. Butler. That's not quite what I meant. I don't see that happening again in this country. It was the history of the world that I was thinking about. The effect of war on children, the trauma suffered by children and how the seeds of sadness and bitterness are carried from one generation to the next."

Mrs. Butler didn't answer. It was a lot to think about, possibly beyond her own education, but it was obvious when she nodded politely and stepped into the store that she was thinking.

Henry was left standing, uncertain of the impression he'd given to the Butler family. He'd have the boys in school, at least James, and he wondered just how open James's mind would be under the circumstances.

Moments later, a flat bed wagon splashed its way

Pollen in the Wind

up to the edge of the boardwalk in front of the store. Lost in thought, Henry didn't evade quickly enough the splattering of mud, by accident or intention, that the wheels of the wagon caused. He stepped clear as Mr. Butler jumped from the seat.

"Still wastin' your time doing nothin' useful?" Butler said.

"Oh, the rain will stop eventually," said Henry, not wanting to open a serious conversation.

"Hmph, you'll be all wet even when the sun comes out."

Mr. Butler brushed past and went into the store to collect his purchases and his family. When he came out, Henry had moved along the boardwalk, ducked a few raindrops and was standing in front of the feed store. Under his breath he was mumbling.

"There is more hope for a fool than there is for . . ." he didn't finish.

"Proverbs 26; 12," said a voice from behind him. It was the voice of a very old man and took Henry by surprise.

"You surprised me old man."

"The time I saw you take to converse with the two small boys suggests you might be our new teacher," he said.

"I am," Henry replied and shared his name. "Mr Butler wasn't too friendly."

"I saw and heard Mr. Butler but a moment ago as he passed you by. I know the man."

"Yes, some people live their lives in sequestered hate. I recall a line from Yeats to that effect."

"He is a bitter man, while we stand in awe and the wonder of life with all its possibilities."

Henry began to laugh. "No, not at you neighbor, but the wisdom you share. Who are you? What has been your calling?"

"My name is Jason, Jason Tuttle," he began. "For years I worked for an eastern newspaper. I covered the world's war fronts. Death and destruction are war's only victors."

"I guess you have to see it to believe it." Mr. Butler came to mind and his exasperating smaller view of life's potential. What would it take for him to change? He was going to have his boys in his classroom. Under the circumstances, that could be difficult if he couldn't gain their respect. He would think more on it. The rain came to an end and the two parted with a mutual assurance that they would meet again.

In fact, they did meet again, breakfast one morning in the Guest Kitchen Restaurant. Jason Tuttle had just ordered and waved to Henry to join him.

"How goes the school teaching business?"

"Nearly ready for the onslaught. It's going to be a new experience for me."

"Nervous?"

"Not really. I'll admit I've wondered a bit about the Butler boys."

"You mean you've wondered about the father. He has the problem. Patriotism to a cause can be both an illusion and a curse. I feel sorry for his young wife. Some people live their lives unable to see beyond a few feet and they have no means of changing. It takes over their whole lives."

"That comes with education if the mind can be opened. What do you think?"

"Ah, the school teacher shows. Are you going to order?"

A week later, riding alone in the land of the big sky, as he'd heard it called, Henry reached the top of a rise that offered him a sweeping view in every direction. He slid to the ground, carefully removed a long cylinder from a leather case that hung from the saddle horn. Then he gently slapped the rear of his horse. He knew she'd not go far. Finding a comfortable spot he sat down and removed what turned out to be a telescope. Slipping off the protective caps, he swept the horizon behind him until he focused on the distant buildings of Butte. After locating what he believed to be the window to his rented room, he gazed at the mountains and the beauty of the country around him. He considered his experiences, how different the view of the landscape appears when you are lifted hundreds of feet in the air in a balloon. It was so different from what you saw immediately around you; a bigger picture.

He hadn't yet put Butler out of his mind and he wondered, as he made himself comfortable in the long grass, what it would take to change his view of things, something that might rebuild a man's pride. There were so many people like Butler; a phonograph with only one tune that was then played from one generation to the next . . . . As a reader, he'd found so much written wisdom on people relationships that mankind had little excuse to still be glaring jealously at each other. He picked a small wildflower and examined it carefully, continuing to speculate. He lay back, dreaming. As a teacher, he wanted better, not just for himself. Slowly his thoughts took shape. He had an idea. When he got back to Butte, he looked up his friend Jason Tuttle.

"Ah, we meet again," said Tuttle.

"Lunch, today? I was hoping I'd catch up with you. School starts next week."

"And you've been worrying about the Butler lads?"

"Well, yes, indirectly," said Henry. "Somehow we've got to deal with their father. Do you think he has feelings of inferiority?"

"Quite possible."

"I understand he's good with horses. No, I'm not jesting." They both laughed, but there was a serious side to his question.

"He's about the best around; was a cavalry officer."

The two spoke a bit longer and from the directions he'd been given, Henry found his way to the Butler ranch. It was not a big one, but it was neat and the house and barn well built.

"My Pa's back in the corral training horses for the Yankee blue-bellies," James said.

Mrs. Butler came to the door at the sound of voices. She'd heard James's words. "He loves horses, but hates who he does it for. Howdy again," she said.

"I . . . I came to see him about my own horse. I'm not sure if I have a problem."

She smiled as James scooted off to tell his Pa. "You can really go on out there yourself. He won't bite." She smiled a sad smile.

Henry did, and conversation for a minute was awkward. Yes, he could see signs of a developing leg problem. It wasn't too serious.

"Beautiful horses you have here."

Butler grunted an acknowledgement. "We make a living."

Henry wanted to make some kind of comment about his work, possibly a bitter pill for a southern cavalryman to be training horses for people that brought so much grief into his life. When he spoke, he picked his words carefully.

"Well trained horses for the men who are securing

safe passage of settlers into the west is a compliment, I'd say."

Butler grunted again. It was James who interrupted any further comment.

"Can I show you my horse, Mr. Marston?"

"I'd like that," Henry replied.

The three of them walked toward the barn. James' horse was a beautiful spotted pony with handsome markings. "Pa and I trained her," he said proudly. His Pa nodded.

As the visit ended, Mr. Butler said he'd treat Henry's horse if he wanted to leave her. "Got one you can use in the meantime. Cost a bit."

They arrived at a fair price and as Henry returned toward town he felt better, perhaps a better understanding of Mr. Butler. He now had a reason to drop out to the Butler ranch another time. He found Jason Tuttle the next day and they considered Henry's visit.

"So what do you think?" he asked, after explaining what he'd learned about Butler. He also had an idea.

"Worth a try. We all feel better when we get outside ourselves. Let me know if I can be useful to you. It would be too bad to see his kids grow up angry over something for which they had had no part. Be a help to his young wife also."

"I'm not sure how to go about this or if any of it is my business."

"It wouldn't be if you tried to confront him directly, Henry. You may just discover something here about human nature!"

"Words from an expert?" laughed Henry.

"No, words from an older man," laughed Jason.

The first days of school came and went. His initial tension was gone. He'd been back to the ranch several times about his horse and he seemed at ease with that situation. About November, as names were being forwarded for various town offices, Henry went to one of the open meetings. Various names came up and when the name of Butler was forwarded, Henry's mind jumped. Now! he thought. He rose to his feet and spoke.

"Here's a man with strong convictions, a man who stands by what he believes in . . . and the best interests of the country . . . has two fine well disciplined boys in school. That should tell us something in itself."

Somebody commented that he was still fighting the Civil War and ought to grow up. It was here that Jason Tuttle spoke, much to Henry's relief. "Yes," he began, "to many the loss has not worn off. It was a tragedy to all of us and it takes some of us a little longer and a little encouragement to see the bigger picture. I would suggest and am willing to risk that what Butler has felt in the past may not be at all the level of his thinking in the days to come."

Henry began to applause and soon the room responded. Hopefully, Butler would be a candidate!

Henry bumped into Butler a week or so after the elections. Butler had won a position to the town council. His boys at school wondered and asked at school if Henry hadn't been more than a private during the war. It was a funny question to ask, but it showed Henry that there was some kind of productive discussion going on at home. He felt good about that and for Mrs. Butler. A chance meeting with Butler was a friendly meeting, in fact, Butler thanked him for his comments and support. They talked briefly about the boys and their school work. Nothing was said of his war convictions, no more than a harmless remark as they parted.

"Sometime you have to see things from a different viewpoint to get the full measure of what's important," said Henry.

"I guess so," said Butler as he stuck out his hand to shake.

Thoughts in the Autumn of Life

There was snow on the ground, the wet sticky kind that creates a delicate tracery amongst the barren branches of the poplar trees. Roaming Bear sat cross-legged at the small opening of his teepee. The buffalo skin flap was open, but he was oblivious to the chill air that touched his wrinkled old face. Roaming Bear was old, a senior member of the Shoshone tribe that traditionally moved across the grass land that would someday be called Wyoming.

He was looking out across the open country, remembering better days, days when there was the laughter of children, the un-intrusive chatter of squaws pounding corn or perhaps even the sounds of a young expectant woman singing. In the quiet of his mind, Roaming Bear recalled the first strange looking wagon of a white man and his family slowly working his way across the rolling contours of the open country before him.

He was younger then, strong and respected for his physical skills and capacity to lead and feed his growing family. So many years had passed since then and there had been so many canvas covered wagons that had crossed the Shoshone's hunting grounds. So many of the buffalo had been killed, too many just for the sport of it. And too, so many of his own people had died at the hands of these un-accepting intruders. The seasonal migration of his people was a thing of the past. Life would never be the same, ever.

He recalled how long ago at evening he had killed a small elk, cleaned and dressed the fresh meat and ridden to the encampment of a white man and his family. He went toward the people in peace willing to share food for the weary travelers. As he approached, the man had a rifle in his hands and eyed him cautiously. Roaming Bear raised his open hand and halted his approach. The man lowered his weapon. Roaming Bear spoke, but his words could not be understood. The man's wife came up beside her husband and smiled and with hands made signs of welcome. The gift was given and by motions and scratching lines in the rich soil a map provided location of a river not far ahead. The meeting was brief, but friendly.

The small family and their wagon, leading a cow tied behind it, moved on the next morning. Roaming Bear never saw them again, but he did see others. By the hundreds they came. There had come, as well as other Indians, men who spoke more than one tongue and efforts to verbally stem the tide had proven futile.

For some reason the people of his tribe were not considered friendly and in time did take up arms to defend and protect their lands. And in time, also, the white man sent mounted black men on horses to raid their villages and wantonly kill men, women and children and even dogs. Roaming Bear had fought back with bow and arrow, spears and sometimes with a captured rifle. But the tide was too great and eventually the white man's rifles could speak many times while their own held only one shot at a time.

Words between the Shoshone and other tribes, as they sought some protection of their hunting grounds, failed. Words proved to be no more than empty promises. Ambition and lust for power seem to be the cause between many peoples.

On this day as Roaming Bear looked across the land before him, he hoped with the snow laying cold on the ground, that his remaining son and small party of raiders would not return too soon to the village. Their tracks in the snow would be followed and again the declining nation of his people would be threatened. The elders of the tribe, Roaming Bear included, had refused, for lack of understanding, trust or appreciation, what the white man had offered when he spoke of "Reservation". A small area of barren land seemed not to be a negotiable consideration. The whole situation was a worrisome problem for which he held no answers, or at least only one small selfless solution. As he sat, he felt the comforting hand of his woman on his shoulder, but that alone would not be enough.

Roaming Bear wondered if in other far distant lands there were people who swept across the earth laying claim to what they wanted for themselves. The Great Spirit had provided land enough for all peoples and food abundantly, asking only that the land be revered and the abundance shared. Yes, too simple a solution, he knew. The hand on his shoulder was firm and squeezed ever so gently and he knew his woman was aware of his thoughts - that enemies may be defeated, whatever the cause, but it is the hatred left behind that never dies.

Branded

Blackie McCartney was a small man, physically as well as mentally. He chewed tobacco and didn't wipe the corners of his mouth when he spit, which he did frequently. Laundry was not a strong suit for him either. For some reason he believed there were shortcuts to wealth that didn't involve all the tedium of day to day effort. He had a lot to learn.

He worked as a hand on the cattle ranch of wise old Walter Carlson for a month, but one day asked for his wages and disappeared. Nobody seemed to know where he'd gone and when you come right down to it, nobody, except Mr. Carlson cared. Deep down, from what he'd seen, he felt sorry for the fellow.

"Blackie, you sure we can pull this off?"

"Hell, yes, got it all figured out. All we need is four or five men for a month, two at the most."

Blackie squatted before a small campfire, a branding iron glowing red in the hot coals. He turned it over a time or two to make certain it was ready.

"I know a couple in town," said his companion. "Red Haskell is one . . . if he's out of jail. Last I heard, they locked 'im up for a brawl at the tavern . . . busted up the place a bit." He began to laugh. "Said he was 'disturbin the peace'. He sure disturbed a piece of the bartender's front teeth. We could get him . . . an' there's the Woody brothers."

"Can they move long horns?" Blackie pulled the iron from the fire and pressed the red hot end into a pine log he'd pulled close by. It burned deep, scattering a small shower of sparks as it sizzled into the soft wood. Then he looked up at the unshaven young man watching. "Chet, I mean, can they move long horns on a round-up?"

"Yeah, I guess, sure! They done it 'afore."

Blackie pulled the smoking iron away from the log and admired the results. "Not bad, eh?" he stuck the iron back into the red coals.

"Cripes, that's the Triangle C brand; the Carlson brand. What you doin' with that?"

"Picked it up when I left," said Blackie. "Now just you watch what happens next." He turned the iron over in the embers as he'd done before. It only took a minute for the iron to heat up again. Glowing red, he pulled it out of the fire and carefully inverted the triangle with the letter C in the center and pressed the hot iron over the top of his first brand. Again it spattered a few sparks and smoked. When he pulled the iron away the new inverted triangle over the first impression made a star out of the original design and the letter C was closed into a circle. He spat off to the side, smiling. "So, now we have the Star and Sun brand."

"Well . . . you dirty dog, you! Damn! That's masterful, that's somethin' else." Chet pranced around the log with the new brand mark, shaking his head. "You son of a . . . man! I see the picture. Yeah, I can get a crew together."

"Another month the Carlson hands will be roundin' up everything on the range and branding anything that ain't got a mark on it."

"Yeah, and turning 'em loose till they're ready to trail north" Chet was beside himself. "You crafty son of a gun, you."

So it was that efforts began to put Blackie's plan

into play. Red Haskell was back in jail, but expected to be out in time for the drive. The Woody brothers were pleased to take part in some easy money. Bill Woody had been fired a couple of years back by old man Carlson himself, so getting even suited him just fine. For the promise of a bottle of whiskey, Chet got a breed to be one more hand.

"We need one more," said Blackie, as the collected group met back in the high country a week later. "We need someone to go to work for the Carlsons."

"They ain't none of us they'd put up with," offered Chet.

"I know," replied Blackie, "but we need someone on the inside . . . someone able to keep us posted on their plans, dates and what railhead they'll be drivin' toward."

With the details of the plan underway, there was general agreement that one more person working with the hands on the Carlson spread would be needed. It couldn't be just anybody, that was for sure. A few names were suggested and one by one tossed out . . . "Can't keep his mouth shut" . . . "No, he'd be too risky" . . . "Couldn't rope a calf if he tried . . ." So it went until a few days later, one of the Woody brothers rode into their hidden camp site with a party in mind.

"Seems to be a drifter, spends a lot of time at the bar and don't talk much."

"Where's he from, Woody?"

"Hell, I don't know, somewhere south of here. I just asked if he knew runnin' long horns. He looked at me, his eyes narrowed an' he just nodded."

"We gotta be sure!"

"I'll see if I can get him drunk, Blackie. Yeah, that's what I'll do." He got to his feet and strode toward his horse. "Be back in a few days, boss." With that, he was gone, slipped out the narrow gap between the two massive walls of the mesa that concealed their camp and rode off toward Mosquero, the nearest town to the Carlson ranch.

"He damned well better be careful. Chet, you follow him and cut him off if he gets in over his head."

"You mean . . .?"

"Absolutely! You're the fastest draw of any of us, an' we can't afford any slip-ups."

Chet bit his lip. He knew he was fast with a gun and taunting another to draw against him so far hadn't been too risky. "If you say so, Blackie."

Actually, it didn't come to that. Woody didn't have to get him drunk and risk spilling information of his own. He found the fellow had come up from Texas and was looking for a short time job before he felt comfortable about going back south. He knew cattle alright, but mentioned in an off-handed way that you could make a better killing with what's traveling over the railroads. Quicker! Said there was a lot of money moving on the rails these days. Yes, he was interested, in as much as Woody seemed willing to share and also willing to meet with the others involved.

Blackie and the boys set up a location where they could meet without revealing their camp, They looked him over, took careful note how he wore his gun tied down and the notches in the brim of his hat. He went by the name of Cassidy, but names of men in such businesses didn't often use their real name; Cassidy would do.

"Use that thing?" said Blackie, spitting off to the side.

"A time or two." Cassidy's face relaxed into a broad grin. "Gonna test me?"

Chet stepped forward, pulled a silver dollar from

his pocket, flipped it a couple of times and said, "Can ya hit it standin' still or do you have to be movin'?"

Cassidy looked at the coin. He winked at Blackie. "If you toss it, which side do you want the bullet to go through?" He then turned to Chet. "Any way you want it, just toss it."

As the group watched, Chet tossed the coin thirty feet into the air, Cassidy drew his pistol and fired twice. His second shot hit the coin and sent it zinging off fifty feet or so before it dropped to the ground. Chet noted that his draw had been smooth and fast. He felt confident that he was just a mite faster. There was no question, he could handle his weapon.

"Coin must have been on edge on my first shot," he said. "That's why I had to shoot twice."

"Oh," was all Chet could say. He turned to Blackie who just nodded.

"Now, this is how it shapes up," said Blackie. "You drift down to the Carlson spread. They're lookin' for hands. If you've had work movin' cattle, which you say you have, the old man will put you on. You'll have to work your back side off. He pushes. And he's a sharp old geezer. Oh, don't go in with your gun tied down. He'll notice."

Cassidy nodded and rubbed his chin, taking it all in.

"We need to know what railhead he'll drive for and when. Simple as that. We'll keep a lookout for you in town. You should know at least a week before they head north . . . be gettin' the chuck wagon set to roll and so on."

Cassidy again nodded. "You got it, Blackie." Mounting, he touched the brim of his hat to Blackie and tipped with his fingers to Chet and the Woody brothers. He turned his horse and rode off in the direction of the Triangle C.

Woody was smiling. "Man, can that bastard shoot! Aren't you glad you didn't have to deal with 'im Chet?"

Chet shook his head and jutted his jaw forward. "Not as fast as me!"

"Now we've got work to do ourselves. Start pickin' up strays. When we collect a dozen or so, we'll brand 'em an' turn 'em loose. When the time comes, they'll all go north and our herd will have the Star and Sun brand on 'em. Every chance we get to find one of their cattle on their own, we'll add another brand over the Triangle C." With a smug look on his face he swung himself up into his saddle. "Let's ride, boys!"

Days passed, busy weeks slipped by and the number of calves and strays the gang rounded up began to add up. Then word finally came early in September that the Carlson spread was ready to drive north. Cassidy reported through Chet that Dodge City would be where they would be going, the end of the week.

The Carlson drive began, close to a thousand long horn, a dozen seasoned hands and the chuck wagon. Old man Carlson himself was going to make the drive.

Shadowing from a distance, five men moved along parallel to the travel of the herd. They screened their evening campfires and ate lean. Then one night, well up the trail, with heat lightning and the rumble of thunder in the distance, the big herd was restless and hard to settle down. Rain finally came and the Carlson hands wearing hooded rain gear couldn't be distinguished from a small group of men that slid inconspicuously amongst the herd. With one major flash of lightning and a pistol fired in the air, a few steer started to run, then the whole herd became a thundering stampede. Blackie's boys cut out a good portion of the running cattle, moving them in a direction off to the side, while the rest of the herd went in a sweeping curve in another direction before control could be re-established.

"We've got a few hours, boy. Let's get our brand on the group we cut out," shouted Blackie. "They won't be comin' lookin' until daylight."

Settled down, the cattle were roped, tied and re-branded, changing the Triangle C into the Star and Sun. One rider from the Carlson camp did come in their direction and when he saw the steer were settled down and hands to hold them, he didn't approach any closer. He evidently presumed them to be men of their own. When the sky began to lighten in the east, men began to urge the cattle into the slow and steady pace that would eventually bring them to the Dodge railhead. Again Blackie and his men were out of sight as the work was carried out by the Carlson hands. Only at night did a couple of them drift over and mix with the herd with the idea that they would cut out a few more. Hopefully, by the time they reached Dodge, the majority of the herd would be carrying a different brand.

"This is where I leave you, boys," said Blackie. "I'm riding into Dodge to register our brand so there won't be any question when we get there as to whose cattle they are. So far this has been a slick operation and should pay off well. Chet, you're in charge! Adios!"

Chet liked the idea of being in charge and didn't hesitate to communicate that he was the one who was in charge. He hoisted his gunbelt as if to add emphasis. The Woody brothers resented being ordered around for no good reason and let Chet know their feelings. Up to this part of the drive, Blackie had run a fairly relaxed operation and felt confident that they would share fairly in whatever the effort provided at the end of the trip. The breed didn't seem to care so long as he was fed daily and the promise of a bottle at the end of the drive was his share. Cassidy, of course, was still a part of the Carlson team and would get his at the end. On his own, Chet began to think that this extra man might not be so fast with his gun after all. He was also glad Haskell was back in jail, so one more to their split of their take would be unnecessary. Except for the breed, each man began to think of what they might be sharing if their number was cut down. Blackie would have been smarter to have remained with his group for another couple of days, but he was getting itchy to complete their effort. Three days later the whole herd reached the stockyard where all the cattle would be sorted out according to brands and counted. For the Carlson hands, the tally proved disappointing.

"Don't worry, boys," said old man Carlson.

"But the brand is not our own," said one of the younger hands.

By the end of the day, a full accounting for the herd had been accomplished and bidders made their offers. Conditions on the trail and the months before had been good for the herd. They had lost little weight en route and brought good bids. Blackie was there, but remained pretty much on the sidelines. When he stepped up to the high bidder, he received a surprise he hadn't counted on.

"The Star and Sun brand, oh, sure, that would be the Carlson herd. We've already paid Mr. Carlson top dollar and he's gone over to the saloon to run drinks for his boys."

Blackie stammered something about the brand, but with money already having changed hands, he knew he'd have to go to old man Carlson if he expected to get anything out of his efforts. He knew, too, he would have to face his own boys and that put more than a little concern in his thinking. At first he wondered how it had come about. Then he suspected that Cassidy was not who he thought he'd claimed to be.

What Blackie learned before he left town was that Old man Carlson had seen the new brand weeks ago and realized when they killed a steer and skinned the animal to look on the underside, that the brand was comprised of one brand over another, otherwise the burn would have been made by one iron with a uniform temperature and a uniform burn on the longhorn's hide. It didn't show on the outside, but was quite evident on the underside of the skin. With that information learned early enough, Carlson had sent a man on to Dodge. The Carlson's would be bringing in two brands, not one.

Somehow Blackie eluded his boys and was nowhere to be seen in Dodge. Cassidy did turn out to be someone other than he'd claimed, and Chet, angry about his loss blamed their problem on Cassidy. Unfortunately, the Woody brothers learned Cassidy's identity as a Texas Ranger after Chet had confronted him. Chet may have been faster on the draw, but was not as accurate. Once aware of the brand changes, Carlson had called in the Ranger to work along with him and he had done just as asked for both sides.

"I'll be going on after Blackie, now," said Cassidy.

"Good. He shouldn't be hard to catch up with."

"What charges do you want to make, Mr. Carlson."

"To me, jail is the wrong place for men like this. They should be put on a work crew under close supervision, road building, the railroad, some place more demanding than sitting in a jail. They won't learn anything just sitting. They need to learn the value of real work. Like it or not, these men will now wear the wrong brand for the rest of their lives."

Where the Trail Narrows

Riding point for a cavalry unit out of Fort Laramie, I found myself somewhat beyond my usual scouting distance from the mounted soldiers. Off in the distance I'd seen what I believed to be a lone Indian on foot, an unusual sight in the wide open country and had decided to investigate. For a moment he disappeared from view, evidently into a gully or natural ditch. Looking back toward the column of mounted bluecoats, I would judge my distance to be no more than two miles away. When I reached the gully I saw my party just a short distance ahead of me. It took only a minute to catch up. There was no effort for the man to run from me.

Although I wore the blue britches with the yellow stripe of the mounted men, Indian scouts did not benefit more than a minimal uniform. My hat was broad brimmed with a scarlet ribbon. My coat was a deer skin with fringes and a few colored beads. As I rode up I realized the man ahead of me was an Indian, a very old man. I spoke to him in my native Crow.

"Hold on, old man, where are you going?"

He stopped, turned to look up at me and replied. He spoke the Blackfoot tongue and his words were understandable.

"You take old men prisoners?"

Obviously in the open country he had seen the unit's dust, recognized the column as unfriendly and had sought cover that would allow him to go his way alone.

"I take no prisoners, friend."

"No Iyeska half-breed is friend to me," he replied proudly. He recognized immediately that my willingness to serve the white man's army spoke strongly against me. "You, with a squaw-man for a father, if you take no prisoners, let me go my way alone."

"And just what is your way?"

"I go the way of all old men in my tribe. I return to my maker. Old men must die or the world grows moldy and lives the past all over again. My trail has grown narrow with the years."

"But you are not that old, old man," I said. "You have many good years to travel."

"I am no longer of this world, young man. I do not understand the world you are a part of," he said, moving to a large rock where he could seat himself. "My links to the past are fading."

I dropped down off my horse and squatted in front of him. There was no question, he was old. His hair was long and gray, his hands gnarled and spotted with the marks of age, his face was greatly creased from both the weather and the wear of many seasons. Although clean, his clothing was old and many times repaired. The fringes of his leather trousers were nearly gone. He wore a feather of an eagle in his hair. Obviously, at one time he had been a proud warrior. Now his only weapon was the knife he carried on a beaded belt. I felt sadness for the old man, but his leaving his village as he had was our custom. He would no longer be a burden to anyone by his quiet departure. I took the canteen from my belt and held it out to him to drink. He smiled.

"One more taste of water will make little difference, but I will enjoy it. Thank you." He drank deeply before handing back the canteen. "Now tell me, young

Pollen in the Wind

man, why do you do what you do?" You have one foot in the white man's world and one in mine?"

"I am the bastard child of a squaw many years ago. I am not wanted in my native world and only used in this one as you have already taken note and called regretfully to my attention. It is the plight of a breed.

"But you work against my people, so you are my enemy." He reached for the knife at his waist.

"Hold old man, your blade is too dull and rusted to cause me harm and your arm no longer the strength of the mountain lion." I put out my hand to prevent his movement, though I believe we both could anticipate the outcome. He relaxed on the stone where he sat, and looked up at me with clouded eyes.

"Do you have a family?"

"Death crept up on my woman years ago. It came as a white man's sickness. Two of my living sons travel in the company of Crazy Horse. I am proud that they do not lay down their arms as did Red Cloud. We all know the odds are against us. Surrender is difficult to accept. The white man's word's are talk that mask the truth. As my enemy you should know."

He spoke slowly, deliberately, looking into my eyes. I rubbed my chin, listening to the old man's words. I understood his feelings.

"So what are we two to do?" he sighed. "For me not to die with honor, against an enemy of my people, leaves you a younger man with the terrible burden of killing your Indian brothers."

"Half brothers," I said, smiling at the old man's thought and wondering which half of me would suffer the most. "There is no dignity in the death of an old man,"I said. "You are coming to your grave in a full age , like a shock of corn that reaches its season."

"Yes," he said, sadly.

For several minutes the two of us sat quietly, again considering our situations.

Off in the distance could faintly be heard the sound of gunfire. I sprang toward the rim of the gully and looked in the direction I had come. There on the plain a battle was taking place. Surprised and caught in the open, the cavalry detachment was surrounded by a circling band of Indians. Somehow, they had concealed themselves until the right moment, perhaps in a gully like the one the old man and I had entered. The bluecoats were down, using their horses as protective cover as the Indians circled ever closer, slowly and effectively diminishing the soldier's ranks. Having traveled farther from our column than might have been necessary, I had failed as a scout to detect the trap the column had entered into. I watched a disaster in the making. It would not take long to happen.

The old man scrambled up the side of the gully to watch.

"Do you see my sons?" the old man asked, squinting through eyes that no longer saw that distance.

"If they have your heart, they are there old man."

He was smiling when I looked at him. I'm not sure it was for his sons or that the pony soldiers were falling. The last man fell as a wave of riders swept across the remaining defenders. The fight was over. The bluecoats had lost.

"Ha!" he said. "Your link with your past is broken. Your weary life can at last stand still." The old man seemed pleased that now the two of us had nothing to look forward to but dying. "We are both unwanted by our brothers . . . and half brothers," he added with a delighted chuckle.

"I am now all that is left of the unit I served," I

Pollen in the Wind

said. "minutes ago I might have been at the height of my career, honored and admired. Now, I am no longer in such an enviable situation."

"And a half breed besides," he said, interrupting and adding to my new self pity. "We travel together in a lonely world. We will decay like the autumn fruit that has mellowed too long."

"But I am not ready."

"Who is?"

"I have more winters ahead, Old man." I slid back down into the gully, followed by the old man. "Death is not something I deserve." For several minutes I lay there thinking I hadn't amounted to very much so far and quite likely would not as a consequence of this tragic affair. I shook my head as if the shaking would clear away such thoughts. "No! I said. "No, I am not ready."

"You are wrong! You have already spent your youth. It is the young who are slaves to dreams and only at middle life does one have all his senses. The old and unwanted are servants of their regrets."

"But my death will interrupt the great experience of living. When I die, it will come with my boots on and the clear blue sky above me. With an unfaltering trust I will then approach my grave."

"You are aging rapidly, my son. Travel on with me together." He put his wrinkled hand upon my shoulder and spoke as persuasively as he could. "We can move on until our weary lives stand still."

"I will travel along the trail together with you until your trail ends. Then I must find my own way."

The old man's face was sad. He had not won his argument. He would have to travel on alone and that, too, was one more rejection. His look asked again. I shook my head. The old man's words held much wisdom, for there is nothing worse in life than to travel alone, rejected, unwanted ... by anybody.

Where the Past is Present

Families have a way of falling apart if there is no communication between members. Wayne and his brother, Paul, had not seen their father in years. With their mother's passing a few months earlier, the family seemed about to go separate ways entirely. It wasn't that they had been a close family before. The senior Mr. Rogers, Henry, had been in education for years and had been a very popular and effective teacher. It was academic politics that denied him tenure and deserved advancement that finally disgusted him. Weary of it, crushed and disappointed, he'd left the University and even home for prospecting in the west. He more frequently sent money home to the family than to visit himself. It was a letter from Wayne that brought Paul to his brother's Indiana campus.

"One of these days there won't be any of our family left," Wayne said after the usual brotherly greetings at the station.

"So, you thought we'd best reconnect to our roots, eh, Professor?" he replied with a broad smile. Paul was the youngest of the two. His academic interests were in history.

"Well, the last cryptic communication from parts west came from Vernal in Utah. Father may have fallen off a mountain by now. His last note to me was more than a few months ago."

Both young men were tall and lanky, like their mother had been. In their late twenties, they were seriously oriented to the focused routine of academic life and research in particular. Research had proven freer of the faculty games their father had suffered. Their parents had set a strong pattern of intellectual curiosity. They fully understood their father's frustration with academic games, favoritism and egos, aware that students, sadly, are subsequently exposed to and learn more than simply classroom assignments.

"We could go see the old buzzard," suggested Paul. "I would guess he's somewhere in the area of the Green River."

"As our family historical authority, Professor, isn't that about the area that turned back the two Franciscan fathers in their search for an overland route from Santa Fe to California?"

"Escalante and Dominguez? I wasn't aware that you knew about such things, brother."

"Ah, yes. I am well read, it's in our blood. What I've read of William Ashley's explorations and writings of John Wesley Powell just a few years back, they both suggest it's an area of considerable geological interest. My field!"

"So, it's not your father you want to see, but a tumble of rock formations?"

"A deductive mind, little brother! Can we make such a journey together at the end of the semester?"

Paul scratched the back of his head. Then he rubbed his hands across his chin, gestures that made it seem as though he was considering a difficult question. "Hmm," was all he said.

"No?" Wayne wasn't sure about his brother, or was he just pulling his leg? He did that. "Perhaps the area's hangout for the Sundance Kid or Butch Cassidy has more appeal to you?"

"The Green River area has a well-known history as part of the Outlaw Trail up through the canyons."

"You've read too many dime novels, Wayne, or is that the thrust of your academic endeavors these days?' Sure, I'll put my life temporarily in your hands and we'll find the father we never really knew we had." He paused. "What if we don't find him?"

"I've written to the sheriffs in Vernal and Dutch John to post a notice and perhaps even keep their eyes and ears open for him."

So, early in June with the end of the University semester, the two young men met again. This time it was, as agreed, to travel west; both wondering what kind of a parent they would find. Each came equipped for a wilderness experience, back-pack, minimal cooking gear, ponchos and a bedroll. They speculated the whole way out what their father would even look like, should they find him. It had been that long.

"Let's see, he'll not have shaved very often. Probably dressed in an old shirt. Remember that red wool one he had on the last time he came home? What'll you bet?"

"I just wouldn't be surprised," laughed Paul.

They weren't. The sheriff at Vernal had run into a fellow named Paul Lynch in the area of Pat's Hole and he knew who Henry Rogers was and would be on the lookout for him. It had taken a couple of months before communication was accomplished and the older Mr. Rogers was at the sheriff's office on the date Wayne had suggested.

"I told you he'd be wearing it," laughed Paul when they saw him.

"What you boys want?" he said. Henry had never been big on hugs or hand-shake formalities. But, he was shaven and looked healthy and fit. His face was sun tanned and his eyes were bright. The red shirt was clean and greatly patched at the elbows. The shirt shouldn't have been much of a surprise. Each of the boys had favorite old sweaters they wore till they were in threads.

"Just passing through, thought we'd say hello," said Wayne, not wanting their coming together to be considered a family crisis. "Been how long, Dad?"

"Never been one to keep track," he replied. "Out here, time comes in big stretches. May even be standing still. You eaten yet?" He'd never been great on casual conversation either, but that seemed to be another family trait.

"Ma used to say, if it hadn't been for her, the men in this family would go off into separate caves to contemplate some esoteric research," said Wayne. "She had been fairly close to the truth, but it never let it upset her marriage. She was patient with all of us. So, Dad, we're what's left of the family. Where do we go from here?"

Henry pulled a rumpled map from his pack and pointed to a location where the Yampa flows into the Green River. "This twist in the river is a place called Steamboat Rock. I think you'll find it of interest." He smiled from privileged information. "Working our way up stream won't be easy."

"Where do you live out here, Dad? asked Paul.

"Have a small cabin, actually several. I move around seasonally, much as people long before any of us came here. Call it a hunter-gatherer lifestyle. From what I've learned so far, human occupation of this area goes back thousands of years."

"I'm ready," said Wayne. as he poured over the old map, his finger tracing the twists and turns of the Green River. "Some of this area must have been near or under sea level at one time."

"Millions of years ago," responded his father.

"Then mountains began to rise, some pretty steeply, exposing various layers of rock from below. Where they broke off, major fault lines occurred, erosion followed, stripping away material that re-deposited in the basin formed at the foot of the new mountains."

"You sound like you're teaching, Dad."

"You'll find this a real classroom, son, the best there is. One reason I used to take students out of the classroom, much to the dismay of my collective colleagues. Observation, study and understanding are possible in the field. No nonsense. Prospecting for gold only made time here possible." He winked and smiled at the puzzled expressions on his sons' faces.

"You mean . . . all the time you've been west, that . . . you've . . . ?"

"There's a lot to see here, boys, so let's move on, eh?"

They finished their meal, gathered their gear and obtained horses to carry them eastward in the direction of the Green River. They followed more a trail than any kind of road through stretches of ground covered with juniper. Phosphate rich formations of rock jutted up before them. Then vertical sandstone flatirons, compressed and bent, thrust dramatically upward, revealing where powerful forces of nature's uplifting pressure had been at work. They made camp along their route and the following day reached the Green River where a local rancher accepted their horses to be held for their return.

Wayne could not get over the varied geology of the area and remarked with excitement about the formations they were seeing. Here was geological history turned on edge so that layer after layer could be examined, layers tilted, bent and carved into a complex landscape. Henry Rogers watched with interest as his sons' expressions changed. For days, the three moved up along the river, portaging some areas, working their way along stretches where red rock canyon walls rose steeply on each side of them. Then followed flat open areas where the Green River meandered lazily around small islands covered with greasewood and salt brush. Varied wildlife was abundant and in their own way questioned these intruders entering their unique habitat. Wayne made sketches and notes in a journal he had brought along for just that purpose. From a distance, a bighorn sheep watched them suspiciously. It was exciting!

"Does anybody live up in this area?" asked Paul.

"Yes, son, a few. I just happen to be one of them. But, that matters little when you're busy."

It was the word 'son' that this time caught Paul's ear and possibly Wayne's as well. He'd said it twice now. For so many years, the family had lived separated lives and with Henry Rogers home with the family so seldom, the concept of father and son had become almost an abstraction, an idea, hardly a reality. He was glad he was here, all three of them together, more of a family than they'd known for years.

"To answer your question more fully, Paul, we will shortly be seeing the artwork of an early people, oh, perhaps several thousand years ago. Some are what are called pictographs, some petroglyphs, dot pecked designs incised in the surface of the rock face, large figures, abstract designs that defy our understanding and meaning. They are the work of an early people hundreds of years ago. Perhaps they didn't actually live right here, we've found so few artifacts, a few stone points, tools and animal bones. But, we'll see a few rock shelters where food was stored. I'll point them out."

Both young men listened with increased interest as their father went on to explain about the great plains people that lived east of the Rockies, people that lived on the meat of the great bison and mammoths before some of these larger species became extinct and they had to rely on smaller game and eventually turned to wild plant life for more of their diet.

"Mammoths?" exclaimed Wayne.

"With reliable water resources, this plateau with its natural diversity, is a natural interface with cultures in three directions. Yes, mammoths, and before we complete our visit, I'll show you a real surprise."

"Dad?" said Paul, increasingly curious about this weathered and vigorous old man who had spent so many years away from home. He savored the sound of the word "Dad" in his mind as he spoke. Henry Rogers smiled, perhaps he too, after so many years, liked more than just the sound of his son's questions. He was still a real teacher, and a father.

"You young fellows are both on college campuses, passing on information about our world to other eager young man and women. Let me suggest to you that apples do not fall far from a tree." He nodded as they listened. He went on. "Text books can only offer so much. Too abstract! We learn in many different ways. Shortly, we will reach a place where the river currents slow as the river curves around a broad sandbar. We'll spend some time there. My camp is nearby. Erosion and periodic flooding, perhaps not in that order, have uncovered an ancient world, a window into the past. It is the kind of thing researchers long to find. I consider myself lucky." He beamed. "A real classroom!"

"We're ready . . .Dad." Paul smiled to himself as they shoved off, working their way upstream.

For a time their effort allowed little chance for real

conversation. Before long, Hank, as he was more widely known in this area, motioned toward the shore. There, they hauled their skin covered bullboat into the shallows and climbed out.

"Look at the bones . . .carcasses! Dad! These are the bones of . . .of huge animals!"

Henry Rogers winked at Paul as he began unloading and carrying gear ashore. "Dinosaurs, Wayne! Here are the back plates of a Stegosaurus, here a baby Stegosaurus. You'll find mostly plant eaters, but also a few predators like the Allosaurus and Ceratosaurus. I've had it all to myself. No staff problems. Not one! Of course, someday others will come."

For a whole week together the boys and their Dad camped along the Yampa and daily explored the local area of the dinosaur bones. It was the uplifting of the layers of rock that had allowed erosion to strip away concealing layers that had once been the river bed. Henry had collected papers in his nearby cabin, writings along with measured drawings he'd made of large and small bone fragments. He had even gathered ones with teeth still embedded in chunks of sandstone. He also had the fine chisels and ice picks that made examination possible. His home was a laboratory in the field. Wayne was ecstatic!

The three talked by fireside during the long summer evenings together and gradually came to know each other, and to understand in each their obsessions with knowledge. For Henry, there was much here yet to be uncovered and protected for future generations. Funds would have to be raised and broader interest generated. Both boys enthusiastically pledged to do what they could toward funds. Yet, the greatest find of all for the two boys, and perhaps, too, for the father, was nothing quite so old as a dinosaur. Dinosaurs never did wear tattered red shirts.

"You've not been just prospecting for . . ." Paul couldn't finish, only thinking the word 'gold' and in the back of his mind, the recovery of an old man's self worth. The boys practically danced around their father at the thought, both realizing that sometimes when you go in search of something, what you find is not at all what you expected. It was going to be hard for them to leave. "I guess apples don't really fall far from a tree," Paul commented, laughing happily as the found family packed their gear.

A Look of My Own

As part of my academic program at one of the Eastern Ivy League schools, I elected to undertake a study of the Indians of North America. Yes, I am Indian, or rather part Indian and a young boyish looking maiden at that. My study to be was not so much their habitat or customs, but more their adjustment and response to the presence of the white man. It naturally would involve quite a bit of history, a subject that is interesting to me, primarily because of my own native American ancestry. As a minority in an otherwise all white college, my collegiate relationships have been relatively few, and are comprised of a small group of men and women from various parts of the world.

I was born in Pocumtuck, a broad fertile valley just west of the Connecticut River in Massachusetts. I should call the place Deerfield, but prefer to call it by the name of its original inhabitants, the Pocumtuck Indians, who knew it as their homeland. Pocumtuck's origin dates well back before the 1600's, possibly to the beginning of time itself. My ancestors hunted in the forests, fished in the nearby rivers and farmed rich soil with crops of maze, beans, squash and tobacco.

Let me begin by saying that New England has been the home to Indians for a very long time. My people lived in dwellings called wigwams, which were dome-shaped enclosures made of bent poles and covered by bark and woven mats. They were portable and seasonally moved from fishing stations to cornfields and in the winter to more sheltered locations. The annual migrations were little different than what my understanding is of our western brothers. As I get into my writing I will, of course record my observations in a journal as I am already doing here.

The history of fighting between white colonists and Indians goes back to 1620 when the Great Puritan Migration brought thousands of settlers to the New World; New World to them, I might add. In 1644 the Mohawk Indians attacked the Pocumtuck settlements and during the years all the way to 1680, during King Philips War, occupants of the valley were killed and homes burned. That wasn't the end of it because the reestablishment of the area as Deerfield continued to experience fighting; King William's War and Queen Anne's War. Unable to resolve differences or the consequences of greed by peaceful measures was little different than some of our own territorial struggles.

In 1704, one raid by French and Indians saw the capture of one hundred and nine whites and much of Deerfield burned again. The captives were hurriedly marched back up along the Connecticut River and ultimately divided into small groups around the area of Lake Champlain and further on toward the St. Lawrence River. I use the white man's designations of these places, for contemporary understanding, in lieu of their Indian names. Adjustments to each other's presence from the start got off on a bad footing. The exercise of judgments are too often self-serving, regardless of race or nation. Our concept of land ownership, for example is quite different than the English people's. The French came into the lands of what is Canada, hunted, trapped and fished. Ownership and settlement was not their original intent, although Quebec did have a beginning. Rivalry between the French and the

English had simply been transplanted here into our own differences.

As a student of history, one point I'd like to make regards belief that Indians, all Indians, are warlike and have little hesitation to attack other tribes, take prisoners and carry on other inhuman actions against each other. The business of taking scalps is one that would most readily come to mind. Let me forward a question as to the humanity of my white brothers who, throughout their history have burned people alive at the stake, have carried out hangings, firing squads, religious Crusades and all the horrors of being held and tortured in dungeons, not to overlook assassinations, poisoning, starving and so on as acceptable practices. Is one more horrendous than another simply because of race? So on that score, I accept the simple fact that we all share a potential to violent relationships with each other when the objectives are strong enough. Only the means stands out as worth noting. Does history record only our excesses? For the most part, people all over the world live, or try to live, rather modest family oriented lives.

Many of the Mohawk Indians were eager to adopt captive children, so I come of mixed blood. My more immediate ancestors were repatriated and returned to Deerfield sometime around 1850. My father was Indian, my mother was white. He remained with his people. So, it was from my mother that I learned some of the ways of Indian life and developed an interest and curiosity about our adjustment to the growing west.

The Jesuits, for a long time, kept records of marriages, adoptions, births and deaths beginning back in the 1730's. I'm sure my grand parentage could be traced back there somewhere. I'm almost certain that if captives were marched north that one of them was a baby or very young child, perhaps carried on the shoulders of an Indian, adopted into the family and taken on the life of an Indian. In many respects the Mohawk way of child rearing was less strict and offered a great many more freedoms and was more natural than the nurture of Colonial children. So, by the time many captives were offered freedom, they had to make a choice. Many decided to continue their Indian life. Women had a place of respect, equality and evidently even a degree of political and economic authority. Even in this day and time I do not find this to be broadly so. It has been observed that native peoples have a great respect for and feeling for the past, basing their wisdom and culture on past experiences and values. White people live in the present and the future, a major difference in their sense of community.

Here I am at the age of 23, interested in the Indians of our west and the rapid growth of that area of our expanding nation. My formal education is nearly behind me and through a small scholarship I am able to undertake sufficient time off campus to collect my observations. Not wanting to prejudice my study, I feel I must somehow separate my findings from what had been the native American experience here in the east to date. As carefully as I could, I began to think through the things I would need, what to expect and a whole long list of things. I felt sure I'd not cover everything. Then I began to cut my baggage to a minimum. I suppose a woman always packs too much. Then I arranged for expenses and finally transportation.

Traveling west, I passed through Chicago, Sioux Falls and eventually across the Missouri River, through what are called the Badlands to a small town called

David K. Richards

Spearfish on the western edge of South Dakota. The last leg of my journey was by stage, a rough and dusty ride, through country much different than New England. South Dakota became a state in 1859. It was shortly after Chicago that I decided that traveling as a woman alone was going to be difficult. Fortunately my boyish figure, dark eyes and sharp features provided a reasonable basis to dress as a young man. Having grown up with five brothers was a real asset. One of my lesser concerns was the softness of my hands. To that end, I decided to pass myself off as a card player. The long travel by train allowed just enough time for me to learn how to handle cards with some degree of facility. I could make a false shuffle, make a pass, slip a card or even force a card along with learning odds and the rules of a number of games including Poker and Black Jack. At the time, I wasn't quite sure it would be a skill I'd need to draw on, but it passed the travel hours.

Spearfish, my choice of destination or starting point, was not much of a town. Getting there, I'd passed through Deadwood, another small town of wooden storefronts and decided as we changed horses that I was not ready for something quite like that. The bank had been robbed shortly before our stage arrived and the sheriff had been wounded in a shoot-out as the bandits had made their get-away. Our driver said this was fairly normal for a lot of the small mining towns that had sprung up. For some, the hard work of mining had given way to the questionable route of banditry. The flood of dime novels back east had drawn just such a picture. Along with the wild life of the cowboys coming to town further south, I suspect they pictured a more romantic twist than was reality. I saw few Indians in any of the towns we passed though and wondered about that. I learned that Indians who by nature can't handle whiskey were another problem.

In Spearfish, I found a suitable room with a tub and decided to take a job in the local hardware store, a two story building crammed full of every manner of household and building materials you could possibly imagine. It was run by a Mr. Coffin, a big greasy man with a handlebar mustache and a loud course laugh. He'd come west out of Ohio some years back. He seemed to delight in calling me, 'Kid'.

"Hey, Kid! You best spend some time lookin' around so you'll know where things are. You handle that?"

"Sure, Mr. Coffin," I'd replied. It wasn't all that hard except when it came to the heavy things, sacks of flour and such. Then he'd give me a hand.

"Kid, you got the muscles of a girl," he'd say, and unknowing, he was right.

I learned quite a bit from the people that came in and began to realize it wasn't just the bandits who were robbing town's people. The very land itself was being parceled out by the government as though it had always been theirs. It came under the heading of 'homesteading'. The local Indians were not a part of the opportunity or the transactions. Mr. Coffin's prices were higher than back east, but some of that might be expected way out here in the middle of the country. He seemed like an honest business man until one evening something very unusual took place. I happened to be working later than normal. I was unpacking some boxes in the back room when there was a knock on the back door. I opened it and was confronted by the ugliest hairy man I'd ever seen. He asked for Mr. Coffin by name. Innocently, I said I could help him. He looked me over from one end to the other, grunted under his breath and jerked a thumb over his shoulder in the direction of his wagon outside.

"I'll need a hand, kid."

Then he came right in, moved a box from in front of a door I hadn't realized was there and opened the door.

"Grab an end," he said and pointed to a long rectangular box with numbers and a man's name on it. Together we hauled it to the back of his wagon. We moved two more and a smaller one that was far too heavy for me to even budge. He handed me a soiled envelope.

"If they's still five a piece and ten to a box, this'll cover it."

I just said, "I s'pose." I didn't know. He seemed to know what he was doing.

When I handed Mr. Coffin the envelope he looked at me funny, but said nothing. It was later that I learned a bit more.

There weren't many women in Spearfish, a few wives, a few tired looking women who worked in the restaurant and a few who worked down the street in the saloon. It was a good ten days before I ventured into that end of town and it just happened that on that day a United States Cavalry unit had made camp nearby. The town, at least for a day or two, had horse soldiers with time off. It seems that although peace arrangements had been reached with the Lakota Indians and Red Cloud, not all the other tribes were in agreement. Raids and some real fights, caused by mining encroachments on hunting lands was at the root of it. That kind of activity sounded familiar.

The saloon was about what I'd heard, read about and expected, crammed with a raucous lot, all drinking, grabbing at scantily clad women or playing cards.

I didn't risk asking for anything to drink. Indians were not openly served anyhow, though I was hardly ready to make my roots known. I watched the card games for a bit and when someone dropped out, asked if I could sit in. It drew a few chuckles, but after a hand or two my playing was taken a little more seriously. No, I didn't cheat, but had a fair understanding of odds. It made a difference. Just listening, I learned a lot. One expression I almost responded to verbally was to the effect that 'the only good Indian was a dead Indian'. There were others as well that triggered further derogatory epitaphs and coarse laughter. It wasn't long before I simply cashed in my chips and moved toward the door.

At another table someone claimed a player was cheating and it caused quite an angry response. When one big fellow called another a liar, everybody moved clear of both of them. They were ready to draw their guns and shoot it out right there until one of the Army fellows present hit the big one over the head with a bottle and ended it. Anyway, I did come out with a few dollars and a small pouch of gold dust that I took the next day to the assayer's office. I was ten whole dollars richer. Mining was at the heart of this tremendous influx of people into this area of our country. It was the gold dust; amazing!

The next day I ran into the Army fellow who had wielded the face saving bottle the evening before. I struck up a conversation with him. They were heading on into Wyoming where they were still trying to chase down some renegade Indians and get them to one of the reservations. From a military standpoint he had a pretty healthy respect for the Indians as opponents. He'd been in several scraps, and not all successfully.

"For the uncivilized savages they were some of

the finest riders anywhere, circling around and around us while we fired and then reloaded. It was at that point that they would sweep in close, fifty or sixty yards away and put three or four arrows in the air before the first would hit its target."

"Really?" I gasped.

"Yeah, kid, but that's going to end pretty soon. One of these days, when we get the new Springfield-Allen modification or even the newer Henrys, it'll be a different story."

"Henrys?" I asked.

He winked. "Yes, siree. We've been using the Spencer, a seven shot breech loading carbine. The new Henry carries a sixteen shot load." He winked again. "Make a real difference in a tight scrap."

I heard his reply, but my mind was going in other directions. I had a few more questions.

"What are the Indians using?"

"Bows and arrows mostly, but a few are illegally trading furs for rifles. Some they pick up after a fight, some they get from traders who are willing to sell the rest of us short; unscrupulous traders. They did General Custer in at the Little Big Horn and a Captain Fetterman before that. It sure takes all kinds of people.

I was sick, knowing in what I had very likely participated. Fortunately the Army fellow changed the subject, introduced himself as Gordon Scovill from Waterbury.

"Connecticut?"

"Right!"

I mentioned Deerfield and he not only knew of it, but a bit of its early history. He asked, "What brings you way out here?"

"Curiosity, mostly. We hear so much back east and have even seen a wild west show. It's hardly like that at all. This is a different world."

Corporal Scovill agreed. He mentioned a chap he'd run into who came from somewhere back in New York State who had come west for some of the same reasons and liked to sketch. "He's done a lot with water color painting; great drawings of horses. He even traveled with us some. Ogdensburg? Is that in New York State?"

We talked further and the next day he was gone. And right the next day I left the hardware store. Mr. Coffin wondered why, so I told him. Other than himself, I wasn't sure he was really helping. That was one time I wished I had been a man. It was then that I decided if I was really going to see Indians, I realized I had two choices, join a war party or go to one of the reservations. Of course I took the latter.

From Spearfish, I decided to travel eastward, to Rapid City and on to Box Elder. I traveled by stage. There I bought a horse and used the balance of my earnings from the hardware store to purchase a number of small items; needles, thread, a few small kitchen knives, soap and scissors. My intent was to travel in the direction of Pine Ridge and to one of the reservations. If I wanted to see Indians, I'd best go where they are. I'd been told there was a reservation about thirty miles south of Box Elder.

It was an easy ride through pockets of grassland, areas where ridges of granite broke the skyline. Spruce and a longer needled pine and aspen seemed to flourish in this country. The sky was the clearest blue I'd ever seen. Really beautiful! Late summer was proving to be an ideal time. Returning east to resume classes was far from my mind. En route, I saw a variety of wildlife, elk, a distant bear grubbing in the earth, and lots of birds. And most exciting, I saw my first buffalo, not one or two, but dozens, big furry beasts roaming across an open grassy area. Mesmerized, I sat on my horse and from the far side of a small grouping I saw several riders, Indians. They rode bareback as I understood was their custom. They approached the buffalo from the far side. Suddenly, the buffalo broke into a run in my direction. I was terrified. Fortunately, another rider appeared from a grove of aspen and rode straight toward the running herd waving a blanket. That rider turned just before he got close and caused the animals to turn back on themselves in a broad sweeping curve. It was amazing! Meanwhile, on the far side, the first two Indians I'd seen, rode right up alongside the stampeding animals. I didn't see it happen, but with bow and arrows they dropped one of the big animals. It fell, first to its knees, then to the ground as the others raced on by. It was over in less than a minute. For me, it had been a moment of real excitement as well as fear. The rest of the buffalo slowed to a walk about a mile further away and seemed to be returning to quiet grazing. The Indians dropped to the ground and approached their kill. From off the far side of a number of large spruce, another Indian came forward dragging what I've learned is a travois. It was simply two poles tied along the sides of a horse with the lower ends dragging on the ground behind. Across the two poles was formed a kind of shelf or platform. Oblivious to me, the men loaded the animal on the travois and moved off to the south. I followed at what I believed to be a safe and discrete distance.

I was, however, taken by surprise, when I found myself quietly in the company of several riders. Evidently we were on our way to their village. I was frightened at how quietly it happened, but was also pleased. They looked at me, but did not speak.

We all eventually rode into the center of a grouping of teepees, poles placed in a circle and gathered at one point at the top forming an inverted cone. They were covered by hides and painted with colorful designs. As housing, they were simple and neat. From a small opening at the base of one teepee a very old Indian came out. In fact, most all of the men I saw were quite old; no young men anywhere. There were explanations by the man beside me, none of which I understood fully. When I held my hand upward in a traditional sign of peace, the old man nodded. When they saw I carried no weapon, hand motions directed my dismounting and I was led to one of the several small fires that burned. Looking around, I was more impressed by a sense of poverty than by any well being. Our curiosity toward each other was mutual, their suspicion understandable. As I stood amongst them, I wondered both how I might communicate my own heritage as well as my gender. As an unarmed young person, I seemed to be no threat to them. The other matter, I solved an hour or so later by watching the women and at one point I took the hand of a little girl and walked in the direction the women had gone. There was some giggling, but by the time we rejoined the others, there was no misunderstanding as to what I was. Word spread quickly and I was subsequently abandoned by the men.

Just before that I had taken a small bundle out of my pack and spread the contents on the ground. With gestures, I indicated them to be gifts. Questioning looks passed between the small group that had gathered around me. The needles and so on were well received, however, I had not anticipated that they would feel obligated to return the kindness. Through motions back and forth, they understood that I had come to learn their language and would need a place to stay. It all worked out rather nicely as we slowly came to accept each other. The old man I'd met initially brought forward a woman whose teepee no longer had a man. I could stay with her. Her name was Songbird. So began my visit with my Indian brothers.

Things went fairly well for a few days. Songbird was a lovely woman, round faced and plump, very pleasant, but also sad. We got along quite well. I must say she kept very busy, busy with food, drying meats, preparing hides, necessary things.

A few days later a group of white men arrived in a wagon, evidently with food supplies and a few blankets, flour and lard. It was a ration that seemed to be dependant on a willingness to cooperate with the agents who brought them. What was doled out hardly seemed enough to last a whole week, which was the next time it was said they would come to visit. These people worked for the Bureau of Indian Affairs. During their stay, I remained in the background and dared not open my mouth. I did listen to them and observed. I found myself disturbed by their manner and hoped that these men were exceptions to the interrelationship between white and Indian peoples. Accepting what amounts to welfare by a proud people was a heart rending experience. It was evident in the faces of the people. I began to wonder if reservation was more a form of prison internment than a freedom to live their lives independently. Borderline poverty is hardly a condition that fosters hope and the spirit of free enterprise. I sat for a long time wondering how I might fairly record such observations in my journal. It was then that it occurred to me that I had gotten myself into the Indian reservation a lot more easily than might be possible toward my getting out. That was a bridge I would have yet to cross.

The children seemed to respond to my being with them and learned very quickly as I struggled to learn their language. I discovered that I had come west without thinking through enough of the problems I might encounter. Too late, we exchanged words back and forth and by the end of the week could exchange a few real sentences. Names and simple greetings came first, then identifying objects, pronouns and a few verbs to give action. We made games out of the process. The old men of the village were beyond their days of fighting. They came and sat as I taught, curious, often smiling at the youthful energy of the children. It was the eyes of the women that were the saddest and there were times when they just quietly shook their heads at what I was attempting. None wept openly, but I'm sure they did.

There was one night that a number of riders slipped into the settlement to see their wives and families. In many cases they carried rifles and had cartridge belts slung across their shoulders. They rode beautiful brown and white ponies. I wondered if the rifles might be some of the new Henry rifles that Mr. Coffin was surreptitiously dealing in. I also wondered if what he was doing was in the long term best interests by continuing the fighting between peoples, or was it greed on his part that simply saw another merchandizing opportunity. I was really confused. I concluded and made notes in my journal to the effect that there are few people in this world who seem capable of making friends out of adversaries without physical conflict. No man came to Songbird's teepee and during the night I heard her weeping softly.

Sometime in the early hours of morning the sound of horses made us aware that the warriors, and that is what they were, were off once more. If I'd been a man, I'm not sure that I wouldn't have joined them.

I spent a third week working with my Indian brothers and would have liked to stay longer, but I had a long ways to go to get back to my studies. I could not help but wonder, if this relationship between white and Indian continued, how our government could ever say they were sorry and make amends. Perhaps governments don't ever apologize. With the black people, it had so recently come to such a frightful resolution, if Appomattox was truly the end.

I must say, that as I slipped off into the hills, guided by one of the old men and a young boy who had learned enough words to be of mutual help, I worked my way back to the white man's world. I was not proud of half of me; painfully saddened in the other half. I could see that a half-breed like myself without the real benefits of kind friends and a real education would be at a loss in both worlds.

One of the last entries I made in my journal, possibly poorly expressed, related not to my original intent to take note of the adjustment and response of the Indian people in the presence of the white man, but was more the reverse of what I'd intended. The white man was not accepting the presence of the Indians, "the damned savages". They were in the way and because of their stubborn resistance were considered as even less human than the black slaves freed by Mr. Lincoln's Emancipation. Our treatment and even our laws confirm our obstinacy to better conditions. I found my own acceptance to all I had learned to be such a strong reaction that I knew my life and the focus of my efforts in the years to come would be forever shaped.